The Bobwhite Doesn't Always Sing

A Novel

By Mary B. Ansari

LeRue Books
www.Lrpnv.com

Dedicated to the memory of Eric,
my son, and to my loving
husband and caregiver, Nazir

Chapter 1
Turning 80

I remember my mom talking about their childhood together. It included attending several funerals of aunts, uncles and other relatives. In fact, one that was most memorable was a double funeral for their Aunt Cecile's in-laws who had died two days apart of unrelated causes. My mom and Aunt Liz always talked about how they stood on their tiptoes to peer into the open caskets. My grandparents didn't shield them from the realities of death being a part of life though. Can you imagine?

On the day before her eightieth birthday, my Aunt Elizabeth Azmi found herself looking back over a life of great successes but there was also a mixture of happiness and heartache. In so many ways Aunt Liz led a sheltered childhood.

Aunt Liz's maternal grandmother was the only close blood relative who lived to be over 80. Of the immediate family, Grandma died at 62, Grandpa 66, and a half-brother, 66 (an uncle I never knew well). Even her son's life was tragically cut short. He was only 30 at the time and it was really a freak accident.

Three of my great-grandparents were deceased before Aunt Liz or my mom were even born. Coming from a family that led such short lives caused Aunt Liz to grow up thinking she would not live to be seventy. My mom only lived to be 40, so Aunt Liz had plenty of reason to think life might be short. I, on the other hand, feel like I'll live a long, long life!

The story is not really that unusual at first. My Aunt Liz loved to write, and she published because of her job, but this was different. When Aunt Liz was sick, I came by to help out and found a story she had written. It's almost like she was trying to get all her frustration, anger and confusion on paper to find some kind of release by telling a story.

I guess she was trying to find closure after my cousin Derrick was killed in an accident. I know she was inconsolable for a long time. She wasn't living nearby so her only source of consolation were her friends because Uncle Arif's health and the treatments he was receiving were making him miserable.

Probably the best way to relate her struggles is in her own words. It's kind of a journal and a story. She was re-reading the story and journaling at the same time. I don't know if she intended for it to be shared or even if it's all true, but it's definitely worth telling. She said she wouldn't mind.

A Birthday AGAIN!

As she gazed out the window at the sparkling, snow-covered trees and glimpses through the low-hanging clouds of her beloved Lake Tahoe, she chided herself for allowing melancholy to interrupt what should be a time of great celebration. Tomorrow her husband, Arif, was planning a drive around the lake followed by a very special evening at their favorite restaurant where they had celebrated so many anniversaries and birthdays.

Chef Henre was preparing some special non-menu delectables for her. Liz was thankful that Arif didn't want to give her a big party, and she made him promise not to give her even a small surprise party.

Why can't I stop thinking about how this day would have been if Derrick, had lived? Would Arif and I feel less alone in facing the challenges of aging if Derrick was still here? Maybe pulled his life together, married and had children? She sighed. "Probably not, she thought almost saying it out loud. In fact, her life could have been even more tragedy-filled.

She almost scolded herself as she thought, "How could I ever forget that I should be eternally grateful that he didn't end up killing someone. If that had happened, would she still be alive? Would she and Arif still be married?"

As she continued to wonder, Arif came into her office. "Well, you'll never guess what!"

Before she could respond, he continued, "The forecast for tomorrow has worsened. The storm that was supposed to split is now scheduled to hit Tahoe directly with snow and high winds. Perhaps we should high tail it to Sacramento."

"Oh, sweetheart, don't forget that I was born in a midwestern blizzard. You know how much I want to have this birthday at Tahoe."

"I'm just warning you that we might end up eating scrambled eggs at home."

"That wouldn't be so bad by the fireplace."

"Oh, okay, it's your landmark birthday," Arif acquiesced. "It seems that it almost always happens when we celebrate your birthday at the lake. I can see us now, snowshoeing into the restaurant. I'm going out to run some errands before the storm."

"Don't forget the bread and eggs, dear."

The interruption didn't break Liz's line of thought. Why did she have to recall those terrible days when she lost both Derrick and her brother and almost lost Arif too? For the most part, she refused to live in the past, but because of some concerning health challenges she and Arif were facing, she felt the need to revisit another time in her life when she had met with almost insurmountable challenges… and somehow survived.

Did she dare allow herself to read what she had written in those difficult years between 1995 and 2009 in her desperate search for closure? The few times that she tried to read the words she had committed to paper, she found it too heartbreaking to continue more than a few pages. Would this time be different? Why was the manuscript beckoning to her?

Hesitantly she walked over to the bookcase and pulled out a binder from the bottom of a stack of papers and binders on the lower shelf. She blew some dust off and walked over to her favorite recliner. As she sank into the chair, she took a deep breath before opening the binder. She quickly leafed through the title and introductory pages and began reading the story that she started writing over 20 years on January 31, 1995.

Even though it had been three and one half years since the dreadful day of the accident that took her son's life, Liz had been unsuccessful in finding closure and for quite some time, something inside her had been telling her to commit the story of her grief and search for closure to paper.

Perhaps that would help to heal the open wound inside her heart and conclude the excruciating grieving process. Being so isolated in her grief had made it doubly difficult to overcome. Everyone said that the first year was the most difficult and that time would soften the pain. In some ways it had, but because of her peculiar situation, closure always evaded her. Maybe I'll call it *Do Not Stand by My Grave and Weep.*

When in 1991 she first returned home from the funeral, it was as though Derrick was still there, 2000 miles away in Missouri, and everything was normal. In recent years he never wrote, so it wasn't unusual for mother and son to be out of touch for two or three months at a time. Because she was more inclined to communicate through letters than by phone, she wrote to him about once a month, knowing that she would never receive an answer. Occasionally, he would call, but Liz was the one who did most of the calling. From 1987 to 1991, she saw him three times, but before that, after her father's death in 1970, she saw him only twice.

Because of this pattern of infrequent contact, it was easy for her to return to Sacramento and pretend that Derrick was still in central Missouri, very much alive. For the first couple of years, this denial worked fairly well, except when she visited his grave and on certain days such as Mother's Day, his birthday, her birthday, the anniversary of his death, and some holidays. Because there was nothing unusual in not receiving letters and phone calls from him, it was almost as though nothing had happened. Also, because no one in Sacramento knew him, except her husband, Arif, who didn't know him very well, it was not unusual for him not to be a part of her everyday conversation. All this made it possible for her to pretend that her son was still alive.

Now, almost four years later, Liz could pretend no longer. Now she was confronted with the terrible and agonizing realization that she would never see her son, her only child, again. In this respect, time hadn't made anything better or easier for her. Because of her isolation, this tortured realization had taken longer than normal to occur.

To make this all easier to understand, it's necessary to explain that, after Derrick was a very young child, Liz didn't raise him but rather that his paternal grandparents had custody and raised him. After a messy and bitter divorce, the court ruled that neither parent was to have custody. Instead, the paternal grandparents were awarded custody.

Liz's former in-laws were accustomed to getting their way, one way or another, as they did in this case. At that time, Derrick was not quite three years old. From then on, Liz never was able to spend much time with him, but, even though she lived many miles away, she always managed to stay in touch. Her parents, Joseph and Anita Springmeyer, lived in the same town as Derrick, so until their deaths in 1969 and 1970, she saw him about once a year and frequently talked to him on the phone when he was visiting her parents' home.

When her father's death followed her mother's death by only 15 months, Liz not only lost her parents, but she lost personal contact with her son for several years. She continued to write to him on a regular basis but didn't see him again until 1977. In 1977, when she returned and saw Derrick, he was no longer the little boy that she remembered, but was a teenager who was two inches taller than her 5'8", had a driver's license and was attending a military academy.

When Arif and Liz left Middletown after her father's death, she fervently wished that they would never have to return. If Derrick hadn't been living there, she might never have returned. In Middletown she and Arif went through the traumatic experience of having her father's home burglarized the day after his funeral. A few weeks later they had the unpleasant task of returning to Middletown to prepare her father's home for sale. It was a home crammed full of furniture, antiques and memorabilia that her parents had collected over many years. Liz and Arif tried to prevail upon her half-brother, Rob, to come from Minnesota to help with the house, but he had numerous excuses for not being able to come. It was Christmas, and they had the overwhelming task of inventorying and packing or selling hundreds of items.

The stress of dismantling the family home was so severe that in the midst of it Liz suffered a miscarriage. Since she had missed only one period, she suspected that she might be pregnant, but it hadn't been confirmed until she miscarried. To Liz the miscarriage was almost a relief because she would have been fearful for the well-being of a fetus conceived and carried during a period of such emotional stress. On the other hand, she was distraught about miscarrying, because when she suspected that she might be pregnant, she felt that a death in the family was being followed by the promise of new life.

Further adding to the tension was that Arif never felt comfortable in Middletown. Because he was a foreigner of Asian birth, so many people living in that bastion of Midwestern conservatism, her parents included, were suspicious of him and his motives and suspected that his marriage to her was a marriage of convenience. Proof of this prejudicial attitude came early in their courtship when a maternal aunt had the audacity to ask Arif how much money he wanted to go back to his native country and leave Liz alone.

Liz should have known that Arif's charm, good looks and intellectual brilliance wouldn't be enough to win over the suspicions and distrust of her family and relatives. A couple of years before Liz met Arif, she took a fourth generation Japanese-American friend and neighbor to visit her family home in Middletown. Liz never forgot taking Joyce to the grocery store where her friend reported feeling as though she were some kind of exotic animal on display in a zoo. Liz was so upset to have exposed her friend to such humiliation, but Joyce, who grew up in San Francisco Bay Area, was very gracious and said that she considered it to be a learning experience.

In fact, in 1957 when her parents took Liz who was an incoming freshman to the University of Missouri to help her move into her dorm, her father took her aside and looking very serious cautioned, "Liz, up to now you've lead a very sheltered life. Now all that's about to change."

Liz was astonished when she saw how worried her father looked and asked, "Daddy, what's wrong? I thought you and mother were proud of me and happy that I was going to Mizzou."

"Of course we are, dear. It's just that you're going to be exposed to different social activities and people from many backgrounds, and your mother and I are worried about you being exposed to drinking and smoking and possibly getting mixed up with foreigners."

Liz was particularly perplexed by her father's comment about foreigners. Where did that notion come from? Liz was never to forget her father's concern. At the university she refrained from smoking and drinking, but after graduation became romantically entangled with a foreign graduate student whom she eventually married.

The longer that trying to wind up her father's affairs dragged on, the more the stress of being in Middletown took its toll on both of them, and they ended up taking their frustrations out on each other. Liz was deeply concerned that even at his young age Derrick would detect the tension between Arif and her. To this day she feels distraught that the only times that Arif and Derrick ever had together were those sad and stressful days. There were so many decisions to be made, and they were being pulled in so many directions that their time in Middletown became a virtual nightmare, one which they wanted to bury forever.

While in Middletown, the one bizarre happening that Liz and Arif never forgot and later were able to laugh about was when an elderly, wealthy, eccentric, alcoholic neighbor asked Arif to come to her home to pick up something that she wanted to give to them. After Liz received Mrs. Levant's call, she turned to Arif and said "That was the neighbor across the street who lives in the pink stucco house with blue tile roof that is unlike any other house in town."

Arif queried, "What's that got to do with her call?"

"Well, dear, Mrs. L has some treasure that she wishes to give us and…"

Starting to look annoyed Arif interrupted "Come on, Liz, spit it out. We have a full schedule today,"

In order not to further annoy Arif, she rattled off, "Mrs. L insists that you be the one to pick up the gift."

"Why me? You're the one she knows."

"Dear, look upon it as an opportunity to meet one of the town's celebrities. Apparently, she was on Broadway in her younger days."

"Oh, okay, this better be something worthwhile. Be right back" said Arif as he looked around for his jacket.

As he left, Liz called after him, "Did I mention that she's a bit eccentric?"

"Who around here isn't?" he shot back."

After Arif was gone almost an hour, Liz became concerned. They needed to meet with the lawyer, the house appraiser and the movers. What could be holding him up?

She looked out to see Arif, a package in hand, running toward the house. He burst in and announced' "Your Mrs. L is some kind of sex maniac!"

He threw the package down in disgust and sat down to get his breath. "Nothing you could have said would have prepared me for what I walked in to."

"Did she greet you in a negligee?" Liz asked.

"On, no, that wouldn't have been such a shock. She opened the door totally naked except for the newspaper she was holding in front of her. Then she proceeded to take me on a tour of her mansion. I was walking behind her on the so-called tour while she kept the newspaper over her front. When we were in front of her bedroom, she started to tell me what beautiful brown eyes and black hair I have. Desperate to make my escape, I looked at my watch and told her we had an appointment in 10 minutes with the executrix."

The scene Arif painted was so bizarre that Liz almost found it amusing. Trying not to laugh, Liz said, "Obviously, that must have worked."

"Not 'til I promised to come over to tell her goodbye. So much for that promise."

"Did I ever tell you that when Mrs. L's brother became senile, he used to write me passionate love letters? He and his wife lived next door to Mrs. L and doted over me as a child."

"That's enough, Liz. I've experienced and heard enough about this neighborhood already. I'll be anxious to see what she bestowed on us."

When it turned out to be an elaborate Italian lace tablecloth for a banquet table along with 25 napkins. Arif sarcastically commented "Just what we always needed."

After making his escape, Arif always referred to Middletown as the Peyton Place or Texasville of the Midwest.

The Bobwhite Doesn't Always Sing

Chapter 2
A Reunion

Liz's trip in 1977 was made under the guise of attending her twentieth high school class reunion, whereas the real reason for the trip was to see Derrick. How difficult it was to return to the town where she had grown up and to no longer have a family home. How strange it was to stay in a motel only a mile and a half from her childhood home. Driving by her former home, she was relieved to see that it was beautifully maintained and looked much the same as she remembered it.

One of the highlights of the trip that she vividly recalls was going with Derrick to visit Mrs. Fulstone who had adopted Liz's father's dog, Ginger, after her father's death. Ginger was very old, but still in good health when Derrick and Liz last saw her. It was gratifying to see what a wonderful home she had with Mrs. Fulstone. Derrick was overjoyed to see Ginger again, and Liz treasures the pictures she has of him with his faithful childhood companion. How often since Derrick's death has she tearfully looked at those pictures and the several others she took on more recent visits.

Liz was so thankful that Derrick was with her the first time, after so many years, that she visited her parents' graves. Derrick was not inclined to spend much time in cemeteries, but he always was good about accompanying her there. Their graves were near the still-vacant portion of the cemetery where Liz's parents and she used to take Ginger for a run. Sometimes, when Liz was visiting, her parents and she would take Derrick and Ginger there. Liz's mother always loved the beauty and tranquility of the place. It was on top of a gentle knoll, which gently sloped into the Missouri woodlands. It seems strange that a cemetery could hold such joyful memories, but that undeveloped part of the cemetery more resembled a scenic park than a burial ground.

When Derrick and Liz made that first visit, in her mind she could see her parents, Derrick as a little boy, and Ginger frolicking on the knoll, which prompted her to ask, "Derrick, do you remember as a little boy coming here with me, your grandparents and Ginger?"

"Yeah. That was some of the best fun I ever had with you and Grandma and Grandpa. And afterwards we'd always stop at the A & W for root beer floats."

"You and Ginger would wear yourselves out running up and down that slope."

"My uncle Matt owns the adjoining land where it becomes wooded. I go there sometimes for target practice." He must have noticed that Liz frowned at the mention of target practice, which prompted him to add, "My dad said that he could never teach you how to shoot."

"And I still don't know how to shoot," she announced proudly.

"Do you want me to give you some lessons?"

"Derrick, stop it! I'm not interested. That's something you and my brother have in common. Rob is a real gun nut."

"I'd like to meet him sometime."

Another treasured memory of that trip was going to Middletown Lakes with Derrick. Most things in Middletown hadn't changed much since her childhood days, but a portion of the lakes had changed beyond recognition. The lakes were a series of gravel pits that had been converted to recreational use. One of Liz's paternal uncles used to own gravel pits and sand and gravel business.

When Liz was growing up, there had been an area set aside for swimming with a bathhouse, beach and playground. She was amazed to find that the beach had been abandoned and was overgrown with weeds and vines. Derrick and she threaded their way through the heavy growth to find the old bathhouse and playground. Upon finding their ruins, it appeared as though they had been abandoned for 100 years. As they examined the site, Liz relived for Derrick some fond recollections of the place. Liz's mother never encouraged her to go to the beach because Liz almost always got infected with athlete's foot there.

Occasionally, however, Liz did go to the beach with her girlfriends, all who were good swimmers except for Liz and her closest friend, Anne.

Looking toward what used to be the swimming area, Liz could see the boarded-up remains of the diving tower sticking up. "There's where my brother, Rob, almost succeeded in drowning me."

Derrick queried, "Are you talking about the diving tower?"

"Yes. I made the mistake of going to the lake with Rob when he was home from college. He told mother that he was sure that he could teach me how to swim. Since no one else had been successful, he wanted to give it a try."

"How old were you?" Derrick inquired.

"I must have been 11 or 12. Anyway he got me to walk the boardwalk to the tower. When I got there, I saw a couple of my friends and was talking to them when Rob came up behind me and pushed me into the water. I panicked when I couldn't touch bottom and got water up my nose and started choking. Somehow, I surfaced, flailed about and started going under again. I could hear people screaming at me to tread water. I was sure I was a goner when someone grabbed me and pulled me to shore. That someone was Rob. That was the first and last time I ever went swimming with him."

Derrick chuckled and asked, "And when did you learn to swim?"

"Not 'til I was a sophomore at Mizzou and was required to take swimming. I had to dive to pass the class, which is the only time I ever did that. As I recall, you had quite a fear of deep water. When you were four or five, I remember taking you to the pool and you wouldn't come in the water with me."

"I had to learn to swim after getting a little looped and falling out of a boat at Scout camp."

"Aren't you a little young to be getting looped? And where were the chaperones?"

"Heck, Mom, around here kids start drinking beer when they're 11 or 12. After curfew a bunch of us snuck out, retrieved the beer from where we hid it, found a boat and went boating."

"Does your grandmother know anything about this? As I recall, she and your grandfather Hoffman are teatotalers."

"You recall that one correctly. Avis doesn't know everything I do. She learned that I broke curfew but doesn't know the rest." Seeing Liz's look of disapproval, he added, "Unless you tell her."

After an awkward pause, Liz was surprised that Derrick wasn't anxious to change the subject. Instead he persisted "Mom, when you were a teenager, did you ever come out here to drink beer or neck?"

"You're right. In those days this was THE place to come for that, but I was more of the studious type and didn't date or party much. In fact, one of my best girlfriends was reported to have said that I was a nice girl but awfully boring. What about you? Do you come here often?"

Derrick flashed an impish grin and answered, "What do you think? I don't think that I was ever accused of being boring. Come on. Ma, were you really that square?"

"Oh, I had my rebellious side, but I reserved it mainly for my negativity toward the Catholic Church in particular and organized religion in general."

To change the subject, she told Derrick about how one of her paternal uncles who owned the lakes was reputed to have thrown a two-carat diamond ring in the lake after his fiancé broke their engagement. When Liz was at the lakes, she always hoped to find the ring and would spend time there, sifting sand.

"Look. Derrick, that's where the dock used to be where daddy would rent a boat and row mother and me to the island for a picnic."

"Yeah, when I was really little Grandpa and Grandma Springmeyer took me over to the island in a rowboat for a picnic."

From there they drove to a portion of the lakes where the summer cabins were located. That part looked the same or better than when Liz was growing up. Derrick showed Liz where his best friend Alex Aquino's parents had a cabin.

As they drove toward the Aquino cabin Derrick commented, "Boy oh boy, do we ever have some hot parties at the cabin when the Aquinos are out of town!"

"And who cleans up the mess you leave?"

"Four of five of us guys come out the next day and help Alex repair the damage."

Liz was thinking about the Hoffman's decision to send Derrick to a military academy and found herself hoping that the experience would instill in her son some much-needed discipline and academic focus. Her reflections were soon interrupted as they came to a stop in front of the cabin. Liz remembered the cabin well, because it had been in Alex's mother's family for many years. Liz had gone to school and been good friends with Alex's mother and had visited the cabin a couple of times as a teenager. Before heading back to town, Liz snapped a picture of Derrick standing by Alex's boat.

Reluctantly Liz attended her high school reunion. When she told Derrick that she would much prefer to spend the evening with him, he said that he personally knew several of her classmates who would be very disappointed if she didn't show up. She went to the reunion with dear friends, Anne and Jeffrey Bishop.

Anne had lived next door and been Liz's best friend through junior high and high school, and Jeffrey had been a neighbor when she was in grade school. After not having seen them for almost ten years, it was wonderful being together again. They drove to the country club in the Bishop's luxurious Chrysler sedan. Jeffrey was a partner in a very prosperous law firm, and Anne was an attorney also. As they approached the club, they could hear the blare of a band. The band turned out to be the entertainment and impediment for the reunion.

Because of the loud music, the evening ended up being extremely frustrating and disappointing for Liz, especially because she could have been with Derrick. Many people attended whom she hadn't seen for 20 years, but the music was so deafening that she couldn't hear what they were saying. Even outside, it was difficult to compete with the din of the band. After a couple of hours, she began to lose her voice and was relieved when Anne and Jeffrey wanted to leave early. The next day Derrick remarked that he could hear the music five miles away.

Six Years Later

After that trip, another six years elapsed until she saw Derrick again. This time he was an adult and was struggling very hard not to flunk out of college. He had a girlfriend, Tammy, to whom he introduced his mother. Tammy seemed really nice and very mature for her age and was majoring in education at Mizzou. Immediately Liz liked her and suspected that she would be a good stabilizing influence on Derrick.

As Derrick drove Liz back to the motel, he inquired, "Well, what do you think of her?"

"So far, I like her a lot. She seems to have a lot of intelligence and ambition and to really like you."

"I was hoping that she would meet your approval." What he said next caught Liz totally by surprise. "But there's one big problem."

"Do you want to tell me?"

He lit a cigarette, drew in deeply, exhaled slowly and said "Well, it's very obvious that her father doesn't like me and doesn't approve of Tammy seeing me."

"Do you know why?"

He fidgeted as he replied, "Not really."

Liz reflected upon how Derrick's grandparents were from the upper echelon of Middletown's society, making Derrick a so-called "very good catch." In the 1950s, the Hoffmans moved from Kirkwood, an affluent suburb of St. Louis to Middletown, where they became a potent financial, political and social force. Little did Liz dream that Tammy's father considered Derrick to be too wild and abusive for his daughter.

Seeing that Derrick was feeling uncomfortable, all she could think to say was, "Well that's a strange one."

By then they were in front of the Holiday Inn. As Liz got out, Derrick said, "See you tomorrow around 8:30 for breakfast."

"Sounds good. Good night, son".

For a number of years, Jill Aquino had been like a second mother to Derrick. Derrick was friends with all the Aquino children and was part of their family for Thanksgiving, Christmas, Easter, birthdays, weddings, and many other days of the year. Because of the double generation gap between Derrick and his grandparents who raised him, he craved a normal family life, and the Aquinos had given it to him. Jill's husband, Raphael, was a physician and had literally sewn Derrick up countless times. Liz was so thankful that her son had such a wonderful second home.

While Liz was in town, the Aquinos made her feel that she too was part of their family. Jill gave an elegant luncheon in her honor to which she invited many of Liz's friends and Liz's mother's friends. During lunch Alex and Derrick stopped by to say "hello" to the ladies. How handsome the two of them were, Alex with his swarthy good looks and Derrick with his classic Germanic handsomeness.

Being former high school classmates, Jill and Liz had a lot of reminiscing to do. It was so wonderful to have re-established contact with her. More than ever, Jill and Liz had a lot in common, most notably that she too had married an Asian, her husband being originally from the Philippines. At that time, mixed racial marriages were almost unheard of in Middletown. Raphael, however, because of his light skin, Catholic faith, and infectious personality managed to win over the ultra-conservative stronghold and eventually became the town's most sought-after physician.

Vivid memories of Liz's 1983 visit include having dinner with Derrick and Tammy at a nice restaurant in Columbia, going shopping with Derrick for some recordings to add to his collection, having breakfast with him and Avis, his paternal grandmother, at the Holiday Inn, and seeing where he worked. He proudly took her on a tour of the park where he was employed, which was located on several scenic acres along a creek. From his enthusiasm, it was obvious that he loved every inch of the park. It was the kind of woodsy place that so much appealed to him.

At one point while they were driving along the creek that formed one boundary of the park. They parked and got out to take one of the paths that Derrick had built to the creek bank when Liz exclaimed, "Derrick, I can't believe it! On this bend in the creek is the very spot when my girlfriends and I used to skinny dip. We would ride our bikes all the way from town to cool off in the creek. Then we would climb the bank to that high spot to dry off and sunbathe."

"Mom, you didn't--not someone as square as you have painted yourself. I think there's a lot that you're not telling me."

"We would come out here every chance we got. Needless to say, our parents didn't approve and would usually find out from the way we smelled from the creek water when we got home."

"Did you ever come here with boys?"

"No, of course not!" Liz said indignantly.

"I'd say that you protest too much," Derrick quipped.

While at the park, Liz took several pictures of Derrick posing by his car with the trees he had planted in the background.

Upon leaving the park, he took his mother to see his aunt, Sue Hoffman, at her horse barn near the park. Sue had always had a passion for horses, so it was evident that, even if she hadn't found happiness in her marriage, she had found some happiness with her horses. Liz had always been fond of Sue and was glad to see her again after so many years. It was abundantly evident to Liz that Sue and Derrick had a really good relationship.

Liz hadn't brought Derrick a gift from Sacramento, and since she wanted to give him something as a memento of their time together, she bought him some stereo equipment for his car. Since she wanted him to make the selection, the two of them went shopping for it before she had to leave. A few months later Derrick woefully told her that his car was broken in and the equipment stolen.

That 1983 visit took on the characteristics of all the rest of their times together. The visits were always very short, usually two or three days at the most, but they were very intense. It was as though the rest of the world stood still for their brief hours together. Derrick, who was always working or had social commitments with his many friends, would reserve the time his mother was going to be in Middletown just for her, and Liz, who was always the busy wife and career woman, would put her other life in Sacramento on hold while she was with her son.

They had so much to talk about, so many things to catch up on and to learn about each other. Their times together were artificial in that they were all good times. Liz always said that she couldn't remember having even one real argument with her son. Obviously, that was because she didn't have the responsibility of raising him. She never had to discipline him or refuse him anything. Even though they had some serious discussions, particularly during the last couple of visits, nothing ever transpired that was ever unpleasant or even close to being an argument.

Because her father had been a native of Middletown and her mother had lived there for 35 years, Liz always tried to stay in touch and visit their close friends when she was in town. Much to her surprise, Derrick always wanted to accompany her on those visits and appeared to enjoy them as much or more than she did. Derrick had countless friends young and old, and he was extremely interested in becoming acquainted with his mother's and maternal grandparents' friends. During those visits, Derrick often would excuse himself to later be found deep in conversation about fishing or cars or football with her friend's husband. He had the enviable capacity of making friends everywhere he went. Liz always said that he didn't inherit that trait from either parent.

In a world that is often hectic and stressful, it was difficult for Liz not to long for those simplistic, idyllic days of being with Derrick. Those days offered a beautiful escape from the real world of coping with a demanding career, being married to an Asian and managing a home. Even Derrick's home resembled more a retreat than a place to live. In 1984, Derrick purchased a run-down shack on ten beautiful acres of Missouri woodland. Over the years, in his spare time, Derrick succeeded in transforming the ramshackle house into respectable-appearing bachelor's quarters. After first visiting the property in 1987, Liz grew to love the place and missed going there intensely.

What she loved about it most was its solitude and lushness with the wonderful pond where a heron came to sit on a branch of a dead tree on the pond's edge and the pheasant, raccoon and deer tracks everywhere. It was heaven to sit in the evening on the small rise by the house watching the fireflies and listening to the frogs and locusts. The place was so rustic and suited Derrick so perfectly.

Derrick was a country boy at heart. He didn't get past his first year of college and hated indoor, office-type work. He also felt strongly about buying American. One time on the phone Liz commented, "We just bought a new car…"

Before she could finish her sentence, Derrick interrupted, "And let me guess. I'll bet it's Japanese.

"How did you know?"

"I know how you liberal Californians are. You avoid buying American-made vehicles."

"You're right--it's a Nissan. We wanted a car that's low maintenance and reliable.

"What about that Mercedes you had? You always said that if you couldn't get ahold of Arif, you knew you could find him at the Mercedes garage."

"That's why we decided to buy a Japanese car, and, so far we're glad we did."

"How about a Ford or Chevy or GM car?"

"Not too long ago we had a Chevy that turned out to be a lemon. Not to change the subject, but I just bought a new pair of Levis. Now how American is that?"

For a number of years Derrick worked for a state park on the outskirts of Middletown where he didn't get paid much and received no benefits. The hours were long, vacations few, and sometimes the work was very demanding physically. When Liz was in town, he would take her to the park to proudly show the birdhouses he had built and hung, the nature and cross country ski trails he had made, and the many trees he had planted. Because of his passion for the outdoors, he worked there for over ten years until he finally left to go to work for an electrical firm in Jefferson City.

After his death, Liz concluded that Derrick was too good looking for his own good. He was tall, slender, and handsome in a Germanic sense and had a most winning smile. He had a way with women which he capitalized on, and his personal life was tumultuous and never stabilized. If only he had settled down, things might have turned out differently. He did get married, but it lasted only a little over a year. More than once he told his mother of his belief that because his parents were divorced, he too was a prime candidate for divorce. Liz didn't know if he knew that his maternal grandmother had also been divorced, and she wasn't going to tell him.

During this period, Liz wrote Derrick every month or two, but he never reciprocated. Occasionally she would try calling him but when after repeated tries, she couldn't reach him, she became discouraged. On at least one occasion, she called Jill to find out if he was all right. Jill assured her that he was fine and was just busy working and having an active social life. Consequently, Liz was pretty much out of touch with what was happening in his personal life. For that reason, she didn't know the details of his breaking up with Tammy or when he met Lynne Hunsaker.

In 1986 Derrick and Lynne were married. Liz never forgot the strange invitation she received to the reception. It was on a postcard. The reception was held in a small town near Middletown after the wedding in Florida. Liz & Arif were not invited to the wedding and because of the short notice, didn't attend the reception. They never met Lynne.

When Arif and she offered to give them a honeymoon trip to Lake Tahoe, Derrick thanked them, saying that he couldn't take that much time off from work at that time and asked if they could take a rain check on the trip. Of course, they said "yes," but, sadly, the trip never happened.

After finishing the first couple of chapters, Liz got up and made some tea. When she looked out the window, she noticed that a few lazy snowflakes were blowing about. She wondered if this was the innocent beginning of the big storm that Arif was talking about? She placed her tea cup on the table by her chair, got comfortably situated in the recliner and resumed her reading.

Chapter 3
1987

In July of the next year Liz planned a trip to Middletown to meet Lynne. All the plans were finalized and when she talked to Lynne on the phone, she said that she was very anxious to meet Liz.

Liz was extremely excited at the prospect of meeting her new daughter-in-law. Everything was proceeding smoothly until a week before Liz was scheduled to depart. Derrick called and began the conversation in an unusually serious tone.

"Mom, there's something I've got to tell you."

"What is it, dear?" she inquired anxiously.

"I don't quite know how to break this to you," he said, his voice sounding strained. "But you won't be meeting Lynne."

Not believing what she was hearing, Liz managed to blurt out, "What? Why not? Derrick, what's wrong?"

"Lynne left me last night," he blurted out.

"Oh, no! Derrick, are you all right?" she asked incredulously.

"I'm still sort of in a state of shock, but I'm alive," was his response.

"What happened? You two always sounded so happy?"

"It's a long story. I can't begin to tell it on the phone."

"Do you still want me to come?"

"Oh, yes, I need you to come more than ever." he said emphatically.

"Then meet me in Columbia as planned."

"Thanks, Mom. I can hardly wait to see you."

"I'll see you a week from today. Don't forget to meet me."

"Mom, you know me better than that." He said somewhat peevishly. "Bye, Mom."

"Love you, son. Perhaps you will have made up by then," Liz wished out loud.

In a state of anxiety, Liz made the trip to lend comfort to Derrick in his loss. She kept praying that both Derrick and Lynne would meet her flight. When she arrived in Columbia where Derrick met her plane, she was relieved to find her son in what appeared to be fairly good spirits.

When she first deplaned, he wasn't at the gate to meet her. Her plane was to have arrived mid-afternoon, but because she missed her connection in Denver, she arrived about 11:00 pm. In those days before cell phones, she didn't even know if Arif had been able to get a hold of Derrick to inform him of her new arrival time. After waiting for about ten minutes in the nearly deserted airport, she decided to overnight in Columbia and connect with Derrick the next day.

She was calling a hotel when someone touched her on the arm. She looked over her shoulder to see Derrick all smiles and looking more than a little sheepish. Apparently, he and a buddy were in the airport bar and didn't realize that her plane had landed.

The entire time they were together Liz was impressed with how well her son seemed to be taking his separation from Lynne. Even though he was thinner than she had remembered and was smoking heavily, both of which she attributed to the trauma of the separation, he seemed to be in a fairly upbeat frame of mind.

Although she didn't get a clear answer as to why they had separated, she was left with the impression that Lynne had cheated on him. It was obvious that he didn't want to talk about it much, and she decided not to pry.

Since he was at loose ends and in a dead-end job, Liz suggested that perhaps he should think of relocating somewhere near her in California or in New Mexico where his father lived or somewhere else where he knew someone. His response was that he would never leave Missouri as long as Avis, his grandmother, was alive. Now that Avis was a widow, he was having a much better relationship with her and felt a responsibility for keeping an eye on her. That he felt such a deep sense of responsibility toward his grandmother was a trait Liz didn't wish to discourage.

Since this was her first time to visit Derrick's new place, he very proudly gave her the grand tour of the ten-acre spread. Blackie, his devoted German Shepard, accompanied them on the tour. Derrick had planted hundreds of seedling trees, many of which were starting to take hold. He had built a diving board at one end of the large pond that occupied the middle of his property. They walked to the far side of the pond where the woods became so thick that one almost needed a machete to cut a path through. They hid in the woods in the hope of seeing some deer, but none appeared. He showed her several outbuildings. One, that had been a barn, housed a Corvette that he was planning to restore.

Derrick was proud of the history behind his house. It had been a bootlegger's shack during the Depression and had the perfect location on a back road deep in the Missouri countryside for such illicit activity.

Seeing that his mother was staring at the shed behind the house that was overflowing with mostly beer and some pop cans, Derrick explained that he had recently hosted a weekend party. Liz thought to herself that it must have been quite a party.

Derrick interrupted Liz's thoughts by announcing, "Now for the inside. The front steps are a little steep, so be careful."

"Don't forget that your mother hikes in the Sierra Nevada where it's mostly straight up."

"Yeah, I'll bet that you can out hike me."

"Since I've never been a smoker, I probably can."

"Somehow, I knew you'd say that. Dad said that you were always nagging him about smoking."

They were standing in the enclosed entry porch where it was obvious that he stored a lot of his camping and hunting gear. He opened the door to the front room. With obvious pride, he ushered his mother in.

"I didn't do a lot to the front room except for adding the pine paneling."

"Which I like very much," Liz interjected. "It adds a certain warmth and coziness."

"Yeah, it was just dirty white sheetrock before. I wish I had some before and after pictures."

"I'm sure that the paneling helps with the insulation also."

"Yeah, essentially this place had no insulation except for what I added. "Come see the bathroom. I completely redid it. Oh, by the way, this is the only bathroom."

Liz was surprised to see how modern it was with all new fixtures, brass faucets and trim and new lighting. "Son, did you do all this work by yourself?"

"All by my lonesome. Would you believe that Lynne hated what I did with the bathroom?'

"What's not to like?"

"Ah, she didn't like my choice of fixtures, lights and wall color. I had done most of the work before she moved in, so I just bought what I could get on sale with my budget. I guess it wasn't fancy enough for her taste."

As they walked toward the kitchen, Derrick cautioned, "I still have a lot of work to do on the kitchen. Also, I have to wait to save up some more money to buy new appliances."

Many of the cupboards had their doors removed, and it was apparent that he was in the middle of refinishing the cabinets. For a small kitchen it had a lot natural light from two windows and a fairly good layout. Outside he had remodeled the front and back porches.

Liz, brimming with pride in her son's work commented, "I had no idea that you had such a talent for remodeling. Have you thought about making a business of it?"

"That's very kind of you to say, Mom, but I'm really not that good. I just like to do things with my hands."

"Derrick, to speed things along, I wish you'd let me help you with some of the remodeling expenses. I'm so proud of what you've done."

"Gee, thanks, Mom, that means a lot. It's good to have your vote of confidence. I'll let you know if you can help. Now that Lynne is gone, my living expenses should drop dramatically."

Because Lynne had taken the stove, TV, and much of the furniture, the furnishings were very sparse. Otherwise the place emanated a rustic warmth, and with some additional furniture, it would be very cozy. Derrick told her of some plans he had for building some furnishings. He showed her a couple of end tables and a coffee table he had made and the dresser he had refinished. Liz left Derrick's cabin in the woods feeling happy that he had a house and land that he took pride in and loved so much.

The highlight of the 1987 visit came when Derrick took his mother to go swimming at a gravel pit on a friend's farm. Liz was not prepared for the crowd of young people, mostly in their twenties and thirties, who were there. There were at least a dozen divorcees with their children and many seemingly unattached young men. With her there, Liz was sure that everyone was on his or her best behavior. Even though the beer was flowing, no doubt it would have flowed a lot harder if she hadn't been present. It was wonderful to meet so many of Derrick's friends and see how well liked he was. After many years, whenever she returned to Middletown, invariably she would meet someone who revealed that they had met before--that they met that wonderful afternoon long ago at the pit.

After the swim, Derrick and Liz returned to his place and had a barbecue. On the way home, they stopped by to see an elderly man, Mr. Mattmann, whose wife was in the hospital. Derrick knew the man from work and was very concerned about him and his wife. It was obvious that he made a habit of stopping to check on Mr. Mattmann and that it was much appreciated.

After years of living alone, Derrick had turned into a fairly good cook. When he refused to let his mother do anything toward getting dinner ready, she made herself comfortable on the steps of the back porch with Blackie, and his cat, Whitie. For the special occasion, he opened a bottle of German white wine. Contentedly sipping her wine, she watched him grill the garlic bread, corn and steaks as she soaked in the August twilight.

The evening was filled with the heavy fragrances and humming and buzzing sounds of summer in Missouri. Again. the heron was sitting in the tall, thin ghost of a dead tree by the pond, and the fireflies were beginning to make their magical appearance. It was a perfect end to a perfect day.

From what Liz could discern, Derrick felt as contented as she.

When he asked her what she missed most about Missouri, she quickly replied, "You and my parents most of all, then my friends from high school, the corn fields, the coming of a thunderstorm, the four seasons, the fireflies, and the singing of the locusts on a hot summer night."

His response was, "I like it here so much that I can't imagine living anywhere else."

She laughed and said, "Now you're talking the way my father used to talk. He thought that Middletown was the most ideal place in the whole country to live. He used to say that you could travel 1000 miles east and be in New York, 800 miles west and be in Denver, 800 miles south and be on the Gulf and 800 miles north and be in Canada. How could there be a more ideal location?"

"Would you ever want to move back here, Mom?"

"No, I like being close to the mountains and the ocean. You're all that's left here for me."

He hesitated a minute and then asked, "Mom, maybe I shouldn't ask you this, but why did you and my dad break up?"

Even though this was a question that Liz had been expecting him to ask for years, she never resolved in her mind how she would answer it. Because she didn't wish to say unkind things to him about his father and how she thought he loved his hobby of flying much more than he loved her or his infant son, she said, "The biggest mistake I ever made was getting married too young. I was only 20 and somewhat spoiled. Your father and I simply weren't mature enough to cope with the challenges of married life and trying to finish college."

"Yeah, I can relate to that. I was 24 when Lynne and I got married and look at the mess I made of it. I sure wouldn't rush into marriage again. Not to change the subject, but these steaks are done, so let's grab some plates," he said as he transferred the meat to a platter.

Relieved that he appeared to accept her explanation at face value, she literally jumped up from the steps and went to help him carry the food to the picnic table. As they ate, twilight gave way to darkness, and the fireflies began their nighttime dances. Fortunately, there were citronella candles at the table to keep most of the mosquitoes at bay.

After dinner they went inside, and Derrick took her down the narrow, creaky stairs to the basement to show her an antique desk that he was refinishing. It was obvious that to him it was a labor of love. Other than a love for the outdoors, Derrick and Liz didn't have a lot in common, so she was pleased to see that they shared an appreciation for antique furniture.

They went upstairs where he looked for something that he wanted to show her. He came out of his bedroom carrying a tattered newspaper, which he said he found in the wall of a room that he was remodeling. The reason he wanted to show it to her was because it was dated 1963, and he thought that she might know some of the people who were mentioned in the bridal section.

Looking through, she recognized familiar local names but didn't know anyone in particular. Sensing disappointment that she didn't recognize anyone, he returned the paper to his bedroom.

One night during her visit, Liz recalled driving down Hannibal Street with Derrick when he said, "Hey, Mom, there goes Alex's girl, Paula Carlson."

"Where?"

"In that car next to us," he said as he reached for a cigarette.

It was dark, so Liz could barely see whom he was talking about.

"She's divorced and has a little boy. She's really pretty and very nice."

"Do I detect some romantic interest in this girl?" she queried.

"Naw, Mom, not really. Maybe if she wasn't my best friend's girl, I'd ask her out."

"I'm sure that there are lots of nice, unattached girls who would like to go out with you."

"Maybe and maybe not."

"Why do you say that?"

"Because around Middletown and these parts, I seem to have a bad reputation," he revealed.

Thinking that he was being facetious, Liz laughed and let the conversation drop.

Derrick was always anxious for his mother to meet his many friends, so one night he took her to one of his favorite hangouts, Burt's Place, for dinner. The proprietor, Burt Shaw, came to take their dinner order.

After introducing himself, he said, "Derrick, I've come to meet your new girlfriend."

Derrick tried not to laugh and replied, "Burt, I want you to meet my mother, Elizabeth Azmi."

"Are you serious? I thought that you had started dating older women." Then he looked at me in all seriousness and said, "You look far too young to be Derrick's mother."

She laughed and responded, "Burt, you really flatter me. If you aren't joking, then you need to get your eyes checked. I am Derrick's mother. It's really nice to meet you."

After she returned to Sacramento, Derrick reminded her on the phone of the meeting with Burt and said that Burt really thought that she was his date. Derrick was really amused by the incident.

1987 Class Reunion

As it did ten years earlier, her 1987 trip coincided with her class reunion. Again, she reluctantly attended, but had a somewhat better time because the music wasn't too loud. She went with Jill and Raphael, who were ready to leave by 10:00, which wasn't too soon for Liz. The next day when Derrick came to pick her up, he found it difficult to believe that she had gone to bed by 11:00 the night of the reunion.

Other highlights of that trip included the four-wheel drive excursion Derrick took Liz on his property and eating sweet corn straight out of the field. Derrick had a clunker of a pickup truck and was very proud of what he could do with it.

Normally Liz thought of central Missouri as being relatively flat but was to learn that Derrick had an extremely steep hill on the back of his property. Because of the difficult access, he drove his mom to the hill through a neighbor's property. Being from the West, she wasn't prepared for a thrill, but her adrenaline was really flowing by the time they made it to the top of Derrick's hill. He was obviously delighted and grinning from ear to ear when he saw that he could give her such a four-wheeling thrill on his property.

As they were exiting his neighbor's farm after the four-wheel adventure, Derrick, knowing how much his mother craved good sweet corn, stopped, got out and disappeared into the cornfield. Soon he returned bearing a big grin and several ears of corn.

"Here, Mom, try this," he said handing her two ears of corn.

"I'll be happy to, after we cook it."

"Mom, you don't need to cook it," he replied as he shucked an ear and started eating.

Even though Liz had been raised in central Missouri, she had never heard of, much less experienced eating raw corn-on-the-cob. Seeing Derrick enjoying it so much, she shucked an ear and sank her teeth into it and blurted, "Oh, Derrick, this is sooo good!"

It was delicious as only fresh-picked yellow sweet corn can be. They happily sat there in the truck and ate two ears apiece.

Upon returning to Sacramento, Liz called Derrick to let him know that she had arrived safely. She was surprised to learn that on the afternoon of her departure he had fallen off a pulley that he had rigged up over his pond and had bruised his kidneys. In his typical macho fashion, he assured her that Dr. Aquino had given him good care and that he would be fully recovered after a few days of rest.

The incident made her recall how Derrick had always been an "accident waiting to happen." Just a few days earlier, when they were taking a ride in the country near his place, he pointed out a bridge where he had totaled his car as a teenager. That revelation came as a total shock to Liz, because no one had ever informed her of the accident. Apparently, he walked away from the accident with only a few scratches, so why should he bother to mention it? When he saw how upset she was about it, his response was, "Mom, you worry too much."

Over the next few months when she called, he complained bitterly about the problems he was having with Lynne and her family. From what he described, their separation had turned very ugly. Although Liz never knew the particulars, he spoke of being harassed and threatened by her father and other members of her family. Apparently, there were many unpleasant scenes over belongings, money, and other unspecified matters.

She thought it strange if Lynne had instigated the separation, as Liz had been led to believe, that she and her family were being so uncooperative in the settlement. Liz felt as though she was missing a major piece of information to help her better understand what was going on. She thought about calling Jill to see if she knew why there was such bitterness on the part of the Hunsakers, but she decided not to.

Deep down, she was starting to suspect that perhaps Derrick had cheated on Lynne. About all Liz could do from a distance with her limited understanding of the situation was to be a good listener and to encourage Derrick to get on with his life. He seemed much relieved when the divorce was finalized, and so was Liz.

After that visit and his divorce, Liz and Derrick became closer than ever. He never wrote, but she did. They stayed in touch by phone every month or two or three, and she saw him more frequently.

Chapter 4
1989

I know the next time Aunt Liz saw Derrick was in the autumn of 1989 when she took a trip to Middletown after a professional meeting in St. Louis. I heard the ride from St. Louis to Jefferson City in a nine-seat commuter plane was really turbulent. They were caught in a windstorm and Aunt Liz was so nauseous she had to hold on to the bottom of her seat. There were no armrests to hold. She told Jill and Alex it reminded her of the time she reluctantly went flying in a Piper Cub with Derrick's father. That was really early in their short marriage.

When Uncle Peter started doing some simple maneuvers, Aunt Liz ended up vomiting all over her seat and the floor of the plane. That was the last time she flew in such a small plane. Ironically, my grandmother, Anita, went flying in the Cub with Uncle Peter every time she got a chance. Poor Aunt Liz and my grandfather were the ones who suffered from motion sickness. Aunt Liz picks up the story about Derrick during this trip.

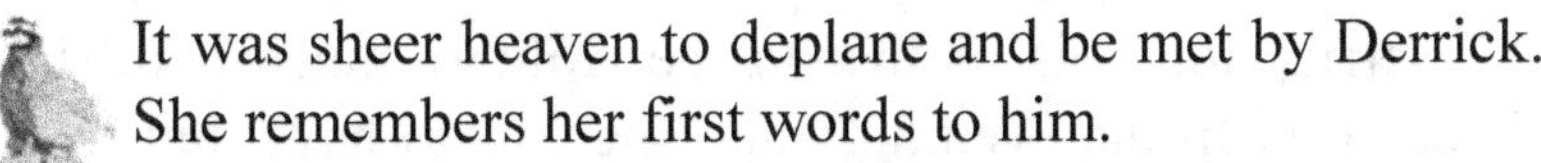 It was sheer heaven to deplane and be met by Derrick. She remembers her first words to him.

"Son, I must love you a lot to fly on that crop duster to see you."

"Why, Mom, what happened? You look a little pale."

"We encountered some really bad turbulence. Hasn't it been windy here?"

"Not too bad. There was a little lightning and some wind--that's all."

Walking toward the parking lot, she observed that Derrick looked a lot older and more mature. The two years since his separation and divorce had left their mark. He still looked very handsome even though he was a little too thin and was dressed as usual in tattered jeans and a faded plaid shirt. He always reminded her of a tall version of Robert Redford or more recently of Hollywood idol, Brad Pitt. This time she knew that she was going to meet his new girlfriend, Paula Carlson, with whom he had been living for several months. She was the young lady he had drawn to Liz's attention on the previous trip.

As they drove from Jefferson City toward Middletown, she could discern that Paula had given Derrick a new outlook on life. After they started living together, he quit his job at the park and went to work for an electrical firm in Jefferson City. The job didn't pay a great deal, but it did offer some benefits. It had been good career move for him. Even though it did involve working indoors most of the time and some paperwork, he seemed quite happy with his new career.

Derrick told her about Paula's little boy, Brad, who was five years old and very sweet but spoiled. He said that Liz wouldn't meet him because it was the weekend, and Brad spent weekends with his father. Brad had some health problems, which probably explained why he was so spoiled.

Derrick took his mother to the Holiday Inn, where she checked in. In the evening when she was to have dinner at his home, she would meet Paula. Derrick went with her to her room, lounged on the bed and watched as she unpacked.

Liz was anxious to show him the latest local history book on the California gold country that she had written. When he leafed through it and commented, "Frankly, Mom, this looks awfully boring," she immediately realized that he wouldn't appreciate having the copy that she had brought for a gift. Derrick's life was all action in the here and now, so she should have known that he would find her historic reference books dull.

Liz was very excited at the prospect of meeting Paula. When they pulled up to the house, she came out to meet them. Paula was even more beautiful than she was in the picture Derrick had shown Liz. She and Derrick made a handsome contrast, her with her long, dark hair, olive skin and sparkling dark eyes and Derrick with his light brown hair, fair skin and hazel eyes. Liz liked her smile and felt that at long last Derrick had found a good woman.

Upon entering the house, Liz couldn't help but notice signs of Paula's presence everywhere. There was furniture to replace what Lynne had taken. Many pictures adorned the walls. There were colorful throw pillows on the sofa and floor and ornaments on the tables and shelves. Her son Brad's toys were neatly stacked in the corner. Liz hadn't seen the place looking so neat and giving off such warmth and charm.

As Liz headed toward the kitchen, Derrick stopped her and said, "Mom, you stay out of the kitchen and leave the work to Paula and me."

Trying not to sound disappointed, she acquiesced, "Well, if you insist."

"Really. mom, there's not room for three in the kitchen."

Liz sat in the dining area where she could see and hear what was going on in the kitchen. Now that Derrick had finished the kitchen remodel, it was the showplace of the house. Noticing the dozen beautiful red roses on the dining table, she stuck her head in the kitchen and commented, "I'm admiring and smelling the beautiful roses. Are they for a special occasion?"

Paula answered, "It's our second anniversary of being together made even more special by you being here."

"Oh my! I feel so privileged to be here to share your special day. I hope I'm not intruding."

Paula was quick to answer, "Liz. we are positively thrilled that you are here." She stopped what she was doing in the kitchen and came over to give Liz a warm hug.

Then she went back to helping Derrick prepare dinner. It looked as though Derrick was more of a cook than Paula, but she was trying very hard. The menu was waldorf salad, flank steak, au gratin potatoes, green beans, and brownies and ice cream. Before they started eating Liz made a toast to the loving couple and wished them many years of happiness together. It turned out to be a lovely dinner, complete with candlelight, music. wine and animated conversation. The whole room radiated with warmth and affection.

In an attempt to preserve the magic of that evening, Liz took pictures of Derrick and Paula in the kitchen and sitting at the table. To Liz it was obvious from their every movement that they were very much in love. That night she went to bed feeling thankful that at last her son had found someone with whom to make a life. The memory of that magical evening was to remain etched in her memory forever.

The next day Liz, Derrick and Paula drove in Paula's car to Kirksville, where Liz's cousin, Joanne, her husband, Bill, and their disabled son lived on a farm that had been in the family for over 100 years. One of Liz's fondest childhood experiences occurred in 1951 when she was 12 years old and went to stay on the farm for a week with Joanne and Bill shortly after they were married. As they drove up the long lane to the farmhouse, so many fond memories were rekindled by the sight of the old barn and Civil War-era farmhouse. She was flooded with memories of how Joanne and she picked wild asparagus along the railroad tracks, and Joanne gave her the thrilling responsibility of collecting eggs from the henhouse and barn every morning.

It was during that week that Liz had her one and only experience of milking a cow. Once was enough as far as Liz was concerned. Liz had loved exploring the loft of the historic barn and playing with the numerous kittens that lived there. Even using the outhouse was a fun adventure for her at that age (except in the middle of the night.) Another novel experience was using the hand pump for the well and pumping the sweet, cold water for household use. She remembered baking her first cake under Joanne's patient supervision. It was a banana cake with chopped walnuts, and they used oleo, the predecessor to margarine, in it. On Saturday night Joanne, Bill and Liz went to town for dinner and then saw the movie ***Born Yesterday***, starring Judy Holliday and William Holden. Now that Liz no longer had a family home in Middletown, in many ways returning to the farm and its childhood memories was like going home again.

It overjoyed Liz to see Joanne, Bill, and their son, Carl. She hadn't seen them since 19 years earlier at her father's funeral. It wasn't long before Derrick started watching the Missouri football game with Carl, and Bill and Paula struck up a lively conversation. Joanne showed Liz all the remodeling that had been done to the house, and then they started looking at heirlooms and family keepsakes. After no longer having her parents' home to return to, everything about the farm took on a special significance to Liz.

Even though Joanne was Liz's cousin, because she was 15 years older, she always seemed more like a second mother or aunt to Liz. It was so wonderful to be with her again. She had heart surgery a year or two before and appeared very fragile to Liz. She and Bill always worked so hard taking care of Carl, who had been physically disabled since birth. They hardly ever got to take a vacation or have any time to themselves, but they never complained.

When Joanne and Liz rejoined the others, they all sat around the kitchen table to partake in Joanne's hot apple cider and fresh-baked cookies whose tantalizing fragrances had permeated the house and fired their appetites. For Liz it was so wonderful to be sitting there with so many of her loved ones. If only Arif could have been part of the scene, she would have known total happiness.

All too soon the magic of the moment was shattered when Derrick remarked that it was starting to get dark and that they should be on their way. Since part of the drive home was on a winding, two-lane road, he was wise to want to get started. Reluctantly, Liz said goodbye to Joanne and her family. Judging from the animated conversation and laughter, Liz wasn't the only one who had a wonderful time that magical afternoon on the farm.

That evening the three of them went to dinner at the Four Corners, which had been "the" place to eat and be seen in Middletown since Liz was a teenager. The place held memories of her first date; of prom night and graduation night; of Sunday buffets with her parents and, after her mother's death, of Sunday buffets with her father and Derrick; of dinner with her father and Arif; of dinner with various relatives and friends after her father's death; of breakfast with Derrick and his grandmother; of dinner with

Derrick and Tammy—oh, so many fond, bittersweet memories.

That evening Paula shared with Liz the problems she had with Derrick's grandmother and the rest of the Hoffman family. Twice she had gone with Derrick to his grandmother's home for Sunday dinner, and both times she had been snubbed and humiliated by various members of the family. Derrick said that it was so uncomfortable that he had promised Paula that he would never again subject her to that treatment.

He added that it wasn't anything personal against Paula, because ever since his divorce it happened every time he took a girl with him to his grandmother's for Sunday dinner. Remembering some daunting experiences with the Hoffmans, Liz assured Paula that she had her complete sympathy and understanding.

Paula was with Derrick and Liz most of the time that visit, but they did go to the cemetery twice by themselves. On the second cemetery visit, Liz remembers sitting in the truck seeking refuge from the chilly, end-of-October wind. Their time together was getting short, so Liz thought she could wait no longer to follow through on the unpleasant responsibility of having to tell Derrick that Arif and she were rewriting their living trust and that he wasn't to be included in the financial distribution of their estate.

She began by saying, "Derrick, there's something I've been meaning to tell you."

Detecting her serious tone, he inquired "Mom, what is it? Is everything all right?"

When she explained the situation about the trust, she added, "Son, I am not at all happy about this, but I don't really blame Arif because he feels that your and my relationship is pretty much one-way." Quickly Liz added, "Don't get me wrong. I don't feel that it's one-sided, but I can understand why Arif thinks it is, since I'm always the one doing all of the writing and calling."

To Liz's relief, Derrick didn't seem to be too surprised to hear about Arif's interpretation of their relationship. He turned to her and said, "Mom, I'm truly sorry that I haven't lived up to my responsibilities as a son. You have my word that from now on I will keep in closer touch." He paused, drew deeply on his cigarette, exhaled and continued. "I never write letters. Quite honestly, the only mail I ever send are my bill payments."

Liz tried to lighten the situation by joking, "I must admit that I thought your writing arm was permanently broken."

Then she told him that Arif had asked her to ask him if there was anything of theirs that he would like to have willed to him. Liz was hoping that he would say that he would like some of the antique china or furniture. After giving it some thought, he responded that the one thing he would really like to have was her parents' antique clock collection. Liz was immensely pleased with his response and felt that Arif would be also. She informed him that the willing of the clocks to him would be included as an addendum to their living trust.

He looked relieved and said, "Mom, I really don't like talking about this. It's too morbid. You're too young to be talking about dying. Someday soon I hope to make you a grandmother. Would you like that, Mom?"

"I'd love it, but you have to find a good wife first."

"And then you can come and babysit."

"You know that I've never pushed you to have children, but, of course, I'm looking forward to babysitting."

"I'll try not to make you wait too many more years. You know, I think my life would have been very different if I hadn't been forced to attend that military academy."

"Oh, in what respect?" she queried, trying not to show her surprise.

"I might have finished college and have a better job. I just hated the discipline of that place and spent years rebelling against it," he said with a trace of anger in his eyes and voice.

"When I used to write to you there, I guess I didn't realize how unhappy you were."

"Well, I wasn't very good about answering your letters, so how could you know?"

"Let's look at the bright side. You seem to like your new job, and it has pretty good benefits."

"Yeah, it's a big improvement in that respect over working for the park. I guess things could be a lot worse, but let's face it, I'm always going to be just a laborer," he said as he lit another cigarette.

"Not everyone can have a management job. I see nothing wrong with being a laborer. Besides, you wouldn't be happy with a desk job," Liz countered.

"Yeah, I always thought I'd like to be a forest ranger, but when I looked in to it, I found out I'd have to have a degree in forestry and still would have to get on a long waiting list."

"Yes, I've heard that those jobs are really difficult to get."

Changing the subject, he said, "Come on, Mom, let's walk over to the graves."

Liz had spent weeks dreading having to break the news to Derrick about his not being included in their living trust. The relief she felt after telling him was so immense, making her wish that she had told him earlier in their visit.

After they visited her parents' graves, he asked her if she would mind seeing where his paternal grandfather was buried. Even though she wasn't thrilled with the prospect, she readily consented. The site was in another cemetery five miles from where her parents were buried.

As they neared the Hoffman plot, Liz's eyes became transfixed on the magnificent oak tree shading it with its remaining autumn leaves. The tree appeared to be at least a century old. Then her eyes were drawn to Theodore Hoffman's marker, bearing the Eagle Scout emblem. Derrick's paternal grandfather was a regional leader in the Boy Scouts, and Derrick inherited from him a love for scouting.

As they stood by the grave, she asked, "Do you come here often?"

"No, Mom, hardly ever, but I wanted to today with you. You know what I like about this place?"

"No. What?"

"I just love the old oak tree next to Grandpa's grave."

She gazed again at the majestic oak and replied, "Yes, it is truly awe-inspiring. It's very beautiful and peaceful here. I'm glad you brought me."

"It just doesn't seem fair," he said pensively.

"What doesn't seem fair?" she inquired.

"Oh, I was just thinking how grandpa never drank or smoked and he didn't live as long as his friend, Jim Brainard, who's buried over there," he said as he pointed to a nearby marker, "who smoked and drank on a regular basis. Also, Grandpa Springmeyer didn't drink much or smoke, and he died young."

"Life isn't always fair in that respect. I think it has more to do with the genes than anything else. Most of my family died relatively young, and they didn't have many vices that I'm aware of."

"I remember that Grandpa Springmeyer was only 66 when he died. How old was Grandma?"

"Only 62," Liz answered sadly as she reflected on all the aunts and uncles, four on my father's side and two on my mother's side, who had died in their forties and fifties or even earlier. "In my youth, I remember attending so many funerals for relatives."

Changing the subject, he asked, "You know what's really strange?"

"No. What?"

"Even though I've spent a lot more time with my dad, somehow I feel closer to you and that I can tell you anything."

"Son, I'm so glad you feel that way," Liz said, trying not to sound too surprised. Since the Hoffmans had raised him, she had always assumed that he felt a closer bond to them and his dad. "It means a great deal to me. I feel very close to you too. I'm glad we're seeing more of each other than we used to."

"Yeah, me too."

Soon it was time for Derrick to take her to Jefferson City to catch her flight home. That time she departed feeling not quite so sad, because now Derrick had Paula to brighten and lend stability to his life. She prayed that Paula wouldn't be intimidated too much by Derrick's grandmother and the rest of the Hoffmans. Little did she dream that the next time she was to return to Middletown, it would be for Derrick's funeral.

Liz was getting stiff from sitting and got up to check to see if Arif had returned from the store. He hadn't, so she surmised that he had run into someone he knew and perhaps had gone for coffee or had stopped by the library. It was still snowing lightly, so he shouldn't have any problem with the roads. She fed the cat, made another cup of tea and returned to her office. So far she wasn't finding her reading to be depressing, and she was anxious to get back to it.

Chapter 5
1990 - Indian Hills

Derrick never visited Aunt Liz and Uncle Arif. After he was no longer living with his grandparents, Aunt Liz invited him several times, but his usual excuse was that he couldn't get away from work. Aunt Liz didn't press too hard for him to come., She knew, to Uncle Arif, Derrick was a painful reminder of her previous marriage. She wanted them to become good friends, but she thought that she had time on her side and that eventually it would happen.

To Aunt Liz, knowing Derrick was synonymous with liking him and she was right. She always thought that if he and Uncle Arif could meet under better circumstances, they would develop a good relationship. With every other visit, it was at the worst of times, like at her father's funeral. The stresses were so bad that she and Uncle Arif were fighting, and even though Derrick was only nine years old, she was sure he could sense the strain between them. This time when Uncle Arif and Derrick met, she wanted the circumstances to be as close to perfect as possible.

My Aunt Liz was patient. She was willing to wait as long as was necessary for near-perfect conditions. And things were becoming better between Uncle Arif and Derrick. Sometimes when Derrick called, Uncle Arif would answer the phone, and the two of them would have a nice chat before Aunt Liz would get on the phone. Progress, slow as it was, seemed to be made.

Little did Aunt Liz know, but when the 1980s ended, her life would never be the same again. The new decade started out on a bad note. In January Uncle Arif became ill.

At first, they thought that it was a side effect of the flu and so did the doctor. After a number of appointments, Uncle Arif was prescribed an anti-inflammatory steroid that Aunt Liz grew to hate. At one point, he was able to get off the steroids, but before long symptoms returned with a vengeance. Larger doses of steroids were prescribed again.

Uncle Arif seemed to experience all of the side effects of the drug that were possible at one time and sometimes simultaneously. That included being hyperactive, he couldn't sleep, then he'd have mood swings and other personality changes and depression. Aunt Liz tried to tell herself that it was "just the medication" but it was hard for her to find any consolation in that explanation.

To add to her distress, Derrick and Paula had a falling out and Paula moved. Aunt Liz was shocked to find out that Paula left while Derrick was recuperating from hernia surgery. As with Lynne, Derrick didn't seem to want to talk about what had happened.

As fate would have it, Aunt Liz heard Derrick's version of the story the last time she saw him before his death, but she wouldn't know Paula's side until much later. Until then Aunt Liz developed some theories about why Paula moved out, and she no longer held Derrick totally blameless. Fortunately, she never asked me if I knew anything.

Aunt Liz was honored to have the hospital library where she worked named after her. Uncle Arif gave a sizable contribution to the hospital where she worked. In September of that year, there was a naming reception in her honor.

When Derrick heard about the naming, he wanted to attend the reception, but Aunt Liz persuaded him to hold off. Derrick was so proud of his mom. He wished he could have been more like her. What he didn't know was that Aunt Liz wanted him to come, but the timing was not good for so many reasons. Primarily, Uncle Arif was not at all well and would have a difficult enough time coping with the excitement and confusion of the reception. Derrick's presence would only make it more complicated. I guess she even asked Uncle Arif not to go through with the reception, but he was adamant about having it.

Two of her cousins from back east were going to attend and would be staying with them. Aunt Liz didn't feel they could handle much more with Uncle Arif being so sick. And besides, no one in Sacramento had ever met Derrick. Many of them were not even aware he existed.

Aunt Liz dreamed of a time when Derrick would come to stay for several days, not just the weekend as he was planning, and be the ONLY guest. A reception with close to 300 attendees plus a sick husband was definitely not the proper stage for his first visit.

Not To mention that Aunt Liz was really apprehensive about how Uncle Arif would react to Derrick's beer drinking and smoking. Derrick was good about always smoking outdoors, but he probably would want a beer once in a while. Beer was something they NEVER had in their house.

So, Derrick got a letter from Aunt Liz (remember, no cell phones or texting at that time). She suggested that at the end of October Derrick and she could meet in Dallas where she would be attending a professional meeting. Then they could drive to Oklahoma to visit her brother. "As the three of them hadn't been together since Derrick was a baby, it would be a most wonderful reunion", she had written to Derrick

The week before the reception, Derrick called to say that he couldn't get off work to attend the reception but that he could meet her in Dallas. I know Aunt Liz was relieved that he wasn't coming for the reception. But she was really excited at the idea of the two of them going to Oklahoma. From what I heard, Derrick seemed excited too. He had a friend to visit in Dallas, so he was going to drive down and spend a few days with his friend (no it wasn't a girlfriend) before meeting Aunt Liz. Derrick told Aunt Liz "it would be a much-needed vacation, the first in over a year." I'm not sure if that surprised Aunt Liz or not.

That fall, Uncle Arif was put on even higher doses of the anti-inflammatory steroids he needed. Unfortunately, he became extremely difficult. If you have read anything about colitis and Chrohn's disease, which is what Uncle Arif's ultimate diagnosis was, it did not give Aunt Liz much hope for a healthy future for him unless he underwent very major surgery. I guess the trip to Dallas and Oklahoma was really the only bright spot for her on the horizon. That was tempered with her concern about leaving Uncle Arif alone for over a week. She was pretty conflicted.

I always admired Aunt Liz too. She was the past president of the society so she had to chair the business meeting. It meant she had to do a fair amount of preparation and stay focused. She told Derrick later that even during that meeting, she had a hard time concentrating on anything but the impending meeting with him. That made him feel pretty good. Aunt Liz was also very worried about Uncle Arif being alone. Every evening she called him and was thankful that he seemed to be coping well by himself. Like I said before, "conflicted".

When she finally got through all the meetings, Derrick showed up a half hour late. He finally drove up in his blue pickup. I guess it was a bit of a surprise to Aunt Liz. She didn't recognize him at first. He had long hair and only resembled the Derrick she knew.

This is where we pick up again in Aunt Liz's story.

As she approached the entry, she ascertained that it was Derrick. After she met him at the entry, he hugged her and introduced her to his friend, Ken Mauer. The plan was for Ken to drive ahead of them until they found the turnoff to Oklahoma. They would have breakfast with Ken at that intersection and then be Oklahoma-bound.

At breakfast, Liz found out that Derrick and Ken had grown up together on the same street in Middletown. Ken had gone on to graduate from Washington University and became a stockbroker in Dallas. Even though he and Derrick didn't seem to have much in common, Liz sensed a very deep bond between them. It was always good to meet Derrick's friends. She found Ken to be more sophisticated than any of Derrick's friends whom she had previously met, but at the same time to be very laid back and likeable.

After lingering over breakfast, swapping stories about Middletown, they said their goodbyes to Ken and began the 300-mile drive to Indian Hills where Liz's brother, Rob, and his wife, Ellen, had lived since 1978. Over the years Liz had visited them in Indian Hills several times, and Derrick had stopped by to see them once on his way to see his father in New Mexico.

It was always a strange sensation to visit Rob and Ellen in Indian Hills, because Liz had been there once before with Peter and Derrick when he was a baby. Indian Hills was the town where Derrick's paternal grandmother, Avis Hoffman, had been born and raised. When Liz was there in 1963, it was to visit Derrick's great grandmother, who still had the family home there.

When Rob wrote that he and Ellen were moving from Minnesota to Indian Hills in search of a warmer climate, Liz was totally astonished. At that time, Rob hasd no idea that Liz had ever been there.

Now Derrick and Liz were driving toward her brother's home and the small Oklahoma town where Derrick had spent so much time as a little boy. Derrick seemed relaxed as though he had a good vacation in Dallas.

After lighting up, he said, "Mom, I can't thank you enough for coming up with the idea of meeting in Big D. Ken arranged a great vacation for me there."

"I'm really glad to hear that. What all did you do?"

"Oh, we just lazed around a lot. Ken has a really nice pad in the suburb where he works. He took me fishing and boating several times. There are some really nice lakes around not far from where he lives."

Yes, I've noticed them each time I have flown into Dallas, Did you go to any good restaurants?"

"We spent a couple of evenings in Old Town eating and partying. In fact, we were there last night."

"That was walking distance from where I stayed. I wish I could have joined you."

"I'm not sure you would have enjoyed the bar hopping and dancing."

"You're right about that."

Since Liz wasn't much of a party person, she always found that side of her son very difficult to understand. It didn't appear to be anything he had inherited from her side of the family or from the Hoffmans either.

To change the subject, she commented, "Derrick, I've never seen you with such long hair. At first I thought you were some Ozark woodsman visiting the big city."

Flashing a good-natured grin her way, he reminded her, "Mom. I thought that you knew that I usually got a haircut only twice a year, before Thanksgiving and sometime in between."

"I guess I forgot because I've always seen you soon after a cut."

"Yeah, well if I don't get it done before Thanksgiving, Avis threatens not to invite me for Thanksgiving dinner. Usually I get one before seeing you, but this time I ran out of time before leaving for Dallas."

"This time you're forgiven. Somehow, I'll get used to it and I love you anyway."

The first part of the drive on the interstate was flat and rather uninteresting, but it started to become scenic the minute they exited the interstate and turned north. It was the end of October, and the trees were at the height of their autumn splendor. After having lived in California for over 20 years, it was a treat to see brilliant autumn oranges and reds that hardly ever are seen in the West. The colors and happenings of that trip were to remain emblazoned in Liz's mind.

It was obvious that Derrick was very proud of the new truck he was driving. He purchased it six months before, and he informed her that he had rolled it once.

"Derrick, what do you mean, you rolled it?" she asked, not hiding her alarm.

"You know how treacherous the gravel roads can be, particularly if you round a corner too fast. Well, I took a corner too fast and skidded and the next thing I knew I was upside down in the ditch," he explained.

"Derrick, when did this happen? Why didn't you tell me?"

He laughed and said, "'Cause I walked away from it with a just few scratches."

"How can you be so casual about something so serious?" she asked incredulously.

He inhaled deeply on his cigarette before replying, "Mom, take it easy. You worry too much. That's why I don't tell you everything."

It was clear that Derrick was anxious to change the subject. It was such a beautiful day and their time together so precious that she tried to stop worrying out loud. Their route took them through sleepy villages and towns. Liz happened to notice a mileage sign for Broken Bow Lake. Rob had often mentioned that Broken Bow Lake was the most beautiful lake in Oklahoma, so she asked Derrick to go out of the way 20 miles to see it. It turned out to be well worth the detour.

In contrast to all the other Oklahoma lakes Liz had seen, Broken Bow was clear rather than a thick muddy red. She could tell it was the kind of place that Derrick liked. They were fortunate to be there on a day when hardly anybody else was to be seen. There were no boats on the lake and no other cars in the parking lot. They lingered for a long time at the spillway watching the clear water rushing over the rocky stream bed. It more resembled a rushing mountain creek than a Midwestern stream. Derrick commented how it reminded him of Current River in southern Missouri where he loved to go fishing and canoeing. He said that he would like to return to Broken Bow next year on a fishing trip with his friends.

They still had another 150 miles to go to her brother's place, so they reluctantly tore themselves away from the lake and continued the drive north. Soon it became more mountainous, which made the trip on the two-lane winding highway very slow. Neither of them seemed in a big hurry to get to Rob's. Liz felt they both knew that they would have their best chance to visit on the road.

Derrick seemed much more serious than Liz had ever seen him. He told her that part of his reason for taking this trip was "to sort things out." Then he started talking about Paula.

"Mom, no woman has ever hurt me the way she did when she walked out on me after my operation," he said as he broke open a new pack of cigarettes.

"I never really knew what happened, but I can't imagine the timing."

"Even when Lynne was unfaithful to me, it didn't hurt so much, but, damn it, Mom, I still love Paula and probably always will."

That was the first time Liz had heard him confirm what she had suspected--that Lynne had been unfaithful to him. He told her how Paula and he were still seeing each other but couldn't tolerate living together. He told her how Paula was overly protective of Brad and really spoiled him. Apparently, they had a lot of disagreements over how best to raise Brad.

Brad was having some kind of seizures that were probably epileptic, so most likely his health problems were not going to go away. Brad's father wasn't paying his child support and didn't help with Brad's many medical expenses. The picture he painted was one of him and Paula still being very much in love but not agreeing on much when it came to raising Brad. Since she felt that Derrick was really opening up with her, she let him do most of the talking.

"Mom, don't get me wrong. I really am very fond of Brad. I just don't want to see him grow up to be a sissy." Then he paused, lit another cigarette and cleared his throat before confiding, "Actually, one of our biggest problems is that one day I would like to have a child, but Paula is afraid to have any more children after the experience of having a child with so many health problems."

This revelation Liz sensed to be the real crux of their problem. Liz placed her hand on Derrick's arm and said, "Oh, Derrick, I'm so sorry! Has anyone else in Paula's family suffered from seizures?"

"She suspects that her great-grandmother did."

"Oh, I was hoping that it was someone on her ex's side."

"No such luck. On top of that, Avis hasn't accepted Paula or any of my girlfriends since Lynne because of her belief that once a person is married, he is married for life."

Liz remembered how Paula had talked about her unpleasant experiences with Derrick's grandmother and the rest of the family. Remembering how intimidating that family could be, she couldn't help but sympathize with Paula.

As they traveled over Winding Stair Mountain, he revealed that he had made provisions for Paula and Brad to be taken care of in the event that something happened to him. Liz couldn't believe that this was her happy-go-lucky son talking. He said that Paula and Brad would inherit his property if he died. At the time, Liz remembered that she didn't take too seriously what he was saying. Never before had Derrick talked to her about anything happening to him. Derrick, who was to turn 30 in January, was just at the threshold of life, so why were they talking about death?

Then Liz thought she knew why. The hostilities in the Persian Gulf between Iraq and the West were just beginning to heat up. Perhaps Derrick thought he would have to go to war. When she asked him, he said it was unlikely that, if the draft were reinstated, he would be drafted, because he was an only child. That made her feel somewhat better, but that conversation marked the beginning of her nagging fear that she was going to lose Derrick.

As they neared Indian Hills, they talked about other things. When he asked Liz what she thought of the Bush administration, she remembers carefully answering, "On domestic issues he's okay, but I don't agree much with his foreign policy."

Knowing his conservative upbringing, she figured that Derrick's and her politics would be at opposite ends of the political spectrum, so she was hoping to change the subject when he surprised her by asking, "Mom, do you go to church?"

"No, I haven't attended church since my university days, but somehow I feel much more religious or spiritual when I'm communing with nature than when I used to go through the motions of attending church."

"I understand where you're coming from. I sorta have much the same approach to religion. Avis is always trying to get me to go to church with her, so about once a year I go with her to keep peace. I think she's the only one in the family who goes much."

He took a drink of water and moved to another subject, "What I really want to do to improve my life is to become a journeyman electrician. What's keeping me is my concern about passing the competitive exam and also the financial and personal sacrifices that it would involve."

Liz couldn't hide her enthusiasm about this career path. "Derrick, that's a great opportunity! I wish you would make it your number one priority. What do you need to do to get things underway?"

"The annual exam is given in January and that would be pretty much my last chance because persons over 31 years of age aren't accepted in the program."

"Well, you can count on me to nag you to make the deadline. It must involve a lot of studying. Also, I can help you some with finances"

"Yeah, I've already checked out some books from the library about it. Thanks for your vote of confidence and offer of assistance."

Learning of this career opportunity for her son made Liz extremely happy.

When they stopped to get gas, Derrick bought a six-pack. He said he figured that her brother and his wife wouldn't have any beer in the house. He was right about that. Her brother used to do more than his share of drinking but stopped several years before. She thought it strange that she should have a son who had such a fondness for a beverage that she disliked so much. With her German background, somehow Liz escaped developing a taste for beer. Her father drank an occasional beer during the oppressively hot Missouri summers, but that was the extent to which she was exposed to beer drinking until she got married. Peter didn't drink that much beer either. Wine was about the only alcohol that Liz could tolerate.

Ever since he was in his mid-teens Derrick smoked and drank beer. He certainly wasn't exposed to smoking and drinking in his home environment, so she concluded that this was his way of rebelling against the strict environment of the military academy, which he attended for two years and hated so much.

It was mid-afternoon when they pulled into Rob's driveway. Liz was apprehensive, because the last time she and Arif visited Rob, he was in very poor health; so poor, in fact, that she wondered if she would ever see him again. Rob was her half-brother and was thirteen years her senior. In his younger days, he had abused his body with too much drinking and several motorcycle accidents. For the last ten years, ever since he had back surgery at the V.A. hospital, he had a number of medical issues and had to use a walker.

In spite of his disabilities, he and Ellen lived on a ten-acre wooded property along the Ozark River. Rob felt that the physical challenges of having several acres to maintain kept him in as good physical condition as was possible under the circumstances. He had owned the property for 12 years, and it was truly amazing to see the improvements that he made to it with his own hands. He cut paths through ubiquitous thorny vines and thickets to all points of the property, including the thick undergrowth by the river. When Arif and Liz were there a year before, Rob's health had deteriorated so much that many of his paths had grown over, which really saddened her. For this reason, Liz was full of apprehension about what was awaiting them at Rob's and Ellen's.

Ellen rushed out to meet them. She and Rob had married in 1975 when she was slightly over 50 and Rob was almost 50. It was Rob's first marriage and her third. Liz credited Ellen with making Rob into a relatively normal human being. Before she came into his life, he was totally self-centered with paranoid tendencies.

He was the cause of Liz's mother's nervous breakdown when she was in her 40s. Liz remembered how he slept with a gun under his pillow when he stayed overnight with her and Peter, and once he wrote a letter to her in blood. His scary behavior caused a lot of problems in her first marriage. Liz's mother always attributed his problematic behavior to her suspicion that he suffered brain damage at birth. Now that Rob was happily married, Liz really enjoyed his company, whereas previously she approached being with him with a great deal of trepidation. How she wished that her parents had lived to see him so happily married.

Ellen and Derrick had met once before when Derrick paid them a short visit in the mid-1980s when he was in Indian Hills to pick up some furniture from his great-grandmother's house. Inside the house, Liz and Derrick found Rob in his favorite chair with his cat on his lap. Much to Liz's relief, he looked a lot better than the last time she had seen him. He greeted her with, "Good to see you, Sis. Who is this handsome young man with you?"

Derrick shook Rob's hand and said, "Hi, Rob. Good to see you again. How are you?"

"Not bad for an old man with one foot in the grave and the other on a banana peel. How's the heart throb of Middletown?"

Derrick countered, "Aw, come on, it can't be that bad. You look in pretty good shape to me. What's this about the heart throb of Middletown?"

"I might look fairly healthy now, but you should be here when I'm having one of my whammies. Anyway, I always tease Sis about you being the heart throb of Middletown."

"What did she ever tell you to give you that impression?"

Rob chuckled and replied, "That would be revealing state secrets. What took you so long to get here?"

"Rob has been looking out the window and pacing up and down waiting for you since noon. You know what a worrywart he is," Ellen interjected.

Liz answered, "Upon Rob's recommendation, I talked Derrick into taking a side trip to Broken Bow Lake. It was wonderful."

"I wish I could have been there with you. It's a jewel of a lake."

Derrick added, "Yeah, I'm going to bring my fishing buddies down here to give it a try."

After putting their suitcases in the two spare bedrooms, Derrick opened a beer, and the four of them went outside to look around. It took a great deal of effort for Rob to negotiate the terrain with his walker, so after a while he and Ellen stayed behind while Derrick and Liz took a tour of the property. Rob had a dog of undetermined breed that took a liking to Derrick. The dog, Buffy, happily accompanied them on the tour. It was obvious that Buffy was missing accompanying Rob on walks around the property and was thrilled to be with them.

Rob and Ellen's land, with its river frontage, was the kind of place that Derrick loved. It had a fishpond, lots of woods and ample river frontage. Also, it had lots of snakes and countless wood ticks. Liz recalled that every time she returned from a visit, Arif had to check her over for ticks. One time they found several in her suitcase. The place was a haven for many kinds of birds. In particular, she loved hearing the bobwhite give its distinctive "Bob White" calls. It was a bird call that brought back many fond childhood memories for her.

By the time they returned from their walk, the short October daylight was fading, and they could smell the tempting fragrances of Ellen's cooking. Liz went to the kitchen to help, and Derrick asked if he could use the phone. From the kitchen she could overhear him talking to Paula.

Because Rob liked to eat early, they had dinner soon after Derrick finished his phone call. Ellen had cooked the meal she usually prepared for company--pot roast, brown gravy, carrots, mashed potatoes, rolls, salad, and toffee bars for dessert. The scene at the table reminded Liz of the setting exactly a year earlier at the farm when she, Derrick and Paula sat around Joanne's table having cookies and cider. As had happened on that occasion, a glow of love and togetherness enveloped the room. It was the first time that Liz could remember sitting at the same table together with her son and brother.

After Ellen's hearty dinner, everyone settled in the living room where the TV was always on. Liz and Derrick were more interested in talking than watching TV, but Rob was absorbed in "Wheel of Fortune." Derrick broke out another beer and went out on the front porch to have a smoke. Liz joined him to find that it was a pleasantly warm evening for the end of October. They had just started talking about Paula, when Rob called, "Sis, when are you coming in?"

"In just a minute," Liz called somewhat peevishly.

Derrick observed, "He sure keeps good tabs on you."

"He's just glad to see us. He doesn't mean anything by it."

"Well, you'd better go in to keep the peace. I'll see you in a little bit."

She reluctantly returned to the living room, and when, a few minutes, later Derrick came in, he asked if anyone would care if he watched "Twin Peaks." Rob said fine, but Liz could tell that he had another program he wanted to watch. Liz had heard a lot about "Twin Peaks," but had never seen it, so she found it somewhat more interesting than the game show. After "Twin Peaks" was over, Derrick took another cigarette break on the porch, and again Liz joined him.

Liz could sense that Rob didn't appreciate Derrick and her spending so much time on the porch, but she didn't care. Rob had always been somewhat paranoid in thinking that people were talking about him, so she was sure he thought that they were sitting on his porch talking about him.

This time Liz talked and Derrick listened. She started out saying, "I really dread going home to the problems caused by the medication Arif's on."

"Mom, you never said anything about any problem with Arif's medication. What's the matter?"

"I know. I don't like to complain. I just keep hoping that it will get better, but so far it hasn't. Rather it just seems to get worse."

"Tell me more about it. I don't understand."

She tried to keep back her tears as she explained. "Arif's whole personality has changed since the doctor put him on large doses of anti-inflammatory steroids last summer. He's very short fused, and he lashes out at me about the tiniest things like some food being burned or not cooked quite right. He takes everything I say the wrong way. Sometimes I feel that I can't say or do anything right."

"Have you talked to the doctor about it?"

Yes, once, about a month ago I called him the day of Arif's appointment. I told him how the steroid medication had altered Arif's personality and that he criticized me and picked fights with me all the time. He seemed very sympathetic and thanked me for informing him. Imagine my distress and dismay when Arif returned from the appointment and said that he was to take a higher dose of steroids!"

"Why do you think the doctor did that?"

"Because, from what I understand, other than surgery there aren't many alternate medications or methods of treating colitis. I've been urging Arif to see another doctor to get another opinion, but he just becomes angry when I bring up the subject. I think it's because he would have to undergo all kinds of unpleasant and painful tests if he changed doctors. Every time he has a colonoscopy it seems to bring on another attack."

"Have you tried to tell him that you realize that he's not himself but that he's really making you suffer?"

"Yes, several times, but it just upsets him."

"Gee, Mom, I don't know what to say. I wish I could help."

"Son, you are helping by being here and listening. I'll get through it somehow--I always do. Right now, my cat is about the only comfort I have at home. I love Arif so much, but now he's not the person I used to know."

"Sis, why don't you and Derrick come in where it's warmer?" her brother called.

"I guess we'll have to continue this conversation tomorrow," she said as she got up to go inside. Derrick followed her in and went to the phone. From the little Liz could hear, she discerned that he was talking to Paula again.

After Derrick got off the phone, Liz called Arif to let him know that they had arrived safely. When she asked him if she had called too late, he said that he was watching TV. He went on to say that he felt fine and was doing well-- somehow she didn't believe him. Then he and Derrick had a short chat.

After the call, she went to her room to unpack the pictures taken at the naming reception that she brought to show everyone. As she passed them around, Derrick and Ellen seemed really interested in each one, but Rob was more interested in what was happening on TV. This really hurt Liz, because Arif had braved considerable criticism from his family to have a hospital library named for her. She felt the least Rob could do was to show some interest in the pictures. Derrick had been so proud and had wanted to attend the reception so badly, but Rob barely acknowledged the event.

That night she went to bed thinking that this was the first night that Derrick and she had slept under the same roof since her mother's funeral in 1969. It was so comforting to know that he was in the adjacent room. Also, if the phone calls were any indication, he seemed to be getting along well with Paula at least from a distance. Through the thin walls of the manufactured home she could hear his cigarette cough. She tried to go to sleep, but she couldn't help thinking about how these were such trying times for both her and her son.

Chapter 6
The Last 28 Hours

What was to be her last full day with Derrick began with a spectacular sunrise. Liz was the first to get up, so she decided to take a walk while waiting for everyone else to awaken. As was her habit when visiting Rob and Ellen, she walked along the country road on which they lived for about a mile. Usually she walked much farther, but that day she didn't want to be gone too long in case Derrick got up. It was a chilly morning, but already it promised to be a phenomenally beautiful day. When she returned to the house, she could hear Derrick in the shower, and Ellen was busy making coffee. It was still early for Rob, who always liked to stay up late and get up late.

Liz offered to make breakfast, but Ellen wouldn't hear of it. She informed Ellen that she would be cooking dinner. In the years that she had been visiting them, it had become tradition for her to cook at least one dinner, complete with Rob's favorite, homemade apple pie. Derrick had never tasted her apple pie or, for that matter, anything that Liz had cooked since he was too young to remember, so she was determined to cook. Reluctantly, Ellen agreed.

Because Liz had washed her hair, she wore it down rather than in a twist to breakfast so it would dry. When Derrick remarked how nice her hair looked down, Rob concurred, which caused Liz to reflect about how men usually like long, flowing hair. Later she disappointed them both by putting her hair up in a twist secured with a barrette.

After breakfast Rob walked about halfway to the river with Derrick and her. He rested on a bench while they walked the rest of the way. The river was barely a trickle compared to the last time Arif and she had been there which had been in the spring when it was very full. It made Liz sad to see the overgrown paths and dilapidated ladders down the steep embankment that Rob used to negotiate in his healthier days to go fishing.

Liz looked for persimmons while Derrick was hoping to catch a glimpse of an armadillo. They found some armadillo tracks, but didn't see one. She told him that she thought they were mainly nocturnal, so perhaps they would have a better chance that evening. Derrick pointed out some mistletoe which was attached to one of the junipers. Liz mentioned how Ellen made beautiful wreaths out of juniper and mistletoe and had sent one to her and Arif last Christmas.

There were a few good persimmons left, but most of them were mashed on the ground. As she was looking for undamaged persimmons, Derrick had a coughing spell. After it subsided, she observed, "That cough sounds really bad. Last night I heard you coughing a lot. I'm sure that all the smoking you're doing doesn't help matters."

"I've had a cold for several weeks and just can't seem to shake it. Normally I don't cough this bad."

To which she scolded, "If you didn't smoke so much, you wouldn't have such a hard time getting over a cold."

He looked a trifle annoyed and said, "It seems to me that you have mentioned having colds hang on sometimes for several weeks, and you don't smoke."

"Ever since I had walking pneumonia in college, they have had a tendency to hang on. For your health's sake, I wish you would quit smoking," she pleaded as she reflected about how much Derrick's father used to smoke and how was always chiding him about it to which he would invariably reply, "We all have to die of something someday."

"One time I gave up smoking for three months, and I got even skinnier than I am now. You wouldn't want that, would you, Mom?" he asked as he lit another cigarette.

"I can see that this conversation is going nowhere. What would you like to do today?" Liz queried.

With the change of subject, he was visibly relieved. He thought a minute and replied, "You know what I'd really like to do?"

"No, what?"

"I'd like to drive by my great grandmother's house to see if it's well cared for. Would you mind doing that?"

"No, that sounds like a good idea," Liz said, trying to sound enthusiastic.

"What do you think our chances would be of going alone, just the two of us?"

"You know Rob won't like it, but I think it would be okay if we weren't gone too long."

"It shouldn't take very long," he assured her.

Before returning, Liz wanted to show Derrick the bamboo grove on the property. It always fascinated her because she never knew that bamboo could grow so far north. She always had thought of it as a more tropical or semi-tropical plant.

On their way to the grove, she could hear a bobwhite singing in the distance. Even though she was with Derrick, it saddened her to be going to all these familiar places without Rob. Close to the grove, Derrick identified some opossum tracks and more armadillo tracks.

When they returned to where Rob was resting, Ellen was there too. When she inquired if there was anything special they wanted to do, Derrick asked if they would mind if he and Liz went to town to see his great grandmother's old home. Quickly Liz added that it would give her an opportunity to do some grocery shopping for dinner. Rob said it was fine with him as long as they didn't disappear for the entire day. In that context, they promised to be gone only a couple of hours.

It was about a four-mile drive from Rob's country place to the community of Indian Hills, a typical eastern Oklahoma town nestled in the foothills of the Ozark Mountains. When they reached town, Derrick thought that he knew the way to his great grandmother's house, but after driving around for about 15 minutes, it became clear that they would have to ask for directions. When Derrick asked someone where Kidd Street was, they found out that they had been looking in the wrong part of town. They both remembered it as being on a hill, but they were on the wrong hill. It turned out that the hill they both remembered was more of a knoll than a hill.

As they approached the house, nothing looked familiar to Liz, but that didn't come as a surprise considering that it was close to 30 years since she had been there. She could sense a great deal of excitement building in Derrick as they parked in front the bungalow-style house. There was a truck in the driveway, so Derrick announced that he was going to see if anyone was home. Liz was reluctant for them to be knocking on a stranger's door, but Derrick knew no strangers. She stayed in the background as he rang the doorbell, and an older man opened the door. Derrick introduced himself as the great grandson of Mrs. Meyers, and she heard the man ask him in.

Derrick motioned for his mother to come, so she reluctantly climbed the steps to the porch. They entered a front room that was crammed with antique furniture and china. The man introduced himself as Chuck Overman and said that he and his wife had bought the house from Derrick's great grandmother's estate over 15 years ago.

When he left the two of them in the living room while he went to find his wife, Derrick exclaimed, "Look, Mom, there's the mate to the antique table I have in my living room! So many pieces of furniture look like Nana's."

"Perhaps they bought the furniture along with the house," Liz observed.

"I hope we get to see the rest of it."

"I don't think that we should overstay our welcome," she cautioned.

"Let me take care of that, Mom. I'll turn on my charm," he said, flashing a winsome smile.

Mr. Overman returned with his wife, Doreen. Although at first she seemed more reserved than her husband, soon she was showing Derrick things that she had purchased from the estate, some of which he remembered and others not. The Overmans had done quite a bit of remodeling, which is probably why nothing looked familiar to Liz. Because Derrick had visited there as a child at least once a year until Mrs. Meyer's death, he vividly remembered every corner of the house.

Soon they were having a complete tour of the place. The entire house was as crammed as the living room with antiques and memorabilia, some from the estate and the rest from the Overman's many years of collecting. It was obvious that the house was in very good hands, and that the Overmans treasured the history behind it. They were given an equally detailed tour of the outside. While they were outside, seeing the area where the fishpond, in which Derrick used to wade as a child, had been, struck a chord of familiarity with Liz. She remembered sitting on a bench by the pond in the autumn sun so many years before. In the distance then and now Liz heard a bobwhite singing its merry song.

Back in the house, Derrick and Mr. Overman were examining something in the kitchen, when Liz heard Derrick ask, "Mr. Overman, would you happen to know where my great grandmother and grandfather are buried? I think I know where the cemetery is, but I have no idea where their graves are."

"Would you like for me to take you there?" Mr. Overman offered.

Liz interrupted, "Mr. Overman, we've taken up far too much of your day already. Just give us the directions--I'm sure we can find it."

"It would be my pleasure to take you there. On the way I can point out where Derrick's great grandfather had his office and some of the houses that he built."

Liz could see how interested Derrick was in seeing everything, so she reluctantly consented.

After bidding Mrs. Overman goodbye, they got in Mr. Overman's pickup truck. First, he drove them through an old part of town where Derrick's great grandfather had built at least ten homes. Derrick didn't recall ever having seen them before. Then we drove through town where Mr. Overman pointed out the old brick building where Mr. Meyers had his store and office until his death in the late 1940s. Derrick remembered having seen the building many years before.

When they arrived at the cemetery, she was glad that they had Mr. Overman to help them find the graves. It was a very large, old cemetery with seemingly many more inhabitants than those now living in Indian Hills. It took Mr. Overman a while to get oriented, but within five minutes he found the Meyers family plot. He stayed in the truck while Derrick and Liz looked around. There were four markers, one for Derrick's great grandfather who died in 1948, one for Derrick's Nana who died in 1975, one for her sister who died in 1968, and one for someone whose name Derrick didn't recognize.

Liz suggested that they should let Mr. Overman take them back to his home where they had left their truck and that, if Derrick wanted, he and she could return to the cemetery to spend more time. He liked that idea, so they walked back to the truck and told Mr. Overman that they were ready to return.

Upon returning to Kidd Street, they thanked Mr. Overman profusely for his hospitality and the tour. She knocked on the kitchen door, and when Mrs. Overman answered, Liz thanked her again for having made a special day even more special. She made Liz promise that they would look her up if they ever returned. Little did Liz suspect that only nine months later she would return alone and not keep her promise.

Back in the truck, she asked Derrick if he wanted to return to the cemetery. His face lit up at the prospect, and he said that it wasn't far out of the way on the way back to Rob's. On their way through town, they stopped at a Sonic and got hamburgers, fries and milkshakes to go and headed back to the cemetery. This time, as they drove through the cemetery, Derrick seemed interested in the old tombstones. There was one kind that resembled an upright tree trunk with a vine entwined around it, which especially intrigued him. When he asked his mother if she knew anything about its origin, she told him that she had seen that style of monument elsewhere, probably in Missouri, but didn't know anything about it.

After driving around a while, they came to the family plot. This time, when they got out of the truck, Liz could hear bobwhites singing in the distance and commented to Derrick about it. "Don't you have bobwhites in California?" he asked, as he dug in his pocket for a cigarette.

"No, not that I know of. I just love their call. It's so happy and upbeat."

"I wonder whose grave this is--whoever it was, she died at age four."

"You should ask your grandmother when you get home," Liz suggested.

"Yeah, I'll have to do that. She'll be glad that we came to the cemetery."

"Where do you want to eat lunch? Those hamburgers will be getting cold."

"Would it be too morbid to sit in the truck and eat right here?" he asked.

"It's not morbid for me if it doesn't bother you. When I was growing up, my girlfriends and I used to picnic in the cemetery in Middletown by the old Chautauqua grounds."

"Mom, you didn't!"

"It was so scenic there that we didn't seem to mind that it was a graveyard." she explained.

The warmth of the truck felt good, because even though it was a warm day for late October, the wind had a nip to it. "What time is it?" she inquired. It was the first time that either of us had thought about time since they left Rob's.

"It's almost 2:45."

"I can't believe it!" Liz exclaimed. "Where did the time go? Rob will be furious."

"Yeah, and we still have to get groceries. Do you know what you're going to cook?"

"I guess I'll have to do something fast like chicken, and I've promised apple pie. Rob has a fit if dinner isn't ready by six."

"I'll make some of my special chip dip, so we can have something to snack on while you're cooking."

"That sounds good. You're quite a cook," Liz observed.

"Well, I have to be when I'm batching."

After eating lunch, they left the cemetery and stopped at the Piggly Wiggly to get groceries. While Derrick was looking for some deviled crab and sour cream for his dip, he found some canned asparagus spears and asked if Liz could put some cheddar cheese over them and warm them in the oven. So far, the menu was tortilla chips and crab dip, baked chicken in mushroom sauce, salad, asparagus topped with melted cheese, garlic bread and apple pie. After they got through the checkout, Liz remembered that she hadn't got the chicken, so Derrick waited out front while she rushed back for the chicken thighs. It was 3:30 by the time they were on the road and 3:45 by the time they pulled into Rob's driveway.

Rob was sitting on the front porch waiting for them. He greeted us with, "Am I ever relieved to see you! I was afraid you had got in an accident. Do you have any idea what time it is?"

Derrick replied, "Sorry, Rob, time got away from us, and the next thing we knew, it was almost three o'clock."

"I'd better get busy in the kitchen," was Liz's only contribution to the conversation.

As Liz went inside, she overheard Rob ask Derrick if he'd like to try out a special gun, one, which he was bequeathing to Derrick. Derrick said he'd like to very much.

Again, Ellen tried to talk Liz out of cooking, saying that there were enough leftovers from the night before for another dinner. Liz was determined to cook, so she shooed

Ellen out of the kitchen. As she was making the pie, she could hear Rob and Derrick target practicing by the pond. Listening to the gunshots made her reflect on how Rob and Derrick had one thing in common, and that was their love of guns.

Rob and Derrick's father had tried in vain to make a good shot out of Liz, but she never had the least interest in guns. She could remember all the arguments her parents had with Rob over his obsession with guns. Now she had a son who loved guns and hunting. Derrick and she shared a love of the outdoors but not when it came to guns or hunting. She was glad that her brother and son were having a good time shooting while she was preparing dinner.

After returning from target practice, Derrick opened a beer and joined her in the kitchen to prepare his crab and sour cream dip. It was very tasty, so Liz munched on chips and dip while trying to get dinner ready by 6:00. Soon it became abundantly clear that it wouldn't be ready until 6:30, so she broke the news to Rob, who tried in vain to mask his displeasure. She could tell that Ellen never had such a late dinner. Derrick helped out by talking to Rob, trying to get his mind off dinner being late. While Rob was in the bathroom, Derrick came in the kitchen and said that to smooth things over, perhaps she should spend more time with Rob in the evening rather than joining him on his cigarette breaks. Liz replied that she refused to be bullied by Rob.

The dinner and evening were relatively uneventful. Derrick filled Ellen and Rob in on some of the events of the day. Because of the rush and Liz's unfamiliarity with Ellen's kitchen, the dinner wasn't as good as she usually prepared, but the apple pie was excellent. Everyone was having such a good time that she felt sure that she was the only one who was unhappy with the quality of the rest of the preparation. Since she hadn't cooked for Derrick since he was a baby, she wanted the dinner to be something very special.

Because Liz had a reputation for making outstanding pie crust, she was surprised to see that Derrick didn't finish his, and inquired, "What's the matter, Derrick? You left your pie crust. Didn't you like the pie?"

"Mom, it was great. I never eat the crust. Got to watch my figure, you know," he joked as he rubbed his stomach. "I liked your pie as much as Avis's, which means that it's really good. I never eat her crust either."

"I wasn't fishing for compliments, but I'm glad you liked it. When you come to Sacramento, I'll fatten you up."

"Do you cook a lot of curry?" he inquired.

"I used to before Arif got sick, but now our meals are pretty bland."

"Curry might be too exotic for me anyway. I have pretty Midwestern tastes."

Getting over his pout, Rob joined in with, "One time your mother made some curry which almost sent me off the planet."

"What do you mean?" Derrick inquired.

Rolling his eyes and grimacing, Rob replied, "Your dear mother said that she was making it mild, but, boy, did it ever set me on fire and almost sent me to emergency. I thought I was going to be the first person in Oklahoma murdered by curry."

Ellen came to Liz's defense by saying, "Honey, stop it! I thought that Liz's curry was wonderful."

Derrick couldn't resist saying to Ellen, "I heard that you tried to kill Rob with oven cleaner once."

Ellen looked sheepish and replied, "Liz, did you tell him about that? Oh, I'm so embarrassed."

Rob chimed in, "Here I was being attacked by super-sized mosquitoes and asked Ellen to go in and get the insect repellant for me. Little did I ever dream that she would mistake the "Off" oven cleaner for the "Off" insect repellent. Immediately after she sprayed me all over with it, I detected a very unpleasant sting that very rapidly turned into an intense burning sensation. I ended up in the hospital for two days with second-degree burns."

"Rob, I seem to recall that not too long ago you were hospitalized for drinking bleach," Derrick mischievously interjected.

Ellen groaned, turned beet red and blurted, "Liz, is there anything you haven't told him about us? He's going to think that I'm crazy."

Liz counter, "Rob's the one who's crazy for drinking from a glass without checking its contents or at least rinsing it out first."

"Yeah, 'round here, I need a taster. What happened is when my dear, sweet, innocent, ever-devoted wife cleaned the bathroom, she was using bleach and forgot to remove the glass it was in from the counter. That time she put me in the hospital over a week."

"The truth is I wasn't done cleaning the bathroom and didn't dream that you would go there for water when you almost always drink cold water I keep for you in the fridge," Ellen countered.

"Who would ever suspect these innocent-looking wives and sisters of trying to kill with oven cleaner, curry and bleach? Very clever on their part I would say."

Derrick chimed in, "Mom told me how you used to call her Pooky in front of her friends."

Rob chuckled and said, "She would try to beat me up whenever I called her Pooky or Twerpy. Can she ever be mean!"

Liz added, "The worst was when he called my friends twerps to their face."

Now Rob was on a roll. "When your dear, sweet mother was in grade school, she used to complain endlessly about a boy who dipped her braids in the inkwell and beat her up after school. Well, let me tell you, one day I went by the school to give her a ride home and, there she was hitting a boy using her closed umbrella as a weapon. When she saw me watching the beating, she announced, "There's my stinkpot brother, Gotta run.""

That was the last time she dared to complain to me about her getting beat up. Then she used to play a game called "king of the mountain" with some neighbor boys on a knoll in our backyard, and she always ended up victorious."

"I wonder if I'd still have a husband if you shared these fables with Arif, Liz retorted.

After everyone had some good laughs, Liz got up to do the dishes, and Derrick dried them. As it turned out, the dinner that night was the only dinner that she ever cooked for her son after he was a toddler.

After the dishes were done, they joined Rob and Ellen in the living room. Rob started telling some of his corny jokes. Derrick joined in and told a few corny and slightly off-color ones. Rob told the story about the time that Avis Hoffman was in Indian Hills for her class reunion and paid him and Ellen a surprise visit.

"Much to my chagrin, I was wearing a pair of jeans with the knees out and had a gun strapped to my waist because I had just finished shooting a snake that was frightening Ellen."

Liz interrupted, "Somehow I was under the impression that that was how you dressed most of the time."

Rob retorted, "Thanks for coming to my defense, Sis. I could always count on you for that."

Ellen added, "Rob was certain that Avis was horrified by his appearance and the gun and probably returned to Middletown to tell all kinds of stories about the incident."

Not to be sidelined, Derrick added "I remember hearing about this from Avis, and she said that she had a wonderful time with you and Ellen." They all had a good laugh over the picture Rob painted of his appearance and Avis's visit. Years later Liz found a picture of Rob and Avis that was taken that day, and Rob hadn't exaggerated about his appearance.

In this manner, the evening passed very pleasantly until Rob turned on the TV at 8:30 and became immersed in a program. Liz joined Derrick for a couple of his cigarette breaks. As they sat on the porch, a strong breeze came up, and Liz mentioned that she thought that she could smell rain. Derrick said that he'd have to stay up until 10:00 to hear the weather forecast. Because the day had been so sunny and clear, they hadn't thought about the possibility of rain.

As the evening waned, Liz began to count the hours that she had left with Derrick. Since it was about an eight-hour drive to Middletown, his plan was to get up at 5:00 and be on the road no later than 6:30. Ellen and Rob were going to drive Liz the 60 miles to the airport in Fort Smith to catch her 10:30 flight to Dallas. That would give her a few hours alone with them.

Derrick decided to call Paula to find out how the weather was in Middletown. He had already called her earlier that evening but seemed pleased to have an excuse to call her again. After talking for about ten minutes, he hung up and reported that it was windy and raining there. Liz inquired if it was cold enough to snow or sleet, and he said that it was in the mid-40s but was supposed to get colder the next day.

It was close to 11:00 by the time they went to bed. For at least an hour Liz laid awake thinking how sentimental the events of the day had been for Derrick and worrying about the weather. Finally, she fell into a fitful sleep. At 2:00 she was awakened by a strong wind buffeting the window. When she got up and looked out, it was so dark that she couldn't see anything but a few flecks of rain on the window. At 3:00 she was awake again, and this time the rain was pounding on the tin roof of the mobile home and against the window.

She tried in vain to go back to sleep, but with the rain intensifying, she started worrying about Derrick having to drive home and Ellen having to drive her to the airport. Ellen was five years older than Rob, which made her close to 70. Liz knew that driving on the narrow, twisting, two-lane Oklahoma roads made Ellen nervous even in the best of weather. Because of his health problems, Rob hadn't driven for several years. He had always preferred riding motorcycles to driving a car.

As Liz listened to the rain and Derrick's cough, she developed a new plan. Since Derrick would be going through Fort Smith on his way to Middletown, if she went with him, she would have an hour and a half more with him and would save Ellen from having to take her there a couple hours later. The rain had made possible what she wanted to do all along. It became very clear that she was going with Derrick, so she got up and started packing.

When Derrick stumbled out of his room after the alarm went off, he was surprised to find his mother already in the kitchen making coffee. When she shared her plan with him, she could tell that he was pleased at the prospect of having her company for even a small portion of his trip. Also, she could tell that he was very concerned about the weather. He went out on the porch and returned to report that it was a cold wind-driven rain, the kind that all too often turns to sleet in the Midwest.

Ellen heard all the commotion and joined them in the kitchen. While Liz was pouring coffee, she told Ellen about her change of plans. Under the circumstances, Ellen agreed that it was a good idea. Her preference would have been that they both stayed until the weather cleared. Liz too wished they could, but she had a flight to catch, and Derrick had already been away from home for a week.

While Ellen cooked breakfast, Derrick and Liz finished packing. Liz could hear Rob shuffling about on his walker, so she knew the time had come to tell him about the change of plans. She kissed her brother good morning on his bald head and proceeded to tell him that she was leaving with Derrick. He looked hurt and said, "Sis, do you have to?"

Liz answered, "Have you looked out to see how hard it's raining? Derrick has to go through Fort Smith anyway, and I don't want you and Ellen to have to make the trip two hours later in this weather."

"Well, okay," he reluctantly agreed. "But please promise that the next time you come, you'll stay longer-- that is, if there's a next time."

"There you go being morbid," Liz responded, not hiding her exasperation. As long as she could remember, Rob was always making out a new will and talking as though he was soon going to die. "When Arif gets better, I'll come for longer, I promise, big brother."

"I'm going to hold you to it."

So that Derrick wouldn't have to worry about stopping to eat until lunch, Ellen insisted on preparing a hearty breakfast. Soon it was close to 6:30, and Liz could tell that Derrick was anxious to be on the road. They had one more cup of coffee and started collecting their luggage. Since there was no room for the suitcases up front in the pickup, Derrick was searching for something with which to protect them from the incessant rain. After Ellen offered a large sheet of plastic, Derrick went outside to tie the plastic around the suitcases while Liz stayed inside with Rob and Ellen.

Rob was saying that he enjoyed their visit even though he didn't see much of them. Liz told him that Derrick and she would try to come to visit them every year or two. Since Rob wasn't well enough to travel, his home was the perfect place for the three of them to have their family reunion.

Derrick came in dripping wet and announced that they should be on their way. He hugged Ellen and thanked her for her hospitality. He shook Rob's hand and told him that he would return soon to go target practicing with him. They convinced Rob and Ellen not to come out to the truck in the driving rain, but they insisted on going as far as the porch. Liz hugged and kissed Rob and Ellen and ran with Derrick to the pickup.

As they were pulling out of the driveway and waving good-bye, Liz had no premonition that it was the last time she would ever visit Rob and Ellen in their home. When she and Arif were there a year and a half previously, she feared that she would never see her brother alive again, but this time he seemed to be so much better that she wasn't as concerned.

As they drove toward Indian Hills, there were signs of the beginning stages of flooding everywhere. The windshield wipers were working very hard. She was wondering out loud if her flight would be canceled, and Derrick was teasing her about being a worrywart. "Mom, you've been away from the Midwest too long. This kind of rain isn't unusual here."

"I'm not worried about my flight half as much as I'm worried about your having to drive all those miles in this storm."

"Relax, Mom. I'm used to it."

Then the conversation turned to Paula. "Yesterday was Paula's and my third anniversary," he said, as he lit another cigarette.

"I should have remembered since I was with you for your second anniversary last year at this time."

"Yeah, Paula was very understanding about me taking this trip and being away for our anniversary."

"Then I have Paula to thank for these wonderful days we've had together. Will you remember to thank her for me when you see her tonight?"

"Sure, Mom. She really likes you."

"And I like her. I'm sorry that you two are having problems."

"Yeah, me too." Then he looked very serious as he said, "Paula asked me to get counseling for my drinking."

Liz tried to conceal her surprise as she inquired, "When did she do that?"

"Oh, shortly after she moved out."

"What was your reaction?" Liz cautiously inquired.

"I went for a couple of sessions."

"Were they worthwhile?"

Inhaling slowly on his cigarette, he said, "I don't know. I guess I'm not convinced that I have a problem. I don't drink during the week, and I never miss work because of drinking."

"And what about the weekends?" Liz inquired.

"Sometimes I get a little happy on the weekend when I'm out with the guys, but that's about all except for my annual fishing trip with the guys to Current River. Then we do get kinda plowed."

"It doesn't sound as though you have a serious problem, but I do know that you don't have to drink every day or even every week to have a problem. Also, it's the kind of problem that can creep up on you. As I recall, you started drinking very young."

Looking a little peeved, he continued, "I think that Paula's the one who has a problem. I met her in a bar, but she's always on me about me having an occasional beer."

"I always thought it would be nice if you could meet someone in a wholesome place like the grocery store, but I guess these days it doesn't work that way."

"Not in Middletown, anyway," he concurred.

"Anyhow, it can't hurt you to get more counseling."

"I didn't drink for a couple a months before this trip, and it didn't bother me. This trip is the first vacation I've had in over a year, so I did a little celebrating in Dallas. When I get home, I'll go on the wagon again."

"I'll certainly support you in that."

"I used to think that a couple a beers had no effect on me until one time a year or two ago when we had a lot of snow and I cross-country skied to town from my place."

"That's a long way to ski," Liz interjected.

"When I got to town," he continued, "I stopped by Burt's Place for a couple of beers. After the beer, on my way home, you wouldn't believe how many times I fell down. I couldn't believe what a difference it made."

"So many people seem to think that they can sit around and drink beer all day without it fazing them," his mother observed.

"Yeah, I guess I used to think that beer was fairly harmless."

"Something that really bothers Arif and me is that so many taverns are located in fairly isolated areas where people have to drive for miles to get to them, which means that after they've been drinking, they have to drive those same miles home. It just doesn't make any sense. It's like handing people a license to kill."

He drew reflectively on his cigarette and said, "Not to change the subject, but I really needed to get away to get my thoughts collected about Paula and what I'm going to do with my life."

"Did you come to any conclusions?" Liz inquired.

"Not about Paula, but I do know that I want to take the examination for journeyman electrician. I see that as my only chance to have a career as more than just a laborer."

"The prospect sounds terribly exciting to me. I'll do anything I can from my end to help you," was Liz's enthusiastic response.

"First I have to pass the competitive exam."

"Is there any way you can prepare for it?" Liz asked.

"There are a few books that I've bought and others that I've borrowed from work."

"That sounds like a step in the right direction. I'm going to nag you about taking the exam."

"That's okay, Mom, I don't mind that kind of nagging."

"What are your thoughts on Paula?" she probed.

"That I love her and probably always will, but I don't know if we can make a go of it. It really bothers me the way her ex won't help with Brad's medical expenses, and Brad's sick all the time. I know I can't afford to pay for it, and Paula just has a clerical job."

"The decision about your career sounds easier even though it's going to involve quite a financial sacrifice for you."

"Yeah, as long as my truck doesn't quit on me, I can get by pretty cheap by myself. Not to change the subject, but I hope Arif gets cured soon for his and your sake, Mom."

"My heart goes out to him to see him suffering so. I love him so much, but what the steroid medication is doing to him and us really scares me. This is the first time in all the years we've been married that I feel apprehensive about returning home."

"Maybe you and he need to see a counselor."

"Arif doesn't place any faith in counselors or "shrinks" as he calls them."

"Mom, I don't know if I can help, but call me anytime if you just need to talk about it."

"Thanks, son. Hopefully I'll go home and find everything much better."

By then the rain was letting up a bit, and they were nearing Fort Smith. She wished to remain suspended in time in Derrick's truck. The reunion, which had been planned and looked forward to for over three months, was about to end. How quickly the good times fly.

Through the fog she could make out the hills on the outskirts of Fort Smith, and the mileage sign read "Airport 2 1/2 miles." She put her hand on Derrick's arm and said, "Well, son, you'd better just drop me off at the entrance to the terminal and be on your way. You have 'miles to go before you sleep.' I guess we both have many miles to go before we sleep."

"I wish I could wait for your plane with you, but I don't think I'll get home until after dark as it is."

"I'm glad that Paula will have dinner ready for you."

He grinned and said, "Yeah, me too."

Liz pointed out the turn to the airport, and all too soon they were parked in front of the terminal. Derrick got out, extricated his mother's suitcase from the plastic cover and carried it toward the front entrance of the terminal. Liz choked back some tears, opened the door and followed him to a dry spot under the overhang in front of the terminal. She thought she could detect that Derrick was close to tears as he gave her a bear hug and kissed her on the cheek. "This is awfully hard," he said huskily. "Bye, Mom. Give Arif my best. I hope he's feeling better."

"Yeah, me too. Bye, son. Remember, I love you and drive carefully."

"Don't worry. I will."

"Give Paula my best. I love you. Take care."

"I love you too. Let's do this again real soon."

"I can hardly wait. Maybe we can do it in Sacramento next time if Arif's better," she choked.

"I'd like that. Well, I gotta get goin'. Call me tonight or I'll call you."

"Okay. I love you, son."

"Even with my long hair?" he quipped.

"Yes, even with your long hair."

He hugged her for the last time and ran through the rain to his waiting truck. She watched as the truck moved away from the curb, through the parking lot and on to the exit gate, then to be swallowed up by the rain and fog. A cold chill gripped her as she stood alone, crying and waving into the emptiness. Then she picked up her suitcase and trudged into the terminal where she had over two hours to wait for her plane.

Before checking in, she went in the restroom to try to compose herself. She had said good-bye to Derrick many times before, but somehow this time was the most difficult. She kept telling herself that the gloom and foreboding she felt were triggered by the stormy weather and Arif's illness.

After getting collected enough to check in, she was amazed to find out that the flights were running on time.

She went to the waiting area, found a seat removed from the crowd, sat down and tried to read the novel that she had brought along. The book was open before her, but she couldn't see the words because of the tears that were still flowing uncontrollably. Numbly she sat there reflecting on the extraordinary reunion in Indian Hills.

All of a sudden, she found it incredible to comprehend that not one picture had been taken. From other trips she had numerous pictures, but there wouldn't be one from this one, which was so special because of it having been a family reunion of sorts. She had forgotten her camera, and Derrick never carried one, but Ellen always took pictures. All she could figure out was that they were so busy every minute they were there that no one had time to think about taking pictures. Of course, there was always next time, but would there be a next time with Rob? Even though he seemed improved, his health was very fragile.

She let her mind recreate the scenes of the previous day. It was a glorious day in the warm October sun and blazing Oklahoma fall colors. It was by far the most unusual day that she had ever spent with her son. On the other hand, the time with Rob had been somewhat disappointing. Even Derrick noticed how Rob seemed jealous of the good time Liz and he were having and how he wasn't interested in hearing about the library naming ceremony. Looking back over the years, she recalled how Rob had always been a little jealous and paranoid. Ellen's positive influence had largely thwarted those tendencies, but they still surfaced now and then.

Finally, her flight was called. After take-off, she gladly allowed her mind to replay to the events of the last three days. Little did she know how many times she would relive every precious second of that meeting in Indian Hills.

Chapter 7
The Next Seven Months

Upon Liz's return, she found Arif to be in no better health but seemingly not any worse. He seemed glad to have her home, and things quickly fell into the abnormal routine that had become normal during his illness. Late the evening of her return, she called Derrick and found out that he didn't arrive home until after dark because of the rain and some flooding. At least it hadn't turned to sleet or snow, and Paula had a good dinner waiting for him.

Things went along fairly uneventfully until about mid-December when Arif took a turn for the worse. He started losing weight at an alarming rate. With a lot of prodding, Liz was successful in persuading him to see another G.I. specialist, who, after putting him through some painful tests, placed him on a different medication. At first it looked as though the medication would help and have fewer side effects. The specialist informed him that it would take over a month to determine if the new medication would be effective. In the meantime, Arif lost 25 pounds, which was weight that he couldn't afford to lose. For the two of them the holiday season was a time of fear and despair. Finally, about mid-January, he became somewhat better.

During this period, Liz talked to Derrick a couple of times. He seemed to be in good spirits and said that he was on the wagon. She encouraged him to refrain from drinking and kept reminding him to find out when the journeyman competitive exam was to be given. He thought it would be sometime around the end of January.

When, during one of the conversations, he asked if Liz knew anyone who had a condo at Squaw Valley and she told him she didn't, he seemed disappointed. He said that he, Alex and a couple other guys were considering going there for a ski vacation and hoped that she would know of a place that they could rent.

Her reply was that as much as she'd love to have him that close, if they wanted to go where the snow was, they should go to Colorado or Utah, because the Tahoe area was in the grip of a five-year drought and the only snow at the ski resorts was man-made. He asked her to send some literature on the Tahoe ski resorts and said that he'd let her know if they decided to come. She told him that she'd have the literature in the mail in a couple of days, which she did. The ski trip never materialized. As far as she knew, they didn't go to Colorado or Utah either. Looking back, she wished that she had been insistent that they come in spite of the lack of snow.

When he inquired about Arif's health, she informed him about Arif's relapse and that he was on a different medication that had fewer side effects. He asked her if that meant that Arif was easier to get along with, and she was truthfully able to say that he was.

Arif and she had planned to go to Hawaii the first week in January, but because of his attack, they had to postpone the trip. They both hated not going because they felt that it would help them get over their depression, but the doctor advised them to stay close to home. Desert Storm began on Liz's birthday, adding to her anxiety.

Derrick didn't call on her birthday, but called a few days later. Because he sounded unusually subdued, Liz immediately asked if there was a problem. He stunned her by saying, "Mom, I know you're not going to believe this, but Paula has started going out with one of my best friends."

"Derrick, I'm so sorry," she uttered. "How could she do such a thing? Is it anyone I know?"

"I don't know if you've met him. His name is Trevor George."

"No, I don't remember the name. When did this happen?"

"I found out about it about the time of your birthday. That's why I'm late in calling. I ran into them at the Four Corners. What a bummer. Christ, Mom, why does Paula want to hurt me this way?"

"I seem to remember that you started dating Paula when she was going with your best friend."

"But that was different. Anyway, it never came between Alex and me."

"You may like to think it was different, but I'm sure that Alex was very hurt by what you did," I lectured. "Anyway, I'm really shocked because I had hoped that you two were getting back together."

Despondently he said, "I'm sick of Middletown and everyone in it."

"Have you thought about moving somewhere else?"

"I can't, Mom. I have my property and my job and the prospect of becoming an electrician. Besides, Avis needs me."

Sensing the futility in trying to persuade him to move, she responded, "I know you enjoy working in Jefferson City. Have you thought about transferring your social life there as well?"

"Strange that you should mention it. I met a girl there the other day who I'd like to ask out."

"Then, why don't you?"

"You know me, Mom. I'm kinda shy."

They both laughed, and Liz said, "I know better than that."

"Not to change the subject, but how's Arif feeling?"

"No great shakes. Much to our disappointment, the new medication isn't helping that much. He's not improving. I wish I could get him to go to Mayo's or the clinic at Cedars Sinai Hospital in Los Angeles."

"Is he still resisting your advice?"

"More than ever. On a more cheerful subject, when are you to take the exam?" she inquired.

"I haven't received the notice in the mail yet. They're supposed to contact me two weeks before."

"If it's to be given at the end of January, that's less than two weeks from now."

"I know. I'd better give them a call tomorrow to find out what's going on."

"Promise that you'll call?"

"Sure, oh nagging mother of mine."

"I'll call you in a week or two to see how you're doing and find out when you're taking the exam. Remember to call if you need to talk to me in the meantime."

"I'll be okay. Just talking about it helped a lot. I think I'll call that girl from Jefferson City right after we hang up."

"Sounds like a good idea. Well, it's getting to be a long call for you. Thanks for the birthday wishes."

"Bye, Mom."

"Take care. Don't forget to call about the exam."

"I won't," he promised.

The next time she called Derrick was the day after his birthday. This time he seemed in much better spirits. He admitted to going off the wagon and having a major celebration for his thirtieth birthday. Since he could sense from the tone of her voice that Liz didn't approve, he asked her if she didn't have even one small vice to which she admitted that she did have one or two glasses of wine a week. Then he changed the subject and said that it was lucky that he had called to check on the exam, because their records indicated that when delivery of the notice was attempted, his mailbox had been knocked down. He then informed her that this happened rather routinely, and he didn't know if it was the result of vandalism or people hitting it by accident as they drove by. That triggered a recollection of seeing his mailbox on the ground the last time she was there. She remembered wondering how a mailbox that was in the middle of nowhere could get knocked over.

Upon telling her that there had been an article in the *Midland Gazette* about the medical library being named for her, he sounded very proud and excited. When Liz asked him to send her a copy of the article, he said that he had saved it for her and would give it to her the next time he saw her. Liz was astonished that he had such an aversion to writing that he couldn't even manage to place an article in the mail. She considered sending him a stamped, self-addressed envelope, but decided instead to ask one of her Middletown friends to send her the article. She wrote to a Middletown friend, who worked for the newspaper, explaining that since Derrick's writing arm was permanently broken, she needed to ask her to send the write-up.

Before hanging up, he told her that he had a date with the girl he met in Jefferson City and that he was going out with her again that weekend. When Liz asked her name, he said it was Linda Gaspari and that she was a waitress in a coffee shop that he frequented. It was a relief to hear him sounding so upbeat. She told him that Arif had taken a leave of absence from work in the hope that a change of routine would be beneficial to his health. She teased him about reaching the ripe old age of 30 and wished him a happy new decade. He promised to call her as soon as he received the results of the exam.

In mid-February Liz and Arif traveled to Minneapolis to visit Arif's older brother, Omar, who was a physician. They went there with the hope that Omar could give them some good advice concerning Arif's inflammatory bowel disease. Omar had a friend, Ryan McPherson, who was a well-respected internist and G.I. specialist, so Omar made an appointment for Arif to see him. After putting Arif through a series of painful tests, Dr. McPherson recommended the route of medication rather than surgery. Much to Liz's consternation, he asked Arif to go back to the first G.I. specialist he had seen and said that he would work in consultation with him. He recommended that Arif go back on low doses of anti-inflammatory steroids in addition to other treatments.

Upon their return to Sacramento, Arif returned to the first G.I. specialist, started taking low doses of steroids again, and followed the other recommendations. Initially, he responded extremely well to this treatment, and for the first time, they both felt very hopeful about the prognosis. In fact, they were so optimistic that they planned a trip to Hawaii in mid-March.

When Liz didn't hear from Derrick about the exam, she called him. Calling Derrick was usually a challenge because he was so difficult to reach. One time she remembered trying to reach him every evening for a week and repeatedly receiving a busy signal. Finally, when she checked with the long-distance operator, she told Liz that she suspected that the receiver was off the hook. When at last Liz succeeded in reaching him, he said that his cat had knocked the receiver off the hook and he had failed to notice it for several days.

This time it took only about two tries for her to get an answer. He told his mother that he expected to receive the results of the exam in a week or two. Again, he promised to call her when he found out. He said it was a really tough test, that over 200 took it, and it would "kill him" if he didn't pass. Hearing him talk so uncharacteristically made her realize how much he had riding on passing.

When Liz inquired about Linda, he said that they were seeing a lot of each other. Liz distinctly remembered him saying, "Mom, she's good for me right at the moment, but she's really not my type." Hearing this disappointed her somewhat, but she was thankful to hear him sounding so carefree again.

He proceeded to tell her that he had rolled his truck again. When, trying to control her alarm, she asked how he managed to do that. He said that he skidded on ice going around the corner near his home but hadn't hurt himself and had inflicted only minor damage to his truck. He said that he still hadn't become accustomed to driving such a lightweight pickup. Turning the tables, he was scolded Liz about worrying too much.

Then he asked to talk to Arif and said that he had a joke to tell him that was not suitable for mixed company. She turned the phone over to Arif and heard him and Derrick having a really good laugh. Listening to them talking and laughing gave her some hope that perhaps her dream of their becoming good friends would materialize sooner than she had anticipated. She hung up feeling upset about his accident but otherwise happy in knowing that things were going reasonably well for him and that he and Arif had such a good chat.

Their trip to Hawaii was very therapeutic. Except when Arif was suspended nearly upside down trying to administer one of his treatments, it was almost possible to forget that he was ill. They had a wonderful ten days playing in the sun and loving each other. It was one of the few happy interludes she could remember during Arif's illness. All too soon, they had to return to Sacramento, but they had a trip to Washington, D.C. to look forward to in April.

On April 1 Liz couldn't wait any longer to find out how Derrick did on the test, so she made what was to be her last call to him. When she expressed surprise at reaching him so easily, he said that he was hard at work on his income taxes. Then he said, "Guess what? I was one of twenty who passed the exam."

"Derrick, that's wonderful! Why didn't you let me know?"

"Honest, Mom, I was going to call you this weekend."

"Son, I'm so proud of you."

"Really, Mom?"

"Of course I am. Why wouldn't I be?"

"Because I've always been kinda a failure, not finishing college or anything."

"Derrick, don't say that," she protested. "You know that I don't feel that college is for everyone. I wouldn't trade you for ten university graduates."

"Thanks, Mom. You're the only one of my family who's really enthusiastic about me wanting to become an electrician. I really appreciate the encouragement."

"Who isn't supportive?"

"My uncle Byron thinks it's a real crazy idea. The rest are lukewarm about it."

"I'm sorry to hear that. I shouldn't say this, but I think that your uncle Byron is a weirdo. I guess they'll never forgive you for not being a doctor or lawyer or engineer."

"You hit the nail on the head. I guess I'll always be the black sheep."

"Don't talk that way." She said exasperatedly. "When do you start?"

"Sometime in early summer. I haven't received my assignment yet. It might be where I work now, but I don't know."

"Would you like it to be where you work?"

"Yes, I really like it there. They treat me really well, and I really like all the people there."

"Derrick, I know that this program will put you under a great deal of financial pressure, so please know that if you get in a bind, I'm here to help. I've never given you any expensive gifts, so I'd like to make up for it by helping you now."

"I think I'll be all right unless I need new tires or something. Thanks for the offer."

It was out of character for Liz to offer assistance without first consulting with Arif, but something inside her made her do it. Arif would have to understand. She knew that Derrick had inherited money from both of his grandfathers, but it was her understanding that it was tied up in some kind of trust fund until he was in his forties. Perhaps the Hoffmans feared that he would squander all his money on fast living. It angered her to think of him having to drive around on bald tires, and it wasn't going to happen if she had anything to say about it.

"Promise me that you'll let me help."

"Yes, Mom, I promise."

"By the way, how's Linda?" she inquired.

"Right now, it's a bummer. We had a fight, and when I call her, her sister answers and says that she's not home. I know she's there and just doesn't want to talk to me."

"I'm sorry to hear that."

"Oh, she'll get over it and come around," he commented confidently.

"Well, I'd better say goodbye before I own the phone company. Please, please let me know when you receive your assignment."

"I will, Mom. I promise."

"Remember, son, I'm so proud of you. Bye, son. I love you."

"Bye, Mom. Love you too."

With those words, they ended their last conversation.

Before leaving for Washington, she wrote to Derrick to reaffirm her offer of assistance. She told him that she didn't want him driving around on bald tires or making other foolish sacrifices to compensate for his pay cut. She couldn't resist saying that one way he could cut his expenses was by cutting down on smoking and beer.

The trip to Washington was a business trip for Arif and a cultural interlude for Liz. During his illness, Arif always seemed to feel better while away from home, and the Washington trip was no exception. When they returned to Sacramento, it was time to start planning their annual sojourn to the Trinity Alps in northwestern California. Since 1984, they had been going there for a hiking trip right before the Memorial Day weekend. Since Arif felt better when he was away, they were looking forward to that particular annual trip more than usual.

Mother's Day came and went without her hearing from Derrick. As their answering machine was in need of repair and they were gone most of the day, she convinced herself that he probably called and tried to leave a message, which, through the fault of the machine, she didn't receive. The other possibility was that now that he was no longer living with Paula, he just plain forgot. In contrast, Mother's Day 1990 had been the best Liz ever experienced, with Arif taking her out to dinner and Derrick remembering to call. It was normal for Mother's Day to come and go without her hearing from Derrick when Paula wasn't around to remind him.

As usual, the days in the Trinities were magical. It pained her, however, to see how little stamina for hiking Arif had. Normally they would average twelve miles a day in steep terrain. That time they did well to hike five or six miles a day. She could sense Arif's frustration with his weakness, but still they managed to have a wonderful time soaking in the beauty of the mountains and the Salmon and Trinity rivers. On their way back to Sacramento, Liz had a feeling of fear and foreboding, which she attributed to having to return to reality after such a carefree and peaceful interlude.

They were home from the Trinities only a few days before Arif made a trip to Los Angeles to see Raj, his dear friend from India, who was visiting his son in L.A. Because of the stress she was under from Arif's illness, Liz was looking forward to having a few days to herself to get rested. Raj had been in the U.S. several months, and she felt so terribly guilty that they hadn't invited him to stay a few days with them in Sacramento.

With Arif's illness, it was practically impossible to have houseguests. At that time, he was administering treatments two and three times a day, which was something that needed to be done in privacy without any interruptions. In November, they had made an overnight trip to Los Angeles to see Raj, but other than that they hadn't seen him. Liz was pleased that Arif was going to visit before he returned to India, At the same time, however she was worried because Arif planned to drive rather than fly. Also, she knew that it would be futile to try to dissuade him from driving because about all they would accomplish would be their having an argument.

Arif left on Thursday, and Thursday and Friday went very quickly for her because most of the time was spent at work. Even though she had looked forward to being alone, almost as soon as Arif left she felt vaguely apprehensive. His plan was to return Monday night in time for their twenty-sixth anniversary on Tuesday. So that she could take Tuesday off, she went to the office and worked most of the day on Saturday. She decided to set Sunday aside for shopping, cleaning house and working in the garden. Sunday evening, she was to attend a house-warming.

When Arif called on Friday, Liz told him that she was having nightmares and feeling really nervous. He told her that he was feeling fine and she needn't worry about him. Because he knew that when she was at home alone, she rarely slept well, he promised to call again on Saturday night to see how she was doing. When he called, she told him that the nightmares were recurring, one of her eyes had developed an annoying twitch and a huge, ugly sore had erupted on her lip. In short, she was a mess. He found it difficult to understand why she would be upset about a twitching eye and a sore and recommended that she sit and relax with the cat. Sensing her frustration at this suggestion, he promised to call the next evening.

After sleeping only about three hours, Liz decided that she would make the best of the one day while Arif was gone that she wouldn't be going to work. When she looked in the mirror and saw the huge festering sore on her lip, she called her friend to tell her that she couldn't attend the house-warming. The sore looked so hideous that she hated to be seen with it even at the grocery store, so she continued to put rubbing alcohol on it in the hope of drying it up.

As she spent the warm June morning in the garden, the sense of uneasiness and foreboding was still with her causing her to conclude that perhaps she had looked forward too much to being alone, and this was punishment for her selfishness. After finishing weeding the garden, she decided to go shopping for items that she rarely had time to look for when Arif was home.

While Arif was away, the only time she felt relaxed was about a three-hour period while she was shopping. It was one of those days when she found almost everything she wanted. She bought a new shade for their bedroom lamp, a pair of shorts and a long tee shirt for herself, a shirt for Arif, a wire basket for barbecuing fish, and lots of groceries and household and garden supplies.

Looking back, it was highly unusual that she didn't call Derrick as she normally did when Arif was away. Her only explanation was that she was so full of foreboding that she didn't want to talk to anyone, not even Derrick. Also, she was working very hard at her office and was immersed in plans for their anniversary. Additionally, she was hoping that Derrick would call her, for a change, as he had promised.

She returned from shopping about 4:00. Around 5:00 the phone rang, and it was Arif to tell her that he was on his way home a day early because he was worried about her. She told him how very much she appreciated his coming early and that she would have dinner ready.

He said to expect him around ten. After hanging up, she tried to figure out what she could cook for dinner without having to go to the store again. She decided upon an asparagus and pasta casserole that Arif liked and his colon was able to tolerate.

By 8:00 she had the dinner ready and she did some reading with Mitsi, their cat, on her lap. For over an hour she remained engrossed in *The Thorn Birds*. Finally, after 9:00, she couldn't tolerate reading any longer because she had come to a portion of the book where everyone was either dying or getting killed in accidents. In her mental state, she found the book to be too depressing, so she put it aside and started watching out the window for Arif.

About 9:30 Liz saw car lights come into view, which turned out to be Arif's. Joyfully, she ran out the door to meet him in the driveway and threw herself into his arms. His kisses soothed her, but before he had been home a half hour, they were having a most extraordinary fight over something she can't even remember. All she can remember is that she was shouting at him, which was terribly out of character for her, and crying uncontrollably. When Arif becomes angry, he rarely screams or yells, but instead he refuses to talk. That night they went to bed with her crying and him not speaking to her. It wasn't until several days later that she realized the fight occurred almost exactly at the moment of her son's death.

At this point. Liz stiffly got up to take a much-needed break from her reading. She knew she needed a break before reading about the funeral. Arif had returned from shopping and the library a while before so Liz and Purky, the cat, joined him in the kitchen. She fixed lunch for the two of them while Arif described the mad scene at the grocery store with people stocking up before the big storm. He bought some champagne just in case they were unable to get to the restaurant for her birthday. They lunched on some chili and cornbread that Liz had made for dinner the day before..

After lunch, Arif said that he was going to build a fire and read a book he had brought from the library. Liz regretted that she didn't want to read by the fireplace with

Arif. So far she hadn't shed any tears while reading, but now she was entering the highly emotionally charged portion of the story. She told Arif that she would join him later on, fed Purky and went back to the privacy of her office.

Chapter 8
June 3 - 5, 1991

After lying awake for several hours, finally toward morning Liz managed to get some fitful sleep. For her it was a workday, so the alarm went off at 6:00. Rather than getting up right away as she normally did, she caressed Arif and told him how sorry she was for making him angry. Much to her surprise, he was very responsive, and before she knew it, they were caressing and kissing, Liz was shedding tears of joy, and then they were making love. It had been years since they made love before going to work. What a beautiful way to start the day!

After their making up and love making, reluctantly she got up to get ready for work. She got out of bed feeling the happiest she had felt for months. With Arif's kisses and caresses, all feelings of anxiety and foreboding had vanished.

Liz was feeding Mitsi when the phone rang. She looked at the clock to see that it was only 6:45. Who could be calling so early? Calls that came unusually early or late always unnerved her. The phone rang again, and this time Mitsi let out a blood curdling yowl, a cry, which Liz had never heard her make. Apprehensively she answered the phone.

An unfamiliar voice said, "Hello. This is Peter Hoffman."

All she could think was that this was a voice she hadn't heard for 28 years since Peter and she were divorced and that something must be terribly wrong.

"Peter, what's wrong?" she gasped. "Has something happened to Derrick?" she managed to utter.

"Yes, I'm afraid so. After a long pause, he continued, "I don't know how to tell you this, but Derrick was killed in an accident with his truck last night about midnight."

Liz started screaming at the top of her lungs, "No, no, it can't be! No, no, please don't let it be!"

Arif heard her screams and came to find out what was going on. She screamed at him that Derrick had been killed. After her initial outburst, somehow she got a hold of herself and said, "I'll be there sometime tomorrow. When is the funeral?"

The voice at the other end said, "I don't know."

Mechanically she said, "Thank you for letting me know. How did it happen?"

"About all I know is that it was a roll-over accident. I'm still in Albuquerque and don't know the details."

"How is Avis taking it?"

"We haven't told her yet. We have to tell her next."

I remember saying, "I hope it doesn't kill her."

"She's really strong. I want you to know that this is one of the most difficult phone calls I've ever made."

"I'll be there tomorrow. Thank you for calling," was all she could think to say.

"When you find out when and where you'll be arriving, one of us can pick you up," he offered.

"Thank you. I'll let you know if I need a ride," she could hear herself saying before hanging up"

Isn't it strange how one phone call lasting less than a couple of minutes can change your whole life? All Liz knew is that, even though recently life had been better, from now on it would never be the same. How often she longed for their life as it was in the late 1980s, before Arif's illness and losing Derrick.

Liz didn't remember much about the rest of that most horrible of days. She did recall that after the phone call, Arif said that it must be a terrible mistake, but she knew it couldn't be. He asked her to call Jill to confirm the information. Liz replied that it was too early to call her, but her main reason for not wanting to call was that she didn't know if Alex had been with Derrick and if Alex had been killed or injured also.

Soon Arif was on the phone making plane reservations. The plan was that she would leave the next morning and he would join her in Middletown on Wednesday. Then she heard him calling Rob and Ellen. Rob had always doted on Derrick, so she knew how the news would devastate him. She couldn't bear to talk to Rob that day.

Somehow, in her hysteria, she waited until 9:00 to call Jill. Her hands shook as she dialed. Jill answered the phone, and Liz heard her voice saying, "Jill, this is Liz."

Jill started sobbing and said, "Liz, what are we going to do?"

Through her sobs, Liz said, "Jill, what happened? All I know is that Derrick is dead. What about Alex?"

"Alex was out of town or he would have been with Derrick. A relative of mine, Dave Ruhlen, was with Derrick, but he wasn't injured."

"Thank heaven for that. Was Derrick driving?"

"Yes." She stopped for a minute before she could go on. "It happened less than a quarter of a mile from his house, in front of my cousin's place."

"I know exactly where you mean. I can picture it. Oh, so close to home!" Liz lamented.

"Dave went to get help immediately, so it wasn't long until the paramedics were on the scene. Apparently, Derrick died on impact."

"How'd it happen?" Liz asked between sobs.

"I don't know exactly, but I do know that the truck rolled and ended up upside down in the deep ditch in front of my cousin's house."

Changing the subject, she said, "Jill, I have a favor to ask. Arif won't be coming until Wednesday, but I arrive tomorrow. Could you meet me in Columbia, and could I stay with you the first night?"

"Don't be silly. We'd be furious if you didn't stay with us. What time does your plane get in?"

Liz gave her the schedule and bid her a tearful goodbye.

The only other thing Liz remembers doing that day was packing. In looking for some appropriate dark colors, she was struck that most of her clothes were bright and happy looking. Prior to Arif's illness, she had worn a lot of black and brown, but after he became sick, he became very sensitive about dark colors and asked her to buy only bright ones. In fact, the previous October they had a major disagreement when she came home with a new black skirt. When his immediate reaction was that she had bought the skirt to wear to his funeral, she told him that she had bought it to wear with colorful blouses. Now it became painfully apparent that she would be wearing the controversial skirt to her son's funeral.

After another near-sleepless night, it was time to get up to go to the airport. Was it only 24 hours ago that the day started so beautifully with Arif and her making passionate love? For the first time, she remembered that it was June 4, their anniversary. Derrick died on June 3, and June 4 was

Arif's and her anniversary. How could they ever again have a happy anniversary?

As they prepared to go to the airport, she tried to persuade Arif not to go to the funeral. She knew that returning to Middletown would be detrimental to his health. He had been advised by his doctors to avoid stressful situations, so why take any chances? For the past 28 years, Liz had been through almost everything relating to Derrick alone, so she could get through this alone too. When Arif insisted on being there, she no longer tried to dissuade him because she knew it was futile. They kissed each other goodbye until the next day.

About all she could remember about the trip to Denver and on to Columbia is that she cried her eyes out. Upon her arrival in Columbia, she was consumed by Derrick's absence even though Jill, Anne, and Lisa, dear friends from her childhood days, were there to meet her. All she could think about was how four years previously Derrick had met her at that airport. It was also at that same airport in 1970 that Liz said goodbye to her father for the last time.

Her friends kissed and hugged her, helped with her luggage and led her to Jill's car. Liz couldn't believe that when they got in the car the conversation turned to everything but Derrick. All throughout the 40-mile drive to Middletown they were making small talk that Liz had difficulty following. Deep inside, Liz knew they were doing it to take her mind off Derrick, but, nonetheless, she deeply resented it.

She wanted and needed to talk about Derrick, and instead they were talking about stupid, inconsequential things. What did she care about what Eleanor Williams wore to the Marshall's anniversary celebration and what Jessica Saunders said at the town hall meeting? How could they be so insensitive to her situation? Apparently, they didn't know how desperately she needed to talk about Derrick. Or was there something they knew that Liz didn't know and they didn't want to be the ones to tell her?

When they got to Jill's house, the others departed and Jill took Liz upstairs to her room. Liz thought about how Jill's home had been a second home to Derrick for so many years. He was as much or more at ease there than he was in Avis's home.

After she unpacked a few things, Jill and she sat on the front porch and had a glass of lemonade and some cake. The day was unseasonably warm for so early in June, and the porch offered a cool reprieve from the afternoon heat.

Jill encouraged Liz to do what she had to do and not to worry about disrupting their schedule. Liz said that she needed to call the Hoffman residence to let Avis know that she had arrived. Nervously she made the call and asked whoever answered for Avis. Soon Avis came on the line and asked Liz to come over. Also, she said that she would like for Liz to join them for dinner. Liz said that she would do both, thanked her and hung up.

After informing Jill of her plans, Liz went upstairs to change. Since the Hoffmans lived only three blocks away, she told Jill that the walk would feel good to her. As Liz walked those familiar streets, she thought about the happy times when she used to walk those same streets on her way to and from grade and high school. When she was a teenager, she used to take her dog for a walk on those same streets, and when Derrick was living at the Hoffmans, she used to walk on some of those streets from her parents' home to the Hoffman's to pick him up.

More recently, Derrick and she had driven down those streets many times together. A more disturbing memory was that she caught Peter Hoffman's attention when he was driving down Macon Street as she was walking her parent's dog in her rather short shorts. That afternoon he called and asked her out to dinner and a movie, Liz accepted and that was the beginning of their relationship.

As she neared Avis's home, she was overcome with anxiety. Almost always when she visited Derrick, they would go there to see Avis. Those meetings had always been very pleasant, but she wondered what was awaiting her this time. Nervously, she knocked on the door, the same door that she had knocked on so many times when she used to go to see Derrick when he was living there as a child. She heard Avis say, "Coming. Just a minute."

She opened the door, and Liz started crying and said, "Oh, Avis, I wish you had never had to live to see this day."

Obviously holding back tears, Avis bravely replied, "Come in, hon. We're all out on the porch."

Liz felt certain that she said "hon", which is how Avis often affectionately addressed Derrick. Avis had to be at least 80 years old, so losing Derrick had to be terribly hard on her. In spite of the bitter divorce, to Liz's knowledge Avis had never said anything negative about her to Derrick, thus allowing Liz to have a near-perfect relationship with her son. For this Liz felt heavily indebted to her.

Liz followed her to the back porch where Derrick and she had sat with Avis so many times. It was a large screened porch, the kind that was so common in that part of the Midwest, and was filled with friends and family, most of whom Liz didn't recognize. It had been so long since she had seen Peter that she confused him with his brother, Matt. After that initial embarrassment, she decided that things couldn't get much worse and tried to relax.

Everyone was telling stories about Derrick. Avis related that Derrick visited her for the last time only a week before on Memorial Day and set up a squirrel feeder for her, which she proceeded to point out to. Peter talked about how he hadn't seen Derrick since 1986 when Derrick visited him in Albuquerque with Lynne. Lynne made a good impression on him, and he was really surprised when they broke up. Matt reminisced about how when Derrick was little, he used to visit Liz's father at the bank and his grandfather would take him to the board meetings. Matt told another story about when Derrick entertained during the summer how Derrick's neighbor Dwayne Ruhlen, the father of Dave Ruhlen who was with Derrick at the time of the accident, would get his binoculars out to watch the naked or nearly naked females diving off the diving board.

Liz told the story about how Derrick told her that the book she wrote, of which she was so proud, was awfully boring. Also, she related how when Derrick was about five, he told her he liked to eat cherry tomatoes because they went diarrhea in his mouth.

They wanted to hear about her visit with him in Indian Hills, so Liz told them about visiting Avis's mother's house and the cemetery. Liz noticed that Avis wiped tears away during her story. Matt related how much teasing Derrick had taken about the article in the paper a few months before about the hospital library being named for his mother. In it, Derrick was mentioned as being her son, which, according to Matt, was the only positive mention that Derrick had received in the newspaper in recent years. Apparently, Derrick's name appeared in the paper quite often for traffic violations.

With the telling of these stories, they were all succeeding in making each other laugh and feel better. The stories continued through dinner and after. After dinner Liz went into the study to return a call from one of her friends from high school. She was hanging up when Avis came in the room and said that she wanted to show her some pictures she had of Derrick. Seeing the pictures made Liz realize that the ones she had were, for the most part, more recent, so she promised to send them to Avis, who seemed pleased at the prospect of receiving them. Then the two of them rejoined everyone on the porch.

Liz took a seat next to Sue, her former sister-in-law, but Sue soon had to leave to answer the doorbell. Then Peter got up from where he was seated on the other side of the room, came toward Liz and sat down where Sue had been sitting. He asked, "Is it okay if I sit here?"

"Sure."

"How was your trip?"

"Fine, considering the circumstances. I cried most of the time."

"Sorry, that was an insensitive question. How long do you plan to stay?"

"Arif's coming tomorrow, and I think we'll stay a day or two after the service."

"Let me know if he needs a ride or anything."

"Thank you. Hey, I want to tell you how totally embarrassed I am for mistaking you for Matt.

Peter laughed and said, "Don't be embarrassed or apologetic. I was flattered since Matt is four years younger than I."

Liz was thinking that Peter looked younger than she had expected. She couldn't see much resemblance between Derrick and him. Perhaps Derrick resembled her more than she had ever realized.

Peter was really trying hard to make her feel comfortable. After some more small talk, he confided, "The reason I never remarried is because I had been such a lousy husband to you."

At what should have been her moment of sweet vindication, she was too numb and grieved to feel anything but emptiness. She wanted to agree with his admission, but lamely said, "I'm sure that you have matured over the years and had become a much better person. I hope I have also."

She wondered if anyone else in the room heard what he said. When she checked her watch, she was surprised that it was almost 8:30, so she said that she would have to be leaving. Sue asked if she would like to join her and her aunt Edna the next morning to do some more cleaning at Derrick's house. Liz answered that she would very much like to, and 9:00 was agreed upon as the time to meet. By the time she walked back to Jill's, it was almost dark, and she was aching from fatigue and stress.

Upon her return, she found Jill waiting for her on the porch. Her husband, Raphael, was there also. Raphael gave Liz a comforting hug. After some small talk they all went inside, and Jill and Raphael waited in the family room while Liz called Arif. Arif said that he would be renting a car in Columbia, so no one would have to meet him. Liz told him that the visitation at the funeral home started at 3:00. He said that he should arrive before then, but that she should go ahead if he was late. They told each other how much they loved one another and said goodbye. It was their twenty-sixth anniversary, but there was no mention made of it. It was an anniversary that forever went uncelebrated.

When she returned from making the call, Raphael said, "Liz, I can't tell you how sorry I am that this time I wasn't able to do anything to save Derrick. He must have died on impact. By the time help arrived, it was too late."

"I know that there was nothing that could be done. Please don't feel badly," Liz pleaded. "You always helped him in so many ways."

"It's rough being a physician and losing someone who was as close to me as my own sons. Derrick was like a son to me. I want you to know that," he said with intense emotion.

"When I used to get upset about his accidents, he always told me not to worry. This time his luck ran out--I guess it was bound to happen." Liz paused to wipe her tears and then inquired, "I haven't seen Alex. How is he taking it?"

Jill responded, "He just wants to be left alone in his grief. After eating dinner, he shut himself in his room."

Raphael added that their younger son, Chris, had been with Derrick earlier the day of his death and was equally upset. Both boys felt as though they had lost a brother. Their daughter, Karen, also had been very close to Derrick and was devastated by his loss.

Upon their asking her how it went at the Hoffmans, Liz reported that after getting off to a rough start, it went very well. She told them that she would be going in the morning with Sue and Edna to clean the house. When Raphael offered her a sleeping pill to get her through the night, she thankfully accepted. How long had it been since she had a decent night's sleep, and when would sleep ever come naturally again?

After showering, Liz went straight to bed and passed out. When she awakened, it was 5:15. Until the waves of grief came over her, it took her a few seconds to realize where she was and why. She lay there until she heard someone stirring at 6:00. Then she showered, got dressed, and went downstairs to the kitchen. As Jill bustled about the kitchen, she informed Liz that Raphael had been called to the hospital to deliver a baby. She poured coffee for both of them and asked Liz what she would like for breakfast. Even though she wasn't hungry, she knew she would need some fortification to get through the morning, so she said that she would help herself to the sweet rolls and fruit that were on the table. Jill was busy preparing a substantial breakfast for Alex who had to be at work by 7:30.

When Alex made his appearance, he folded Liz in his arms and tried to comfort her. Liz had never seen Alex, who was always so vibrant and handsome, look so distressed and haggard. Both Alex and Derrick were very good-looking, Alex, being tall, dark, and handsome, and Derrick, tall, fair and equally as handsome. Liz suspected that the pair of them broke a lot of hearts.

Huskily he said, "Just when, for a change, things seemed to be going right for Derrick, this had to happen. He was so excited about training to be an electrician. On top of that, he was really on a roll with the women. I hadn't seen him so happy for years, and then bam and it's all over," he said visibly fighting back his tears.

"The last time I talked to Derrick, I kept telling him how proud I was that he passed the exam. I hope he knew that I really meant it."

"I think he did," Alex responded. "He talked about you a lot."

"Breakfast is ready," Jill interjected.

As they sat down, Alex admitted to having a sleepless night. He gulped down some coffee, eggs and bacon and apologized for having to run off to work. Similarly to Derrick, Alex had never finished college and was employed as a skilled laborer on highway construction. At age 30, he had never married and, at the moment, was living at home. He said that he wouldn't be working the next day, the day of the funeral, and that he'd be at the visitation in the afternoon. He hugged Liz again, kissed his mother and hurriedly departed.

Liz was picking at her breakfast and drinking more coffee than usual when there was a knock on the kitchen door. When Jill answered, a man in his late thirties or early forties entered. Jill said, "Chad, I'd like you to meet

Elizabeth Azmi, Derrick's mother. Liz, I don't think you've ever met my brother, Chad."

Chad smiled and extended his hand. "It's a real pleasure to meet you. Jill speaks of you so often. Are you here to visit Derrick?"

Jill quickly interceded, "Oh, dear. I forgot that you've been out of town and hadn't heard." By then, she was fighting back her tears. "Derrick's been killed in a rollover accident in his truck."

"What? I don't believe what I'm hearing," he blurted. "Oh, Mrs. Azmi, I'm so sorry. Please, please forgive me."

Numbly Liz replied, "That's all right. I'm sorry to have to make your acquaintance under such awful circumstances." The reason Liz had never met Chad was that he was 15 years younger than Jill, so he had been just a baby when she graduated from high school.

Chad had a quick cup of coffee, picked up what he had come for, and, again, with profuse apologies, departed, after which Jill and Liz consoled each other for about a half an hour. Then Liz called to make reservations at a motel for that evening for Arif and her. When she visited Derrick, she had always stayed at the Holiday Inn. Because it would be too sad for her to stay where Derrick had come to pick her up so many times, she had to find somewhere else, which wasn't easy in a small town like Middletown. Fortunately, there was a new motel that had a vacancy.

It was getting late, so she said goodbye to Jill and departed for the Hoffman's. As she walked the three blocks to Derrick's grandmother's place, she tried to focus on the beauty of the warm June morning. It was an almost cloudless day, and already it felt as though the temperature was close to 70. It was the kind of day that usually inspired happy thoughts and activities, but today was different, so drastically different.

When she arrived at Hoffman's, Sue answered the door and led her to the kitchen where several of the family were already gathered. She informed Liz that her aunt couldn't join to help with the cleaning, so Peter and Byron, her youngest brother, would be going. They waited about five minutes for Peter and Byron and then departed. Derrick's place was about ten miles from Middletown, half of which was on country roads. Because of the many intersections and twists and turns, when Liz went there with Derrick, she was always hopelessly lost soon after leaving the main highway.

Liz sat in front with Sue, who was driving. First she asked if it was going to be an open-casket visitation. Because Derrick had died of a head injury, she thought perhaps it wouldn't be. No one seemed to know for certain, but they thought it was to be open-casket. It was some consolation to know that she probably would get to see her son again.

Next Liz asked if Derrick had been drinking before the accident to which Byron sanctimoniously answered, "Yes."

All she could think to say was, "Thank goodness no one else was hurt."

Peter agreed, "If it had to happen, I guess it's best it happened the way it did."

"Because of Derrick's fondness for having a good time, I never encouraged him to move to California where the party life style seemed to be so common. I just didn't think it would be a good influence on him." Liz remarked.

Byron's smug response was, "Some people manage to find the fast life no matter where they live."

Peter broke the ensuing silence by saying, "I hope you'll like the casket I picked out. It's very simple and sleek--kind of like a gun barrel."

Liz's mechanical reply was, "That sounds nice. I think Derrick would like that."

Then she inquired what was to be done with Derrick's dog and cat. Sue said that she had already found them good homes. It made Liz sad to think that she would never see them again, but she was glad that they had gone to good homes.

As they went around a corner, Sue slowed the station wagon and said, "Up there is where it happened."

Numbly Liz asked, "Can we stop?"

"Sure," she said and pulled over to the side of the road. They got out, walked a few feet, and then Peter said, "That's where the truck landed."

Liz looked at the part of the ditch to which he was pointing and was astonished at how innocuous it appeared. It looked very grassy and soft. There were no signs of the accident except possibly some skid marks on the road, which brought back memories of the many accidents Liz used to read about in the Middletown paper that were caused by skidding on treacherous gravel roads. Looking up, even without her glasses, she could see Derrick's house across the field. He almost made it--another quarter of a mile and he would have been there. He died so close to home.

"He wasn't wearing a seat belt," Peter said huskily. "I wonder if it would have made a difference."

"I meant to ask you about that before. I guess we'll never know," Liz uttered between sobs.

As they got back in the station wagon and drove the short distance to Derrick's, everyone was pretty well overcome with emotion. Liz couldn't help wondering if Derrick would still be alive if he had been wearing a seat belt. Perhaps, as he had so many times before, he would have walked away relatively unscathed, or perhaps he would have survived but have been badly or even permanently injured.

As they rounded the corner and started up the long driveway, she thought that she couldn't face going there without him. Out of the corner of her eyes, she could see the row of trees that he had planted. They had grown considerably. As they climbed the rise to the parking place under the tree near the house, everything looked so lush and beautiful beyond description. All Liz could think was that only three short days before Derrick had been there. Sue was pointing out the portion of the two-acre lawn that Derrick had mowed on Sunday before he went on his fateful outing. It seemed so strange not to be met by Derrick's one-eyed dog, Blackie, but she was very thankful that Blackie had got a good home with Sue's neighbor.

It was time to get out of the station wagon and go inside. Liz's head was throbbing, and she was having trouble seeing through her tears. They entered the sun porch where on the previous visit Liz had been greeted by Whitie and her mewing kittens. She had taken a picture of the kittens climbing into the feedbag. As she shared these memories with Sue, Sue said that just a couple months ago, she finally got Whitie spayed, because she knew that Derrick would never get around to doing it.

From the sun porch, they entered the living room. Upon entering the house, immediately it was apparent that already a lot of cleanup had been done. There were boxes stacked in most of the corners, and some items of furniture were gone. Why the hurry Liz wondered? She felt cheated because she was hoping to see the house just as Derrick had left it. Sensing her surprise and disappointment, Sue told me that she, Matt, and Byron had done a lot of work on Tuesday morning. Because the house was fairly isolated, she explained that they were worried about it being burglarized.

Before starting the cleaning, Sue and Peter showed her around. From a window in the living room, she caught a glimpse of a partially decomposed deer head on the porch roof. No doubt it was the remains of a deer that Derrick had shot the previous November. Seeing it made her recall how much Derrick used to look forward to going hunting every November and to Current River on his annual fishing trip in July.

Derrick had moved his desk where the dining table used to be. It was a good place for the desk because from there he could look out over the pond. The rest looked pretty much the same as she so vividly remembered. A myriad of memories almost overwhelmed her. She heard herself ask Sue what she could do to help. Sue said that the refrigerator needed cleaning and that she would appreciate it if Liz could clean it while she and Peter tackled the Derrick's bedroom and Byron finished mowing the lawn.

When Liz opened the refrigerator, it looked as though it hadn't been cleaned since Paula moved out. She could see that it was going to take some time. The kitchen was the brightest and most cheerful part of the house, and it felt good to be there occupying herself with something mundane. After finishing the refrigerator, she mopped the floor. She was finishing up when Peter came in to ask her if she would like to have some framed pictures of ducks that were still in their original packing. She thanked him and explained that they would be difficult to take back to Sacramento. When she inquired if there was something smaller that she could take as a memento, he told her to help herself.

As she looked around for something small that would remind her of him, her attention was drawn to an unusual drawing hanging on the wall. It was of Derrick in a hunting blind focusing on a deer with a rifle that had a crooked barrel. She looked to see if the drawing was signed but couldn't find a signature. She asked Peter and Sue if they knew who had done it, and they said they didn't. Because no one knew who had drawn it, Liz decided against taking it. Instead she selected a coaster set and holder with ducks on it. Since Derrick had belonged to Ducks Unlimited and used ducks as the decor in his living room, she felt it would be an appropriate memento.

When she asked Sue if there was anything else that needed doing in the kitchen, she asked Liz to join her and Peter in the bedroom. The bedroom was piled high with clothing and dirty laundry. Seeing Sue and Peter going through a large box of sweaters, she commented, "I had no idea that Derrick had so many beautiful sweaters."

Sue replied, "Oh, yes, Derrick could be quite the spiffy dresser when he wanted to be."

Then Peter found a yellowed newspaper in the corner of the closet and said, "Hm, I wonder what this is. The date on it is hard to read--I think it says 1963."

Thinking that it looked familiar, Liz said, "Let me see that."

Peter handed it to her, and soon she recognized it as the newspaper that Derrick had shown her when she was visiting in 1987. She shared with Peter and Sue how Derrick had shown it to her and asked her to look through it to see if she recognized any of the names in it. Peter laughed and said, "Would you believe that Derrick had all the Middletown phone books back to 1980 neatly filed in his desk drawer?"

"No, if I had known that, I would have asked him for one. I still have the one from when my father was alive. Fortunately, people here don't move very frequently, so their addresses and phone numbers don't change often."

Peter commented, "He was quite the pack rat."

"So I'm finding out," Liz replied.

"Well, are we ready to take some of these things back to the house?" Sue asked.

"Could I take just a minute to walk down by the pond?" Liz inquired.

"Sure, go ahead. We have to round up Byron and load these things into the station wagon," she replied. "Take your time."

Even though it was past 11:00, it was so shady that there was still a lot of dew on the grass. Liz was wishing that she had worn some old shoes so she could walk to the other side of the pond where Derrick took her to see animal tracks. The pond was glistening in the sun, and in the distance, she thought that she heard a bobwhite singing. She hurried to the other side of the pond where it was quite muddy. She couldn't go very far without ruining her shoes, but she did see deer tracks and what appeared to be raccoon tracks. From that point she had a marvelous view of almost all of Derrick's property. He had been so proud of his place and loved it so much. Liz had grown to love it too. What was to become of it she wondered?

She could see Sue and Peter loading the station wagon, so she slowly walked back to the house, trying, as she walked, to memorize every detail of the landscape.

"Ready to go?" Peter asked.

"Not really, but I know we have to."

"You're welcome to come back before you leave."

"Yes, I'd really like for Arif to see this place. He's heard so much about it."

"By the way, when's he coming?" Peter asked.

"He should be here before we have to go to the funeral home."

"Does he need someone to meet him?"

"No, he's going to rent a car."

They pulled away from the house, and everyone was quiet as though lost in his or her own thoughts on the ride back to town. Liz was feeling sorry for herself and Sue. Among Derrick's aunts and uncles on the Hoffman side, Sue was Derrick's best friend. When the rest of the Hoffmans criticized him and treated him as a black sheep, she always stood up for him.

They parked in the garage, and Peter started carrying the boxes of Derrick's belongings up the steps to the attic above the garage. Avis came out to see how they were doing and said that sometime soon she would ask Alex to help her go through Derrick's belongings to sort them out. As far as Liz knew, she never solicited Alex's assistance in sorting through Derrick's things. Perhaps they still lie undisturbed where they were placed in the attic that day.

The only item from Derrick's home that wasn't put in storage in the garage attic was a magnificent head of a male deer that had been mounted on the wall of his living room. Avis suggested that it would be appropriate to hang it in Derrick's former bedroom. It was apparent that she wanted it mounted there immediately and that she wanted all of them to participate in the placement and mounting.

As they carried the trophy upstairs, Liz thought about how she used to visit Derrick in his room when he was a child. Unlike the rest of the house, it had an almost rustic, woodsy environment with its open beams and knotty pine walls. It suited Derrick so perfectly, and he used to proudly take her there to show her his toys and model airplanes. For years Liz used to bring him model airplanes as gifts, and he and she spent many happy hours assembling them there.

Derrick's former room was so large that it easily accommodated the buck's head with its impressive antlers. It was the first deer that Derrick had ever shot, and he was very proud of it. Avis reminisced about how every time she saw the head she used to reprimand Derrick for shooting such a magnificent creature. Liz too found it distasteful that Derrick could shoot a deer, but she also felt gratified that the trophy of which he was so proud would hang in his room.

When Avis announced that Edna had lunch ready, Liz inquired what time they were planning on going to the funeral home. Avis said that they should be there by 2:30 to have some time alone with Derrick before the visitation, which started at 3:00. Liz told her that she would probably have lunch with Jill and then go to the funeral home with Arif. If Arif should be late, she would walk over in time to ride with them.

After having lunch with Jill, Liz felt the need for another shower. It was time to dress for the visitation, so she put on something somber and joined Jill on the front porch where she was waiting for Arif. When Jill inquired if Arif and she had any plans for dinner, Liz said that she was certain that Arif would want to have dinner with her and Raphael and their mutual good friends, Anne and Jeffrey Bishop, from Jefferson City. Jill said that she would make the arrangements with Anne and Jeffrey.

As it neared 2:30, Liz became concerned that if she waited much longer, she wouldn't have any time to be with Derrick before the visitation. Consequently, she asked Jill to wait there for Arif while she went ahead to the funeral home with the Hoffmans.

When she reached the Hoffmans, everyone was ready to go. As they drove the mile and a half to the funeral parlor, Liz felt very apprehensive concerning what was about to happen. She longed to see Derrick, but at the same time she was terrified at the thought of seeing him in that setting. Everyone in the car was silent and appeared to be lost in thought.

Soon she found herself standing with Sue in front of his casket. He looked very peaceful and handsome but different with his hair shorter than usual and no mustache. Liz was thankful that he wasn't wearing a suit because that would have been totally out of character. Instead, he was wearing a white dress shirt. Even though she couldn't remember ever having seen him in a dress shirt since her father's funeral, it seemed far more appropriate than a suit. How young he looked, far younger than the last time she saw him. There was no sign of any head injury. How could an injury be so fatal and not even show? Matt had said that his medulla had been severed.

From behind she could hear Peter asking if she liked the casket. she answered that she thought it was perfect for Derrick. She stood there thinking how 22 years before her mother had laid in repose in the same room at the very same spot. How thankful she was that her parents hadn't lived to see this day. They idolized Derrick so much that his death would have devastated them.

Liz was jolted from her thoughts by the sight of two men approaching the casket. One looked very pale and dazed and was leaning on the other for support. She moved away to where Sue was seated and asked her who they were. Sue told her that the one who was being supported was Dave Ruhlen, who was riding with Derrick at the time of the accident. Dave appeared still to be in a state of shock, so she didn't attempt to talk to him. He and his companion didn't stay long, but Dave's despair overwhelmed the room and everyone in it.

She could feel herself chilling and shaking, so she went out in the sun to try to warm up. Everyone said that it was a warm day, but she couldn't feel any warmth in it. She was wondering why Arif was so late and kept watching for him in vain. When people started arriving for the visitation, reluctantly she went back inside.

Among the first to arrive was her cousin, Joanne, and her husband from Kirksville. With them were Liz's cousin, George, and his wife, Thelma, from Alabama. Upon seeing them, Liz broke down and wept. Witnessing her despair, they took Liz to a side room and tried their best to console her. It reminded Liz of how Joanne was with her at the hospital when her mother died. That branch of her mother's family had always been there for Liz when she needed them. Little did Liz know that after the funeral George would make a comment to Arif about the Hoffmans that would end up having traumatic repercussions for Liz in her search for closure .

It was time for Liz to join the receiving line, so she asked her cousins to keep an eye out for Arif and to let her know when he arrived. The receiving line had already formed. Sue told Liz they had saved a place in line for her with the casket on one side and Avis on the other. She mechanically took the designated place as people started pouring in. Many of them were from Jefferson City where Derrick had worked. Liz recognized a few of Derrick's friends. She could hear Avis asking them if they had learned anything from Derrick's death. All Liz could think to say to people she didn't know was, "Hello. I'm Derrick's mom. Thank you for coming."

About a half an hour into the visitation, Joanne came to tell her that Arif had arrived and was in the side room. As soon as Liz finished talking to an old acquaintance, she excused herself from the line. Upon reaching Arif, she kissed him and anxiously asked how he was feeling. He said that he was fine and had a good trip, but that the plane was over an hour late. Liz told him that she regretted having to leave for the funeral home without him to which he replied that she should do what she has to do. After chatting briefly with Anne and Jeffrey, she excused herself to rejoin the receiving line.

Seeing several friends of her parents, she thought how ironic it was that she hadn't seen some of them since the last time she stood in line in the same room for her mother's visitation. Her father's visitation had been a couple blocks away at the Catholic funeral home. She saw so many people whom she hadn't seen for 30 years or more. She didn't recognize her high school Spanish teacher until she heard her introduce herself to Peter. When a man about Liz's age hugged her and said that he was a hunting buddy of Derrick's, Liz didn't realize that he was one of her high school classmates until she heard him introduce himself to Sue.

Whenever she thought that she couldn't endure another minute in the line, she glanced at Avis and gathered courage from her example of strength. If at 80+ years of age she could stand in that line for three hours, Liz had no justification for leaving.

As Derrick's friends filed by, she could smell alcohol on some of them. Several of them commented, "He sure lived fast." Strange, Liz thought, that she should hear these words over and over. It made her think of a book that she read as a teenager entitled *Knock on Any Door*, where the hero "lived fast, died young and had a good-looking corpse." It seemed that Derrick was always living on the edge, and Liz didn't realize it.

One of the more bizarre incidents occurred when Liz's parents' former housekeeper, Cynthia, appeared and started trying to explain to her why she had divorced Liz's uncle. Cynthia had met her Uncle Phil at Liz's mother's funeral, and apparently fell in love at the first sight of his flashy, ultra-expensive sports coupe. Shortly before Liz's mother's death, Cynthia promised her that she would continue to keep house for Mr. Springmeyer if anything should happen to her.

Ironically, Liz's mother hadn't been in her grave more than a few months before Cynthia married Phil and moved to Minneapolis, abruptly leaving Liz's grieving father without a housekeeper. The whirlwind marriage lasted less than two years, and Cynthia had been married twice since. Under those circumstances, Liz was not happy to see her and told her that it was not the appropriate time or place for an explanation.

Another vivid memory from the visitation was that of seeing so many pretty girls crying over Derrick and kissing him. When Paula came through the line, Liz's heart went out to her. Several members of her family were assisting her through the line. Because the line had to keep moving, all Liz could do was to embrace her and sob with her, and then she was gone.

One of Derrick's friends surprised her with a black and white picture that he had taken of Derrick and Derrick's dog, Blackie, just two weeks earlier on a fishing trip. It was a real action shot of him and his dog along a creek, beautifully capturing the zest that Derrick had for life. He and Blackie are standing on some rocks in the creek bed with creek bank and Missouri woods in the background. Blackie is looking up at Derrick with adoration. Everything in the picture was so typical of Derrick and the life he lived and loved. The friend thoughtfully brought several copies of the picture, enough for all the relatives. It is one of Liz's most treasured pictures of her son.

After the visitation, Liz spent some more time with Derrick. Out of the corner of her eye, she was aware that Arif and Peter appeared to be having a cordial conversation. After they finished, Arif joined her with Derrick. All Liz could think was, "Why, God, do the three of us have to be together like this? Why couldn't it have been as she had hoped and dreamed? Why did time have to play this cruel trick on them? Why did time run out?"

It was difficult to leave Derrick, but it was late and time for them to get some dinner and check into the motel. Liz's relatives from Kirksville and Alabama were leaving to return to Kirksville that evening, so Liz and Arif hugged and kissed them and bid them farewell. Upon departing, they said that they would see them again the next day at the funeral.

The plan for dinner was for them to meet Jill and Raphael, Anne and Jeffrey, and another dear friend, Diane Nelson, at the Four Corners. In vain Liz was wishing that they could go somewhere that didn't hold so many memories, but in Middletown there wasn't anywhere else to eat that was very good.

After checking into the motel and changing into something more comfortable, they made the short drive to the Four Corners. When they arrived, the place seemed more jammed than usual. We were shown to a table that was adjacent to the table where Derrick, Paula, and Liz had sat on her last visit to Middletown. How painful it was to sit there and look back on that happy night.

Everyone was in a mood for drinks before dinner. As Liz sipped her wine and looked around the room, she recognized Mrs. Sheaves, who had been a dear friend of her parents. Liz excused herself and went to talk to her. In her effort to comfort Liz, she told me how she had learned to cope with her husband's death. Mrs. Sheaves and Avis were such pillars of strength and courage. Liz wondered why she couldn't be more like them?

Upon returning to the table, Liz was pleased to see that Arif, Raphael, and Jeffrey were having a good discussion.

She half-heartedly joined in the conversation with Jill, Anne and Diane. Shortly after they ordered their meals, she thought that she heard Paula talking to Jill. She turned and saw Paula standing on the other side of Jill. She looked pale and was visibly trembling as she clutched her drink. After saying goodbye to Jill, she approached Liz who got up and embraced her.

Liz introduced her to Arif and they exchanged brief pleasantries. Paula's first words to Liz were, "Derrick would be happy that he died drunk. All the time I knew him, I dreaded getting a phone call that he had been killed in an accident. I just knew it would happen. I thought about writing you, but I didn't know if it would do any good."

All Liz could think to say was, "I wish you had. I've been sitting here seeing the three of us at the adjacent table."

"Yes, this place is full of memories. Derrick and I were getting back together. I was going to move back in this week." She stopped briefly to brush some tears from her eyes. "How long will you be here? I'd really like to talk to you."

"We're flying out Friday afternoon," Liz informed her.

"I'll try to see you before then. Take care."

As she turned to leave, Liz said, "Paula, I've never had a chance to thank you for letting Derrick be with me in Oklahoma on your third anniversary. I shall treasure that time with him forever."

Through her tears, she said, "He told me what a wonderful time you had and thanked me for you. He talked about it a lot. I know that it meant a lot to him too."

"You're not just saying that to make me feel better, are you? I like to think that it meant a lot to him."

"It did--it really did," she reassured Liz.

Taking her hand, Liz squeezed it and said, "God, help us all to get through this. Bye, Paula."

"Bye, Liz. Take care."

Chapter 9
June 6 - 7, 1991

That night Liz fell into a fitful sleep in Arif's arms. It felt so good to have him hold her, but even having him there didn't stop the pain and tears. She could feel the pillow becoming wet from their incessant flow.

The sleeping pill that Raphael had given her worked. Arif was ill and up all night which was worrisome, but because of the pill, she was able to doze off again. The next time she awakened, the sun was out.

As she put on her black skirt and black blouse, Arif commented that he knew when she purchased the skirt that she had bought it to wear to a funeral, except he thought that it would be his. Since Liz didn't know what to say, she told herself that it was the medication making him react that way and tried to ignore it.

They went to Jill's for breakfast. As they were eating, Jill mentioned that she had heard rumors that Derrick had left two wills. This prompted a flashback for Liz to the previous October when Derrick and she were driving from Dallas to Indian Hills. At the time she hadn't paid much attention to what he had said about taking care of Paula and Brad, but now she remembered that he has said something about leaving his property to them.

Because Liz was anxious to get to the funeral home to spend as much time as possible with Derrick, she was having a difficult time concentrating on what Jill and Arif were saying. Finally, she interrupted and said that she wished to spend some quiet time alone with Derrick at the funeral home before the service.

Liz and Arif were the first to arrive at the funeral home, so that gave her an opportunity to say goodbye to Derrick in private. Arif stayed with her for a short time and then went outside. For several minutes she stood transfixed by his casket, not willing to believe what was about to happen. There were several pictures and small mementos that some of his friends had placed in the casket. She could think of nothing to add to the collection. She touched his hair, face, and hands, but didn't kiss him. She felt so numb and helpless standing there. What would she do when in a few hours she no longer even had this much left?

Soon the Hoffmans arrived, so while they were with Derrick she stepped aside and passed the time reading cards on floral arrangements. One card in particular caught her attention. It was on three red roses and read: "A red rose for each year that we were together." The card was unsigned. After drying her eyes, she found the arrangement that Rob and Ellen had sent. In spite of a memorial having been established with the Boy Scouts, there was a veritable sea of flowers.

The service was to be held at the funeral home. She wanted Arif to sit with her, but he wanted to sit with her cousin George, so Liz took a seat in front with Sue. Soon she was aware of the funeral home becoming very crowded, with people being seated in several side rooms and on the front porch. Later she learned that over 600 people attended the service, which was an impressive turnout for a weekday. A few minutes before the service was to begin, several of Derrick's friends approached his casket en masse and wept. One friend stopped and said to Sue and her, "I keep thinking that Derrick will sit up in the casket and say, 'Okay, folks, the joke is over.'"

Sue responded, "Funny, I was thinking the same thing."

Liz tried in vain to persuade Arif to sit in front with her, but he said he would be more comfortable sitting with George. As the service was about to begin, she took her place by Sue. Liz was wondering if it was going to be a traditional service in keeping with everything so far that had been very traditional. Again, she found herself chilling and having to control herself from visibly shaking. She felt, in spite of the warm weather, as though she hadn't been able to get warm since Monday morning before that fateful phone call.

Through much of the service, Sue and Liz silently wept and clutched each other's hand. She could hear the minister characterizing Derrick as happy-go-lucky, such a free spirit. He went on to say that Derrick wasn't concerned with things that worried most people, such as income tax. Strange, she thought, that he should use that example when Derrick was involved in preparing his tax return the last time she talked to him. It seemed that everyone knew a different Derrick. He talked about the many friends Derrick had, both young and old. He was right about that.

After the first few minutes, she found herself having a difficult time concentrating on what the minister was saying and allowed her thoughts to wander. Judging from the size of the crowd in attendance on a weekday, to her it was clearly evident that Derrick had touched many lives. What greater tribute could there be to his short life, she reflected. He wasn't a success in the traditional way of having a university degree and high-paying job, but he was truly blessed with many friends. If only he had a good marriage and a more stable personal life, this tragedy might not have occurred.

The service turned out to be very traditional. Liz found herself wondering how Derrick would have wanted it. Perhaps he would have wanted the service at his place on the lawn by the pond and to have his ashes scattered at his favorite local fishing hole or on Current River. She was disappointed that some of Derrick's friends weren't asked to participate, but, all in all, it was a very nice service.

Her next recollection was of being at the cemetery for the interment. Everyone gathered under the majestic oak tree that Derrick and she had admired just a year and one half before. As they were shown to their seats, all she could think of was her previous visit with Derrickc. She could see Derrick standing underneath the tree, his light brown hair blowing in the autumn wind. That day had been chilly, whereas this was a truly magnificent day, all sunshine and warmth. It was the kind of day that was more typical of the end of June. It was the kind of day that Derrick would have gone fishing. It was a day that one tends to associate with summer recreational activities rather than a funeral. Liz remembers commenting to several people that day that the weather outdid itself for Derrick.

Again, Arif didn't want to sit up front, so Liz was seated next to Peter. She thought about how sad it was for Peter for he too had never had any other children, and he lived alone. In recent years, Liz had been fortunate to see Derrick almost once a year, whereas Peter hadn't seen him since 1987. She thought about how people kept saying that losing a child is about the worst thing that can happen to a parent. She thought how much that grief must intensify if that child is an only child. Why does life have to be so cruel and unfair?

Liz joined close family, each placing a yellow rose on top of the casket. That was about all the Liz could remember about the graveside service. This couldn't be for real. She felt as though she were acting out a scene in some tearjerker melodrama.

Before Liz could comprehend, the service was over, people were leaving and it was time to leave Derrick to be interred. As Arif started helping Liz toward the car, a middle-aged woman came up to them and identified herself as the person who had brought them dinner on Christmas Eve 1970 when they were in Middletown after Liz's father's death preparing his home for sale. She had come to an estate sale that they were having and, seeing how much they had to accomplish in a very short time, she was concerned that they wouldn't have time to get a decent dinner. Like an angel, she brought them a hot, home-cooked meal, which they had never forgotten. For several years, they stayed in touch with Sheila at Christmas but hadn't heard from her in quite some time.

Sheila went on to explain that she now lived in Jefferson City and had read of Derrick's death in the local paper. Her heart went out to them, so she came for the service in the hope that she could be of some comfort. There she was, again like an angel, trying to console them.

She told them that she had gone through a divorce, and then moved to Jefferson City to try to start a new life. There she met the love of her life and lived happily with him until he was diagnosed with and died of some rare form of cancer. Now, once again, she was alone, but she felt much richer emotionally and spiritually for having had such a special love, even though it was for a short time. She said that she hoped that someday Liz could look back on her short time with Derrick as a blessing.

Liz couldn't believe that the same person who, as a stranger, brought them food in a time of need was there again in a time of even greater need. They hugged and blessed each other, and once again went their separate ways. Liz went through the motions of talking to many people at the cemetery, but her only vivid recollection is of the emotional reunion with Sheila.

After leaving the cemetery, Arif, Liz's cousin, George and she returned to Jill's house where several people gathered after the funeral. When Liz mentioned that they were expected at the Hoffman's for lunch, she could detect that Arif was none too keen on going. Reluctantly, he consented and he, George, and Liz went there together. After they arrived, Liz became separated from Arif and George and went to the kitchen to see if she could help with anything. Sue and Edna accepted her offer of assistance, and she carried some of the trays to the table that was set up for a buffet.

As she placed the last tray, she overheard Avis telling the story behind the three roses and the card reading, "A red rose for each year that we were together." She said that the roses were from Tammy, and that Tammy couldn't attend the visitation or funeral because her husband was so jealous of Derrick. Liz should have known that the flowers were from Tammy, but she was unaware of what had happened to Tammy and that she had a jealous husband.

After going through the buffet line, Liz gravitated to the porch where Derrick and she sat the last time they visited Avis together. Matt and Peter were there along with an obviously distraught woman who was showing them some papers. When the introductions were made, Liz realized that this was Derrick's other girlfriend, Linda Gaspari. She was very tall and slender with olive complexion and long dark hair. She was good looking in a callous sort of way. Liz judged her to be about five years older than Derrick. Later, Arif, who also met her at Hoffman's, made the comment that it looked as though Derrick had found her in a whorehouse. Liz couldn't help but agree with his observation.

As Liz sat down, she was shocked to realize that Linda was passing around her love letters from Derrick. Deep inside she felt a piercing envy because this woman had a whole stack of letters from her son while Liz didn't have any. No wonder he didn't have time to send a newspaper clipping to her or to call her. Glancing at one of the letters, Liz could see through her brimming eyes that it was signed "Your love slave, Derrick." Liz didn't read any of the letters because somehow it seemed to her a violation of something terribly personal. What could possibly be her motive for passing them around? Liz was starting to feel ill.

Linda obviously had Peter's and Matt's full attention and apparent sympathy. Liz's thoughts started drifting. She thought about how the day before she had overheard Matt Hoffman say that there was only one person in the whole world that he knew of who didn't like or love Derrick and that was Paula. Even though Liz was keenly troubled and disillusioned by Paula's recent actions toward Derrick, she felt that Paula must have considered her actions to be justified. After all, Liz had heard only one side of the story.

Linda was not making a favorable initial impression on Liz. She was telling everyone how she had been with Derrick earlier the evening that he was killed. She said that he wasn't drunk and that he had asked her to marry him and that she had consented. She was saying that she was going to quit her job as a waitress where she had met Derrick because she couldn't face returning to the memories there.

Peter excused himself and returned with a carved wood box that he gave to Linda. It was the same box that Liz had seen the day before at Derrick's when they were cleaning the bedroom. Peter had discovered the box in the closet, showed it to Liz and Sue, and informed them that it contained materials for making marijuana cigarettes. At the time, Liz chose to forget the incident. Now it was apparent that the box had special meaning to Linda. Instinctively, Liz found herself disliking Linda and feeling that she couldn't have been a good influence on Derrick.

Lunch was served buffet-style in the kitchen. As Liz went through the motions of eating, she listened to those around sharing more memories of Derrick. Soon Arif entered and said that they should be going. Liz excused herself and told Arif that she needed to say goodbye to Avis.

As Liz was looking for Avis, Sue's husband approached her and said that Paula had requested that he ask her to try to rescue the picture that she had drawn of Derrick. He said that she wanted Liz to have it. The picture he described was the one of Derrick with the crooked-barrel gun and the deer that had intrigued her so much the day before. Liz told him that she didn't know if she would be returning to the house or if the picture was still there, but that she would see what she could do.

She found Avis in an adjacent room and emotionally said, "Avis, we have to be going, but first I want to thank you from the bottom of my heart for raising Derrick the way you did so that he and I had such a wonderful relationship. I can never thank you enough."

She smiled bravely and said, "I'll always keep flowers on his grave for you."

Liz took her hands and replied, "I know you will, and I'll send you all the pictures of Derrick that I have."

She looked me steadfastly in the eye and said, "I'd like that."

"I pray that God helps us all to get through this. Goodbye, Avis."

"Good-bye, Elizabeth. Thanks for coming."

After they returned to Jill's, Liz's cousin George departed for Kirksville. He had come to the funeral alone, because the evening before his wife had suffered a bad fall. Naturally he was anxious to get back to Kirksville to see how she was doing.

After George's departure, Liz and Arif chatted with Jill and Raphael for a while. Jill showed them a notice from the Jefferson City paper printed in large, bold letters "In memory of Derrick M. Hoffman, Sherson Electric Co. will be closed on June 6th, 1991." It was overwhelming for Liz to know that such a large employer would shut down for an entire day in Derrick's memory.

Since they had about four hours before dinner, Liz felt that they should try to see a few people whom they hadn't had a chance to see. First, they drove by Mrs. Edward's house and were fortunate to find her at home. She had been a dear friend of Liz's parents and was the mother of one of Liz's best friends. Now she was in her mid-eighties and still living in the same house where Liz had spent so much time as a child.

Upon opening the door, she was obviously surprised and thrilled to see them. She led them to the back porch where they had a nice visit. For Liz walking through her home was a journey back in time. Everything looked exactly as it used to look 35 years before. Her home was filled with antiques much the same way that Liz's parents' home had been.

Even though Mrs. Edwards appeared to be very frail, she said that she had just come in from doing some gardening. Immediately she started apologizing for not having attended the visitation or funeral because she "just couldn't face the Hoffmans."

There was so much antagonism that existed between the Edwards and the Hoffmans when Liz was growing up. She found it difficult to comprehend that those emotions were still so strong. Liz had long since forgotten the cause of the feud, but obviously at least one party still carried a grudge. After they said goodbye to Mrs. Edwards, Arif commented that he had talked to several people who didn't care for the Hoffmans.

They had seen Liz's cousin, Maxine, at the funeral home but only briefly, so they stopped by to see her and her brother, Bill. Bill had been seriously ill for about five years, and Maxine had cared for him as she had cared for her mother and father before. Maxine spent much of her youth caring for her ailing mother, and despite being very good-looking, she never married. She and Bill lived in the family home that they had shared with their father after their mother's death.

As Maxine took them into the living room to see Bill, Liz thought of the many times that Derrick and she had visited with them in that same room. While Maxine and Liz caught up on family happenings, Derrick and Bill usually talked about baseball or football.

After they visited them in 1989, Derrick made the comment that Bill was just sitting around waiting to die and that he would never want to be like that. Liz chided him for his insensitive remark and commented that one never knows what challenges will be dealt by life. At least Derrick had been spared the challenge of coping with old age and poor health.

They found Bill looking exceedingly frail but in seemingly good spirits. Seeing Bill looking so fragile must have been quite a shock to Arif who hadn't seen either Maxine or Bill since they visited in Sacramento in the early 1970s. The conversation centered mostly on Derrick and their memories of the visits he and Liz paid them over the years. Seeing how frail and exhausted Bill was, they didn't stay long and departed feeling very depressed about his condition.

That evening they drove to Jefferson City with Jill and Raphael to have dinner with their good friends Anne and Jeffrey Bishop. They met at Anne and Jeffrey's home for drinks and then went to a private club for dinner. The Mark Twain Club's quiet dignity and elegance was a welcome relief from dining in the boisterous atmosphere of the Four Corners. Samuel Clemens seemed to preside over the club from his imposing portrait, which was prominently displayed on the center wall. Liz hadn't been in the club since she lived in Middletown, and it was a relief to be somewhere that didn't remind her of Derrick.

Inevitably the conversation turned to the events of the day. Everyone had heard rumors that Derrick had made a second will. Also, there were rumors that there was a third girlfriend which caused Liz to comment, "To quote Alex, 'Derrick was really on a roll with the women.'"

She continued, "When I discovered the unsigned card on the three roses, my first thought was that it was from Paula because she and Derrick had their third anniversary of being together last October. Apparently, I was wrong because Avis said they were from Tammy.

Jill added, "Tammy's husband, who was a policeman, was very jealous of Derrick, so much so that the previous Fourth of July he had Derrick arrested for some minor offense, and Raphael and I bailed him out of jail. Because her husband was so jealous, Tammy couldn't attend the funeral, so she sent the roses instead." Jill sighed and dabbed some tears.

In character, Derrick had neglected to mention the incident to his mother. Liz sadly reflected out loud, "I remember being bitterly disappointed when Derrick broke up with Tammy ostensibly because of her father's intense disliking for him."

Then Jeffrey, who by then was a little drunk, enviously made the comment, "Derrick was quite the stud."

After that insensitive comment, Liz excused herself and went to the ladies' room. Anne went with her, but they didn't discuss Jeffrey's comment. Instead, Liz told her that if there was anything about which she could be thankful, it was that things went so smoothly between Arif and the Hoffmans. Because Liz wanted to stay in touch with Avis, she was relieved that relations had improved. Knowing how hard the feelings had been, Anne was both surprised and pleased to hear that things had improved. She said that she had been happy to see Arif and Peter having such a cordial conversation at the funeral home.

Upon their return to the table, the conversation turned to reminiscing about the old days. Arif and Raphael kept each other company while Anne, Jill, Jeffrey, and Liz talked about their youth in Middletown. The excellent wine was the catalyst for some welcome light heartedness and laughter. It was the first time Liz had laughed since she lost Derrick, and it was to be the last time she would laugh for many weeks.

She still had some things relating to Derrick that she wanted to do in the morning. Arif was aware that she wanted to visit Derrick's place, so he recommended that they go early to get there and leave before anyone else arrived. They got up at 6:00, had breakfast, and were on the road to Derrick's by 7:30. Liz had asked Jill to write the directions so they wouldn't get lost. As they neared the property, she pointed out the site of the accident to Arif. They stopped briefly. As she pointed out Derrick's property across the cornfield and through the trees, he commented that he had no idea that the accident had occurred so close to home. He also found it difficult to understand how anyone could have a fatal accident in that ditch. They didn't linger long because they were anxious to get to the house.

As they started up the driveway, Liz could see the Hoffman's station wagon and a truck parked there. They couldn't believe that they had started working so early. Arif wanted to turn around and leave, but Liz prevailed on him to keep going. As they parked the car, he said that he would look at the outside, but not go inside. Liz insisted that he see both.

When Sue came out to greet them, Liz informed her that they were going to look around a minute and then be on their way. At that moment, Peter opened a window to talk to them. He said that they were getting ready to clean out Derrick's desk and inquired if they would like to help. Sensing Arif's discomfort, Liz said that they would look around outside first.

As they walked toward the pond, Arif said, "Let's get out of here."

"Please let me show you the place before we go. I want you to see it," Liz implored.

"Let's make it fast. I don't like what's going on here."

"What do you mean?"

Irritably he said, "I don't want to talk about it now. Just keep moving."

It was another spectacular summer day. Derrick's place glistened in the early morning dew and sunshine. Only a week ago, just 168 hours ago, Derrick left his place to go to work for the last time. Just a little over 100 hours ago, he was here. Now this unlikely assortment of people was here for their diverse reasons.

As they hurriedly toured the property, Liz said a silent goodbye to the pond, to the heron's tree, the wild animal tracks, the trees that Derrick planted, the bird houses that he had built, the picnic table, the tree in front of the house, the storage shed, all the landmarks that Derrick loved so much and of which he was so proud. Who would live here? What would become of this place? She knew it was none of her affair, but the place had become so much a part of her.

As they approached the house, Sue came out to put a box in the station wagon. Liz asked if they could take a quick look inside before leaving. As she took them in the house, she expressed disappointment that they couldn't stay longer. When they entered the kitchen, Peter was there going through the desk. He had set aside some pictures of Derrick and Liz and one of Derrick's dog that he gave to Liz. She thanked him and explained that they had to be going since they still had the cemetery and several other places to go before their early afternoon flight. As they walked through the living room toward the front door, Liz noticed that the picture that Paula had drawn of Derrick was no longer on the wall. She could sense Arif's mood worsening by the minute, so she felt that it would be unwise to inquire about it.

Sue and Peter accompanied them to the car and wished them a good trip home. Liz and Arif thanked them for all they had done in making the funeral arrangements. When Arif offered to pay for the funeral, Peter said that Derrick's insurance would take care of it. As they drove away, Liz was overwhelmed with the sudden realization that she would never see her son's place again. She abandoned herself to grief, and Arif expressed his frustration with her insisting that he see the property in spite of Sue and Peter being there.

Arif's mood darkened by the time they returned to the motel to pack. He revealed that on the way to the Hoffman's after the funeral, George had commented that he didn't see how Arif could tolerate going to their house. Arif went on to say that she was acting and being treated as a long-lost member of the Hoffman family, which he found to be inappropriate. George's comment had managed to tilt Arif's mood from that of outward tolerance toward an awkward situation to one of unacceptance nearing disgust. And this was only the beginning as Liz was to learn over the following months.

Finally, as Liz was packing, she reached a point where she could cry no more. All she remembers is throwing away the black skirt and blouse that she wore to the funeral and wishing that Arif had taken her advice and stayed in Sacramento.

On the way to the cemetery, though she could feel Arif's growing frustration, she vowed that she wouldn't let it mar her visit to Derrick's grave. There were only a few precious minutes to be spent at the grave. As they approached the grave, she felt that she was hopelessly trapped in an unending nightmare. Why couldn't she wake up to life before June 3 or better yet to life before Arif's illness?

Because of the warm weather, the flowers on the grave were starting to wilt. The humid air was heavy with their fragrance. Arif stood by her at the grave for a short while and then said that he would wait for her in the car. Liz must have stayed by the grave for fifteen minutes, asking Derrick why he had to leave her and how was she to cope with both his death and Arif's life-threatening illness? Over and over again, she asked God what she had done to be made to suffer so. As she walked numbly away from the grave, she knew that it would be many months or perhaps even years before she would return.

They drove the five miles to the cemetery where her parents were buried. It had been 21 years since Arif had been there with her. All her recent visits had been with

Derrick. As they tried to pull out the grass that was starting to obscure their grave markers, Liz realized that this was the first time she had visited her parents' graves that she hadn't shed tears for them. This time her tears were for Derrick and for the abysmal situation in which she found herself.

As they drove back toward town, Liz tried to collect herself before stopping at the funeral home to pick up some papers. When they arrived, David Hirsch, the owner and a close friend of Matt Hoffman, was there. He gave Liz the material they wanted and tried to console them. When he suggested that they might want to attend Alcoholics Anonymous, Arif asked him why. Liz still remembers the shock she felt when he said that he thought that AA might be helpful because Derrick was an alcoholic or on the verge of being one. With this revelation, Liz asked herself, "Why didn't I know? Why didn't Jill tell me? Why didn't someone tell me?"

After departing from the funeral home, Arif tersely asked her if she had anything else she wanted to do before leaving. Liz hated to leave without seeing Paula, but with Arif under such obvious stress, she decided not to say anything about trying to see her. Instead, she told him that the one thing she wanted to do was to drive through the park where Derrick had worked for so many years. On their way to the park, they stopped for lunch at McDonald's. Even that McDonald's held memories of the time Derrick and she stopped for breakfast there on our way to the airport in Jefferson City.

It was a glorious day in the park. Liz had always wanted to show it to Arif. The trees that Derrick had planted were shimmering in the brilliant sun, and Liz could see through her tears some of the birdhouses that he had constructed and hung. So many features of the park were the result of

Derrick's labor of love--many of the trees, the trails, bridges, and picnic benches. Derrick would have been pleased to see it looking so beautiful. After driving through the west end of the park, Arif interrupted her thoughts saying it was time to go.

With Arif absorbed in his own thoughts, the drive to Columbia was agonizing. Inside the terminal, Liz's morbid thoughts focused on how 21 years ago she said goodbye to her father for the last time in that terminal. As they approached the gate, her eyes found the hotel phone from which she was placing a call when Derrick met her 3 1/2 years earlier. "Why, God? Oh, why, God, is all this happening?" was all she could think and ask.

Liz wiped away some tears and checked to see the time. Somehow she got through the last two chapters without going to pieces. Yes, she was going to continue reading after checking on Arif. Looking out she could see that the weather was rapidly deteriorating. It wasn't a day for a walk.

She and Purky joined Arif by the fire to find him asleep with his book on his lap. Liz warmed herself by the fire for a few minutes, made a phone call, did 15 minutes on the treadmill and headed back to her office. She would read another couple of hours before fixing dinner.

Chapter 10
June 8 - August 20, 1991

Liz and Arif arrived home late Friday evening, so she had the weekend to try to recuperate before returning to work. To complicate matters, Arif informed her that he needed for their life to return to a normal routine because he was scheduled to try out a new medication the next week. Inwardly, Liz knew that at the time she was incapable of giving him the normal life that he needed to make the experiment with the new medication a success, but also she knew that, under the circumstances, it was pointless to ask him to wait a week or two. Ever since he had been on steroid medication, trying to reason with him had been very difficult.

A memory of that wretched weekend was finding the book she had been reading the night of Derrick's death, *The Thorn Birds*, on the table exactly where she had left it. To Liz, her own life had taken on all the aspects of the tragedies of that novel. Even though previously she had found the book difficult to put down, she knew that now, because of what happened while she was reading it, she could never finish it. Consequently, she threw it away.

Too soon Monday came, and she wasn't ready to face returning to the office. In addition to exhaustion and sleeplessness, she was still suffering from a cold that she had caught while in Missouri. She called the office and informed her staff that she would try to return on Tuesday.

Monday was the first day that Arif seemed to be in a somewhat better mood. When he seemed interested in her romantically, somehow, she put aside her grief and responded to his advances. After some coaxing, it felt wonderful to surrender herself to passion and to be wanted by him again. After the loving, she took advantage of his good mood and asked him to take her to Donner Lake for the day. Since the idea of an outing appealed to him also, Liz packed a picnic lunch and their swimsuits, and they headed toward the Sierra.

On the way to Donner, Arif stated that he wanted to make it very clear that she was not to have anything to do with any of the Hoffmans ever again. Since, with the exception of Avis, Liz had never had contact with any of the Hoffmans, she didn't consider his demand to be too unreasonable except for Avis. Over the years, she had always maintained at least minimal contact with her. Usually, when Liz was in town, Derrick and she would visit Avis at her home or take her out to lunch or breakfast. Liz had written Avis a sympathy card when her husband died. Avis had stopped by to see Liz's brother Rob in Indian Hills.

Feeling somewhat shaken, Liz replied, "But I have promised to send the recent pictures I have of Derrick to Avis. You know that."

"Apparently, I haven't made myself clear. I mean no contact," he responded, his eyes flashing angrily.

"But Avis is old," Liz pleaded. "She's my son's grandmother, and she raised him as best she could. What I appreciate most is that she didn't say anything to him to turn him against me. I don't see how it could hurt to write her a thank you and to send the pictures."

"If you must send the pictures, send them to her through Jill. Did you ever stop to think that people might not want the pictures?"

"I know that Avis and Jill want them. They told me so," Liz retorted.

"I would prefer that you have no contact with Paula either. It was obvious that there was something ugly going on about there being more than one will that I don't want you involved in under any circumstances. You were either too stupid or blind not to see what was going on and played into the Hoffman's hands by helping with the cleanup of the property."

Unsuccessfully trying to hold back her tears, she stammered, "But I had to go there for Derrick's sake and my own sanity,"

"Don't you see that they wanted you there as a witness?"

Incredulously Liz asked, "What do you mean?"

To which he replied, "They needed you to witness that there was no second will."

By this time Liz's tears were flowing uncontrollably. "I'm sorry, Arif, but I was too grieved to see beyond my emotions," she said between sobs. "I don't know what ulterior motives, if any, were at play. All I know is that I had to go there. And I don't see any harm in my writing to Paula."

"Have you written her?"

"No, but I was thinking about it."

"I strongly prefer that you don't. I don't want you to have any more involvement in that messy business. And I don't wish to have to discuss this painful topic again. Have I made myself clear?"

"Yes, I don't entirely agree, but I'll try to understand. Arif, why can't you see that I love you, and I'm not trying to hurt you? I'm just terribly confused right now and need to have contact with people who were close to Derrick. Please, please try to understand."

"You have Jill to call and write."

"Jill doesn't write, and I can't be calling her all the time."

"I love you, Liz, and I feel that by your dwelling on things, you're hurting yourself and me also. I don't stand a chance of getting well with you moping around all the time. Can't you see that I'm fighting for my life?"

"I'm sorry, darling. I'll try to do better. Really, I will," she promised. "Let's find a place to eat lunch and swim."

So they spent the rest of the day feverishly pursuing their lost happiness. They had lunch on the banks of the Yuba River and went from there a few miles to Donner Lake for a swim. Even during the warmest part of the summer, the icy waters of Donner Lake are so cold that it's a challenge to remain in the water for more than five minutes. On that early June day, the water was numbing, but in her frame of mind Liz didn't care if swimming in such freezing water wouldn't be good for her cold. She threw herself into the icy water and pretended that nothing had happened. It was the first swim of the summer, and it was cause for rejoicing. She tried to pretend that all was well with her and Arif and in Missouri.

Returning to work was even more traumatic than she anticipated. As she walked down the hall toward her office, she saw a colleague who innocently inquired if she had a good vacation. How could it be that she didn't know? After explaining to her what had happened, Liz had to seek refuge in the restroom until she conquered her tears.

Ordinarily, at the hospital, news traveled with lightning speed. What had gone wrong with the grape vine in this instance? What had Arif told them when he called about her having to go out of town? Upon entering her office, Liz told the staff what had occurred and asked them to make certain that all the staff were aware of Derrick's death, so that she wouldn't have any more explaining to do.

Liz was grateful to learn that the receptionist hadn't made any appointments for her until the next day. After a few minutes, she informed her staff that she was going to close her office door, go through her mail and try to get organized.

As she went through things on her desk, she found the anniversary card on which she had been working. She had forgotten all about it. When she had been in the office the day before Derrick's death, she had worked on the card while eating lunch, but for some reason had left it unfinished. Traditionally, Liz wrote poetry and created a card for Arif for special occasions. The card for their June 4, 1991 anniversary had only "Happy" written on the front. Obviously, she was intending to write something to the effect of "Happy Anniversary, dear Arif," but had made a mistake in lettering and for some reason hadn't corrected or finished it. The poem inside was complete and was the saddest she had ever written. Through tears she read what she had written only ten days before:

This year I must confess

That because of all the stress
A happy poem I cannot produce.
I've tried, but it's no use.
As your best friend, companion, and wife,
I pray that soon you get a new lease on life.
I long for the way things used to be,
When we went through life so happily.
Happy, happy anniversary, my dear.
May this be the beginning of a better year.

All Liz could think was that she must have had a premonition when she was writing the card. She recalled how vaguely restless and disturbed she had felt that day. It was a card that went unfinished and an anniversary that went uncelebrated.

Her first day back at work was extremely draining. Much to her astonishment, she discovered that she couldn't see to read the print in the telephone directory, which previously she had always been able to read without wearing reading glasses. At the time, she didn't worry too much about the deterioration in her eyesight because she figured that it was caused by extreme fatigue and stress and was only temporary.

After work that day, Arif informed her that their friend Raj from India would be arriving the next day to stay for a day. The thought of having company was overwhelming, but she tried to be cooperative. She thought about how Raj wasn't even aware of Derrick's existence, much less his death.

When Arif told Raj about Derrick, Raj brimmed with sympathy. In fact, having Raj there turned out to be comforting. He was able to give Liz some of the sympathy that Arif seemed incapable of giving. His visit was marred by the news about Derrick and Arif's obvious ill health. After Raj and his wife had shown them such a wonderful time in India, Liz felt badly that his visit was under the worst of circumstances. She regretted that he couldn't stay longer, so she would have someone she could talk to about Derrick.

At work Liz's supervisor, who was the CEO, was leaving on a long-planned, one-month vacation in Australia. Since Liz was the vice president for administration, during his absence she was under more than the normal amount of stress, exacerbated by the close of the fiscal year. At the time, she recalls resenting having so much additional responsibility while she was grieving. In retrospect, however she came to understand that it was extremely beneficial for her to have had a multitude of responsibilities to meet at home and work to help take her mind off her inconsolable grief.

About two weeks after their return from Middletown, Liz returned from work one day with a smile on her face and greeted Arif with a kiss and said "Sweetheart, I'm pleased to report that today is the first halfway normal day that I've had in weeks. Oh, it feels so good! I hope that you had a good day also."

He looked at her strangely and announced, "Your cousin, Maxine called to let us know that her brother, Bill, had died. So much for normalcy!"

Liz collapsed in a chair and was silent.

Arif went on, "I hope you're not getting any ideas about going there to help?"

Numbly Liz answered, "No, Arif, I wasn't thinking that. You know how close Maxine and I are, but there is no way I could go to Middletown to attend Bill's funeral and try to console Maxine. Under the circumstance, I would be totally useless. Fortunately, Maxine has a cousin and niece close by to help her. I'll call her after dinner." Liz could see waves of relief washing across Arif's face.

Much as Liz had feared, Arif's experiment with the new medication was a failure. His physician felt that the only alternative was to go back to using anti-inflammatory steroids along with the other treatments they had recommended.

Less than three weeks after Liz lost Derrick, the son of one of her colleagues committed suicide by jumping off a bridge. Attending the funeral was out of the question for Liz. When she apologized to her friend for not attending, the friend was most understanding. After that, Liz felt very thankful that Derrick died instantly in an accident rather than by committing suicide or being shot or being immobilized by an accident.

After her friends and colleagues in Sacramento learned of Derrick's passing, Liz received many offers of support and sympathy cards. Knowing how skeptical of counseling Arif was, Liz's best friend at work offered to pay the fees for her to go to a counselor so that she wouldn't have to tell Arif that she was seeking professional help. Even though she didn't accept her extremely generous offer, Liz was deeply touched by her friend's concern for her well-being. Eventually Liz did seek counseling, but with Arif's consent.

One card in particular made a lasting impression on Liz. It was from the daughter of a dear friend who had died a couple of years earlier from brain cancer. On the card her daughter wrote, "Elizabeth, my heart is with you. The pain you feel must be unbearable. I think it takes a long time to get over a loss. I still grieve for my mother. In fact, I was in a card store the other day and came across this card. I don't think the card is so pretty, but I love what it says and I hope it is true. I wrote it down to read over my mother's grave and now I pass it on to you":

"Do not stand at my grave and weep.
I am not there, I do not sleep.
I am a thousand winds that blow,
I am the diamond glint on snow,
I am the sunlight on ripened grain,
I am the gentle autumn rain.
When you wake in the morning hush,
I am the swift, uplifting rush
of quiet birds in circling flight.
I am the soft starlight at night.
Do not stand at my grave and weep.

The Bobwhite Doesn't Always Sing

I am not there, I do not sleep.

American Indian"

Prior to receiving her card, Liz was unfamiliar with this well-known bereavement poem in which she found great comfort. One Saturday in late June while she was doing some overdue gardening, the poem took on special meaning when she heard a bird call that she had never before heard in California.

In disbelief she listened to the familiar song--it was without a doubt the call of a bobwhite. She dropped the hoe and started walking in the direction of the call. Her eyes were drawn to the low bushes near a pine tree from where the song appeared to be coming. She could hear the bird but was having trouble seeing it. It continued to sing for about five minutes and then she heard some rustling sounds as though it was moving away. She still couldn't see it clearly. Its call carried her thoughts back to Indian Hills where Derrick and she had listened to the bobwhites. Somehow just hearing that bird made her feel as though Derrick was with her.

As soon as the bird stopped singing, she rushed into the house to consult her bird book. According to the book, bobwhites are not found in California. For over a week, she heard the bobwhite every day in the early mornings and before dusk. Several days later at the grocery store she saw an ornithologist friend from Sacramento State University who had written extensively about birds of California. When she told him about the bobwhite calls, he seemed puzzled and said that as far as he knew there were no bobwhites in that area of California.

That summer Liz spent a lot of time sending acknowledgments and looking through recent pictures she had of

Derrick and getting copies made of them. Much to her surprise, Peter sent several pictures of Derrick in his casket. Liz wasn't aware that any pictures had been taken at the funeral home. He looked so young, handsome and at peace in those final pictures.

One day when she was writing acknowledgments, she was looking up an address in their address book and discovered that Derrick's entry was covered with a heavy label. Seeing his name deleted so completely sent shock waves through her. She never mentioned the incident to Arif because there was no point in doing so. She was being overly-sensitive and she knew it, but, nonetheless, it wounded her to the quick.

In July she sent Jill a large envelope of pictures to be distributed to her, Alex, and Avis. When Liz called a couple of weeks later, Jill reported that Avis seemed very pleased with the pictures. She added that Sue was having a really hard time dealing with Derrick's death. When Liz asked her how Paula was doing, she said that Paula had been talking to Alex a lot and that they were both having a difficult time dealing with what had happened. She related that the week after Derrick's death, Alex played in a softball game that was dedicated to Derrick's memory. It was a game that Derrick was to have played, and the team felt that Derrick would have wanted the game to go on, so they played it for him.

When Liz asked Jill what was happening with Derrick's property, she said that for a while Alex had considered buying it, but decided against it. The last that she had heard was that Peter was going to keep it and rent it out. To Liz's inquiry about whether she had heard any more about a second will, she said that as far as she knew those rumors had quieted down.

Then Liz asked her what she had wanted to ask since she left Middletown. Liz said, "Right before we left Middletown, we stopped by the funeral home. David Hirsch was there, and he shocked us by saying that he thought that Derrick was an alcoholic or on the verge of being one. Jill, is that true?"

"I never thought of Derrick as an alcoholic. In fact, I never saw Derrick drunk. He seemed to have a good record at work. I know that he and Alex would go out with the boys and drink, but boys will be boys, you know. In Middletown there's not much for them to do but party. Alex does his share."

"Last year when I saw Derrick, he told me that Paula asked him to get counseling for his drinking."

"Did he do it?" Jill inquired.

"Yes, he said he got some counseling, and I encouraged him to get some more. He didn't think he had a problem, but I told him that a person didn't have to drink every day or even every week to have a problem."

"I think that David Hirsch would consider all of Derrick's and Alex's friends to be alcoholics. Don't be so hard on yourself, Liz."

"Thanks, Jill, but I can't help feeling guilty for not realizing what was going on."

"You know, I think that Derrick never fully got over Lynne. Did you know that she remarried three weeks before Derrick's accident?"

"No, I hadn't heard that. I have reasons to believe that he was deeply in love with Paula, but with Linda Gaspari and perhaps someone else in the picture, I must admit, it's all pretty confusing."

"Well, I don't think that Derrick was an alcoholic."

"Thanks, Jill. You always make me feel better."

She hung up feeling somewhat relieved that Jill, who was much closer to the situation than she, hadn't detected that Derrick had a drinking problem.

That summer Liz had several health problems. Normally, she was very healthy, but recent events had taken their toll. In addition to her deteriorating eyesight, she had a bladder infection and a traumatized tooth and was starting to go through menopause. The dentist reported that she was grinding her teeth apparently as a result of all the stress she was under. Little did she know that the stress was about to get worse.

Around the end of July she received word from Ellen that Rob had taken a turn for the worse and was in the hospital. When she called Rob, he sounded really weak but optimistic. Ellen said that they were awaiting the results of several tests before a diagnosis could be made. Liz told Ellen that it was difficult for her to leave Arif because of his illness and promised to keep in close touch by phone. Deep inside she had a total dread of returning to Indian Hills where she had experienced such a wonderful time with Derrick. She knew that it was purely selfish, but Indian Hills was the last place in the world that she wanted to go. Somehow she wanted to preserve the treasured memories she had there by not returning to find them gone.

As the weeks passed, and Rob remained in the hospital, it became increasingly evident that she might have to go. Finally, the dreaded call came from Ellen. She called to tell Liz that she felt that Liz might always regret it if I didn't come soon. Liz promised her that she would be there in two days.

Chapter 11
The Return to Indian Hills

When Liz confided in Arif concerning her reasons for dreading going to visit Rob, he was very sympathetic. In fact, it was he who suggested that it might be easier on her emotionally if she stayed in a motel rather than at her brother's home where she had spent her last days with Derrick. The idea appealed to Liz, so she called Ellen to explain her reasons for wanting to stay in a motel. At first Ellen seemed very surprised and disappointed but, in keeping with her character, she was completely understanding.

After assuring her that she would spend all day and evening with her and Rob, Liz made a reservation at a motel that was about a mile from the hospital. Liz's departure from Sacramento was complicated by their having out-of-town guests and Arif's unstable physical condition. The flight to Dallas was very traumatic bringing back memories of having met Derrick there only nine months before. As they flew over the outskirts of the city, she could see several lakes, some of which she was sure that Derrick had boated on and fished. In the distance, she could see the downtown skyline and knew that one of the tall buildings was the hotel where Derrick had picked her up to drive to Indian Hills. More than anything, she dreaded landing at the Fort Smith airport, where she last saw Derrick alive. She prayed for the strength to face that unwelcome ordeal.

After less than an hour in Dallas, she was soon again airborne, this time heading toward Fort Smith. The 250-mile trip took an hour in the small, propeller-driven commuter plane. As it touched down, she thought about all the trips she had made to that airport under much happier circumstances. She first traveled to Fort Smith in the late 1970s and had been averaging a trip there every other year.

A worried looking Ellen met her at the gate and informed her that Rob was eagerly awaiting her arrival. On the way to the car, Liz stood for a moment where Derrick kissed her goodbye, but she tried not to let on to Ellen that she was undergoing such an emotional struggle within. Ellen said that Rob was doing a little better, and she and the doctor were discussing the possibility of moving him to a nursing home. For the past couple of years, Ellen had been having trouble caring for him at home, particularly when he fell and couldn't get up by himself. Consequently, even before his current illness, Liz had feared that it might be necessary to put him in a VA hospital or some other long-term care facility.

Before going to the hospital, they went to the motel where Liz checked in and left her luggage in the room. Since she was anxious to see Rob, she didn't take time to change. As they drove to the hospital, she saw some familiar landmarks which lead her to believe that where she was staying couldn't be too far from Derrick's great grandmother's former home. She had a feeling that it was within walking distance.

When they entered Rob's room, his face literally lit up with delight. He looked very pale and much thinner, but his eyes were shining with happiness. Seeing him so overjoyed made Liz glad that she was there. Even though Rob and she had a lot of differences over the years, they had become much closer after Ellen had transformed him from a selfish bachelor into a caring human being. Also, he was the only close blood relative that she had left.

That first day Liz brought Ellen and Rob up to date about Arif's condition and described in detail the trip to Middletown for Derrick's funeral. Because she felt inhibited in talking about Derrick to Arif, she found herself talking about almost nothing else that first day with Ellen and Rob. It was the first opportunity she had to talk about Derrick extensively with anyone who knew him since she left Middletown.

Because it was a Sunday, she felt fortunate that she was able to see Rob's physician. He explained that Rob had a weak heart, a kidney infection, and was bordering on liver failure. He told her that Rob's condition remained serious, but that he hoped he would be well enough to be moved to a nearby nursing home very soon. After talking to him, she felt somewhat optimistic about her brother's condition.

As evening came, Rob was having a hard time staying awake, so Ellen and Liz kissed him good night and left the hospital. When Ellen dropped her off at the motel, she said that she would meet her the next morning at 8:00 for breakfast. As soon as Liz got to her room, she called Arif to let him know that she had a safe trip and about her visit with Rob.

After she hung up, she went to the motel office to see if they had a city map. They gave her one, and she went back to her room to study it. At first she couldn't remember the name of the street where Derrick's great grandmother had lived, but she remembered that it had the same last name as a friend of hers who lived in Oklahoma City. Yes, that was it--Kidd Street. On the map it appeared to be about a mile and a half from the motel. If she set the alarm for 5:30, she could walk to Kidd Street and be back to meet Ellen at 8:00. With that plan, she went to bed immediately in hope of getting some much-needed rest.

Restless with anticipation, she was awake when the alarm went off. After taking a shower, she was relieved that it was light enough for her to start walking. From the motel the route was a little circuitous, so she kept the map in hand. She felt somewhat conspicuous walking through the small-town residential neighborhoods so early in the morning. It was a warm, humid beginning to what promised to be a very sunny, hot August day. She couldn't discern if the sweat she was generating was from the heat or from the intensity of her emotions.

About three blocks from her destination, she was greeted by the familiar call of the bobwhite. As she made her way toward the house on Kidd Street, hearing the bobwhite's distinctive call made her feel as though Derrick was with her, at least in spirit. As she rounded the corner and the house came into view, in her mind's eye she could see Derrick's dark blue truck parked in front of the house and Derrick approaching the front door and knocking. In spite of it being a different season, everything looked almost the same to her as it did that October day only nine months before. How incredibly her life had changed since then.

With tears streaming down her cheeks, Liz walked past the house to the end of the block, turned, and walked by the house again. Since it was too early to knock on the door and disturb the Overmans. she started walking back to the motel. All the while, close by she could hear the bobwhite gaily singing.

Her reservations for returning to Sacramento were for a Wednesday afternoon departure. Tuesday and Wednesday mornings before Ellen came to pick her up, she repeated the same walk. Each time as she approached the Kidd Street house she felt as though she had Derrick with her. Each time she listened to the song of a lone bobwhite. Kidd Street was the only place she heard a bobwhite on that trip to Indian Hills.

After the first day, Liz tried not to talk about Derrick too much with Rob and Ellen. In spite of his drowsiness, Rob and she had the best visit that they had experienced in years. Rob appeared to be in good spirits, was eating quite well and was constantly joking with the nurses. For that reason, Liz was quite puzzled when on Wednesday morning the doctor asked to speak with her alone.

As Dr. Bradshaw approached, he looked extremely serious. He began by saying, "Mrs. Azmi, I've done all I can do for your brother. His kidneys are failing, and so is his liver. All of his veins have collapsed, so we can't give him any more IVs. Now it's just a matter of time."

For a minute Liz was speechless. Then she managed to stammer, "D--Dr. Bradshaw, I--I thought you were hopeful. I'm due to leave for th--the airport in just four hours."

"I had some hope until late yesterday. I'm really sorry. There's nothing more I can do here, and he's in no condition to be moved to Tulsa. I seriously doubt that anything could be done for him there either. I'm sure you're aware that your brother has a multitude of chronic medical problems."

Liz's thoughts were wildly jumbled, and she was having difficulty following the conversation. "What should we tell Ellen?" Liz sobbed. "What should I do about going home?"

He led me to a chair in a quiet corner and said, "Mrs. Azmi, your brother could linger quite a while. My advice is that you should leave as scheduled, and I'll tell your sister-in-law in due time."

"Dr. Bradshaw, I can't believe this is happening. I lost my only child in an accident just two months ago, my husband has a life-threatening disease and now this. What's going on?" she blurted.

"I'm so sorry, Mrs. Azmi," he empathized. "I didn't know about your child or your husband. I wish I could do something to help."

"I appreciate your being so honest with me, Doctor. I'm so thankful that I came and that Rob and I had such a wonderful visit."

"Yes, that will give you a lot of comfort later on."

"Well, I better get back to the room."

He squeezed her hand and said, "Please don't hesitate to call me at my office or at home any time."

"Ellen's the one I'm worried about."

"I'll stay in touch with her after Rob is gone."

"I'd really appreciate that."

"May God bless you."

"Thank you, Dr. Bradshaw. Thank you for being so honest with me."

Instead of going back to the room, Liz almost ran to the chapel and fell to her knees before the altar. Since her arrival, she had spent some time in the chapel each day praying for Rob's and Arif's recoveries and for her peace of mind. This time she prayed for the courage to face Rob and Ellen as though everything was normal. She prayed that she wouldn't break down and tell them that it was hopeless. More than anything, she prayed that Rob's end would come easily and peacefully.

In a trance Liz made her way back to Rob's room where she found Ellen trying to feed him his lunch. He seemed unusually drowsy and not interested in eating. He said that he guessed he was so exhausted because he hadn't slept much the night before. Liz stayed in the room for a while with Ellen while he dozed and then returned to the chapel where she cried and prayed for about a half hour. Before returning to Rob's room, she went to the restroom and splashed cold water on her face in the hope that Rob and Ellen wouldn't discern that she had been crying.

Back in Rob's room, she found both Ellen and Rob napping. Because she was having chills, Liz went outside to try to warm up. Even the intense Oklahoma heat didn't warm her. As she walked around the hospital grounds, she wondered how she could break the news of her brother's impending death to Arif. She was beginning to feel as though she was under some kind of deadly siege. When she talked to Arif the day before, she had painted a picture of Rob possibly being moved to a nursing home.

When Liz looked at her watch, she realized that in a half hour Ellen and she would have to leave for Fort Smith to catch the flight. The thought sent another chill through her. As she walked toward the room for her last visit with Rob, she said a silent prayer.

Entering the room, she found Ellen awake but Rob still sleeping. Ellen seemed surprised when Liz informed her what time it was, so she agreed that they should try to wake Rob. With difficulty, they brought him out of his deep slumber. His first question was, "Sis, how soon do you have to leave?"

"I'm afraid very soon," Liz heard herself say.

"I really appreciate you coming and leaving Arif under the circumstances. Be sure and thank him for me."

As Liz looked at Rob, she could see that he was having trouble staying awake and focusing on her. She smiled and said, "I'm so glad I came. I can't remember when we've had such a good visit. I'm sorry that I wore you out with it."

Much to her surprise, Rob was dozing off again. Ellen commented that she hadn't seen him so exhausted to which Liz replied that he said he had a restless night. They waited as long as they could, and then Liz leaned over him and said, "Rob, I'm afraid it's time for me to go."

He stirred, opened his eyes, and looked at her intently. "I really wish you didn't have to go, Sis," he said.

"Me too, but Arif is waiting for me. I'll call you tomorrow."

He didn't seem to be able to concentrate on what she was saying. As Liz leaned over to kiss him, he was falling asleep again. She planted a loving kiss on his forehead and said, "Good bye, my stinkpot brother," which was in reference to the conversation Rob and she had the day before about how when she was little she used to refer to him as her stinkpot brother and he called her Pooky and a twerpie. She used to hate it when he called her by those names. Now how Liz wished he would say, "Bye, Pooky." But he didn't.

As she left the room, Liz turned for one last look. Rob was sound asleep and looked totally at peace. It took a great deal of restraint not to abandon herself to tears. Instead she had to concentrate on talking to Ellen. How ironic it was that this was the first time in recent memory that when she was saying goodbye to Rob he hadn't been morbid and said that they would probably never see each other again.

As they drove to Fort Smith, she thought about last October when she made the same drive with Derrick in the driving rain. That day she kissed Derrick goodbye for the last time, and today she had kissed Rob goodbye for the last time. All her close relatives were either dead or dying. Even Mitsi, her cat, was dying. Shortly after they returned from Derrick's funeral, Mitsi had been diagnosed with an incurable tumor in her nose. Because Mitsi was such a comfort to Liz during Arif's illness, the thought of losing her was almost more than she could bear. Was it her fate to pay for her sins by being left to face this cruel world all alone?

What had she done to deserve the hell in which she was living?

Ellen was saying how sorry she was that Liz didn't get out to the house this time. When Liz promised her that she would stay with her next time, Ellen said she was anxious for her to meet their new dog that Rob was so crazy about. Liz was hoping that Ellen couldn't detect how preoccupied and distressed she was.

Somehow they made it to the airport without Liz breaking down and crying. In vain she encouraged Ellen to drop her off in front rather than waiting with her for the flight. After checking in, Liz asked Ellen to wait for her at the gate while she went to the restroom. On the way to the restroom, Liz sought out the place in front of the airport where she kissed Derrick goodbye. As she stood weeping in the exact spot where they had stood nine months before, for one beautiful moment she could feel Derrick hugging her.

With her reverie soon broken by her flight being called, she rushed back to Ellen and promised her that she would keep in touch daily by phone. Liz hugged her and told her to let her know if she was needed. As she looked back at Ellen waving goodbye, she thought of all the times she and Rob had been there to see her off. She could envision him standing there holding on to his walker with one hand and waving to her with the other.

On the flight from Fort Smith to Dallas, she was too much in a state of shock to even cry. As they took off from Dallas and she caught a glimpse of the downtown skyline, the tears returned in full force.

During the four-hour flight to Sacramento, Liz found herself regretting that Derrick and she hadn't spent more time with Rob on that final visit. Ordinarily, when she visited Rob, she spent all her time with him. It was unfortunate that Rob had felt neglected by her spending so much time with Derrick. At least she had somewhat made up for it with this visit.

In vain she tried to read, but either she couldn't see to read through her tears or she couldn't concentrate. Finally, she had a glass of wine in the hope that she could fall asleep. That didn't help either. Nothing could prevent the tragic events of the past months from flooding through and overwhelming her mind.

When Arif met her, he instantly discerned from looking at her swollen eyes that something was very wrong. Even though she had planned to wait until morning to break the news about Rob to him, she decided to not wait. Upon hearing the prognosis, he stared at her in disbelief and commented that whenever they started to get back on their feet, some other tragedy befell them. That echoed Liz's thoughts precisely.

That night Liz was so exhausted that all she could remember was falling into bed and awakening to Arif's anxious voice saying, "Wake up, Liz. I hate to tell you this, but there's a message for you on the answering machine from Ellen's neighbor saying that Rob died at 12:30 last night."

Liz struggled to wake up. It had been days since she had slept so well. It was daylight, and Arif was in his robe. "What?" she asked in disbelief. "It can't be. The doctor said that he could last quite a while. I shouldn't have come home."

"It's almost seven o'clock, so you'd better get up and see if you can get a hold of Ellen."

"Before I call, we should decide if I'm going back."

"Do what you think you should."

"We had such a good visit. I feel that it was more important to be there when I was than for a funeral."

"I agree. If Ellen's children are going to be there, perhaps it won't be necessary for you to go."

When she talked to Ellen, she told Liz that Rob died in his sleep and that three of her children were flying in that day to be with her. Much to Liz's relief, she agreed that there was no need for her to return for the memorial service. Ever since Arif's illness, Liz felt as though most of her prayers had gone unanswered, but this recent one had been answered. Immediately she said a silent prayer thanking the Lord that Rob had died in his sleep and that she didn't have to return to Indian Hills.

Chapter 12
September 1991 - December 1992

After Rob's passing, Liz was under so much strain and Arif was on so much medication that their disagreements escalated. Soon she learned that the less she mentioned Derrick and Rob, the better her chances were for maintaining some semblance of domestic tranquility.

As she found it increasingly difficult to cope, she finally started seeing a counselor. Even though, on the surface, it appeared that it should be easy for her to use the counseling services at the hospital, because of the nature and sensitivity of her management position there, it seemed more prudent to seek help elsewhere. After four sessions, however, she felt that she was getting little or no relief, so she stopped going. Liz didn't know if the problem was with her or the counselor or both. Perhaps they just weren't a good match.

She had gone to a woman who had been recommended by a psychiatrist friend. During the first counseling session, Liz explained to her that she was seeking solutions for coping with her grief and with her husband's drug-related mood swings. Liz was very emphatic that she did not consider leaving Arif as an option. Apparently, this mind-set frustrated the counselor, and, for this reason, she and Liz never found any common ground. Anyway, it wasn't working, so Liz decided to stop wasting time and money. She was desperate for contact with someone who knew Derrick well. It was then that Liz made the decision to try to establish contact with Paula.

In order not to anger Arif, Liz wrote to Paula using her office address. Having no idea how her letter would be received, Liz's hands trembled and her heart pounded loudly in apprehension when, ten days later, she received a reply. She had very much feared that perhaps her letter would be unwelcome or upsetting to Paula. Much to her relief, Paula wrote that she was so glad that Liz had written and that her letter gave her great comfort in her grief. That contact marked the beginning of a deep friendship between Paula and her, which helped Liz tremendously to get through the next several years.

One of Liz's greatest disappointments is that she had been deprived of the possibility of having Paula for a daughter-in-law. Although she would never be her daughter -in-law, Liz was so very thankful to have her for a friend. No matter what happened between Paula and Derrick, she believed that they both loved each other intensely. Also, Liz felt that Derrick would be very pleased that she and Paula developed such a close friendship.

If she had lived in Middletown, Liz felt that she would have completed the grieving process and accepted Derrick's death much more quickly. In Sacramento it was far too easy to lapse into the delusion that nothing had happened to Derrick. On the surface, nothing in her daily routine was changed by his death. Because of Arif's illness and drug-induced sensitivity to talking about Derrick or Rob or anyone else who was ill or dead, Derrick rarely was a part of their conversation. Derrick was Liz's other life, and she could not accept the fact that that life no longer existed. Letters to Paula replaced her monthly or bimonthly letters to Derrick. Every time she wrote to Paula, Liz felt as though she was connecting with Derrick.

When after three months, Liz's eyesight hadn't improved, she went to see her ophthalmologist. Upon examining her, his first observation was that her vitreous floaters had increased dramatically. He seemed quite disturbed about the drastic and unexplained deterioration in her vision and referred Liz to a specialist at UC Davis where she was diagnosed with a retinal pucker, Fuchs Dystrophy, and a cataract.

Since, as far as she was aware, no one in her family had any of these eye problems, Liz began to feel that her eyes were her shock organ and the stress she was under was the cause of most of her visual problems. Even though most of her eye problems could be addressed with surgery, she feared slowly going blind if she couldn't get out from under the constant stress. Now she better empathized with how Arif felt when he said that all her morbidity was causing him great harm. Somehow she had to find a way of creating a more healthful atmosphere at home. Out of desperation, she continued trying to pretend that nothing had happened in Missouri.

There were many times the first year when she couldn't pretend that everything in Missouri was normal. In October, when she attended a professional meeting in San Diego, it brought back all the memories of the meeting in Dallas a year earlier. The Hyatt was the convention hotel at both locations, so even the layout and decor of the lobby in San Diego reminded her of the lobby where she had met Derrick in Dallas. Whenever the meeting was held in the East or Midwest, she visited Derrick and/or Rob enroute. Consequently, the meeting per se reminded her of her visits with them.

Immediately after the trip to San Diego, Arif and Liz went on a windjammer cruise in the Caribbean. With Arif's health problems, Liz was very apprehensive about doing anything so exotic, but he was looking forward to it so much that she was hoping that it would do him more good than harm. They flew from Sacramento to San Juan via Dallas. En route, Liz realized that it was exactly the same date as the year before when she flew to Dallas for the meeting and to meet Derrick. As they started their descent into Dallas, the coincidence caused her to burst into tears. In vain she tried to hide her tears from Arif.

Arif asked, "Why the sudden burst of tears?"

Liz had a difficult time getting ahold of herself and finally managed to say, "Seeing the Dallas skyline..." She stopped, blew her nose and continued between sobs, "The skyline, the Dallas skyline is a reminder that it was a year ago today I flew into Dallas for my last meeting with Derrick. Then she surrendered to more tears.

"Liz, stop it!" Arif commanded. "You're making a scene."

"Unlike some people, I don't know how to turn grief on and off. I wish we were changing flights in Denver instead--anywhere but Dallas."

"There you go being morbid again. I so hoped that this trip would be an escape from your baggage," he retorted.

The cruise really agreed with Arif. In fact, it was the most normal he was during the entire three years of his illness. Upon returning home, he seemed to be doing very well until the middle of December when another attack started almost exactly one year to the day of his last severe attack. Again the attack was relentless for almost a month, during which time he lost over 25 pounds. During the attack, about all he could tolerate eating was beef and potatoes. With Arif's relentless illness, the entire holiday season was a nightmare. In consultation with his doctor in Minneapolis, his local doctor put him on mega doses of anti-inflammatory steroids, and finally the symptoms let up around mid-January. It pained Liz to see him so thin, and her great fear was that he might never be able to regain the weight he had lost.

During that period, the constantly overcast, foggy weather added to their gloom. Of course, the holiday season brought with it memories of Derrick, Rob, and her parents-- all her lost loved ones. One happy moment came when a good friend from Middletown, Diane Nelson, called her on Christmas Eve. It was the first time since their high school days that she had called Liz, and her timing couldn't have been better.

When Liz saw her in Middletown while they were there for the funeral, she brought Liz up to date on all the challenges and disappointments in her life. In the short time they spent together, it became apparent that the saga of their lives contained many common threads. In many ways, Diane, more than any of her other friends, could fully understand the pain she was suffering. For that reason, her call on Christmas Eve helped give Liz the inner strength to cope with the downside of the season.

One Christmas card Liz received was from Darlene Sheaves, who had been a dear friend of Liz's parents and was the mother of one of her close high school friends. She enclosed a long letter with her card. It was a letter full of sympathy and encouragement. In it she wrote that Avis had asked her to let Liz know that a very nice middle-aged couple had rented Derrick's house and that they just loved it. It made Liz sad to think of anyone else living in his house, but, at the same time, it was comforting to know that someone was living there who appreciated the special attributes of the place. Liz didn't let much time elapse before she wrote to Mrs. Sheaves to thank her for conveying Avis's message and to send her best wishes to Avis.

In January 1992 her fifty-third birthday was the saddest that Liz had ever experienced. With Arif on mega doses of steroids, his mood swings were intense. On birthdays past, Rob always sent a card and called and Derrick sometimes called. As was customary on her birthday, Liz had taken leave from work, so Arif and she could do something special. That year they couldn't think of anything they wanted to do or anywhere to go. The weather was as gloomy as their mood.

After driving around aimlessly, they stopped at a mall for lunch and some window shopping, took in a movie and later went to their favorite restaurant. The only birthday card she received was from their insurance agent. When, at work the next day, her staff presented her with a birthday cake and card, Liz was so touched that she cried. A few days later she received a belated card from Ellen.

Two weeks later was what would have been Derrick's thirty-first birthday. It was on a Friday, so Liz's strategy for getting through the day was to bury herself in work at the office. About midway through the morning, a beautiful floral arrangement was delivered. It was from Jill and Raphael. Their thoughtful gesture helped her to know that she was not alone in her grief that day.

A couple of hours later a comforting letter from Paula arrived. Liz arrived home from work to find a letter from Anne Bishop. In all the years since she had left Middletown, Liz could count on one hand the letters Anne had written to her making it difficult to believe that she would hear from her on Derrick's birthday. Since there was no mention of his birthday in the letter, Liz was sure that Anne didn't know about it but somehow sensed that her long-time friend needed cheering up.

That evening she called Jill, and they both had a good cry on the phone. When Liz told her about Anne's letter, she too was surprised about the timing. The next day was the first of February, and Liz was extremely thankful that January was behind her.

The next extremely difficult period began in mid-May and lasted for about a month. Liz dreaded Mother's Day not because of her memories of what Derrick had done for her on that day, but rather because she was no longer a mother. Derrick had called her on Mother's Day in 1990, but it was unusual for him to do so.

After 30 years of being a mother, the intense agony she experienced was the realization that she was no longer, and never again would be, a mother to anyone alive. Of course, she would always be Derrick's mother, but that was past tense. When, that particular Mother's Day, Liz was in the grocery store, and someone wished her happy Mother's Day, she started crying. Never before could she remember a stranger wishing her happy Mother's Day, although she's sure it had happened, and because Derrick was alive, it didn't make an impression.

That first Mother's Day inspired Liz to compose the following lyrics to the melody of "Those were the Days, My Friend:"

Those were the Days, My Son

Once I had a son,
Whose life had just begun.
He laughed and sang the nights away.
Yes, once I had a son,
Whose life had just begun,
When, suddenly, he was taken away.

Those were the days, my son.
We thought they'd just begun.

We laughed and passed the days away.
Those were the times, my son,
We thought they'd just begun,
When, suddenly, you were taken away.

That's how the story ends.
Yes, it's so sad, my friends.
Suddenly Derrick was taken away.
It's so sad, my friends,
That's how the story ends.
Derrick was suddenly taken away.

Soon after Mother's Day was Memorial Day, which didn't depress Liz too much but made her wish that she could put some flowers on Derrick's grave. Just a few days after Memorial Day was the first anniversary of his death. Liz and Arif had plans to be in the Trinity Alps on that day. Since Liz couldn't be in Middletown, the Trinities seemed the best place to be that day. She sent money to Jill to purchase flowers to place on Derrick's grave. On the bouquet was a wide ribbon bearing the inscription: "Son, you were my sun."

June 3 was a beautiful spring day in the Trinities. Derrick was in her thoughts every step of the way on their long hike to Granite Lake. Arriving at the alpine lake, she thought how much Derrick would have loved to go fishing there. She derived great satisfaction from being able to spend the anniversary of the loss of one who loved the outdoors so much in the wilderness celebrating nature. In the high country, it was a day of celebration of the coming of spring. The spring flowers were bursting forth, the aspen and willows leafing, and the birds and insects cavorting in the warm sun. The north side of the lake was still engulfed in massive drifts of snow, and waterfalls from the rapidly melting snow were crashing down the granite cliffs into the emerald waters below. It was an awesome display of renewal in the high country.

The next day was their twenty-second wedding anniversary. Arif began their breakfast conversation with, "Sweetheart, I want to thank you for not burdening me yesterday with your grief. I really appreciate it."

"I thought perhaps you were unaware of the anniversary and what I was going through."

"For the most part, you seemed lost in thought all day, so I would have to be completely insensitive not to know that something was wrong. Thank you for keeping your misery to yourself. Now I hope we can go on to joyfully celebrate our special day."

For Liz that anniversary and the ones since have been bittersweet because of their coming just one day after the anniversary of Derrick's passing. "Arif, I want you to know how difficult it is to make the transformation from melancholy to being joyful overnight. How I wish we could change the date of our anniversary!" she exclaimed.

"Now that's a stupid idea if I've ever heard one," was his curt reply.

"And why do you say that?"

"Because things get better after the first year, that is, if you let them." he said with finality.

That was the first and last time that changing the anniversary date was ever discussed.

Shortly after their return from the Trinities, they had to put their beloved Mitsi to sleep after her year and one-half battle with the malignant tumor in her nose. Watching that ever-growing open sore on her nose for over a year was truly heartbreaking. Fortunately, she didn't seem to suffer much until shortly before they had her euthanized. During Arif's mood swings, she was the only one Liz could turn to for comfort. Almost every evening Liz would lie on the sofa, and Mitzi would take her place on her chest. Soon she would lull Liz to sleep with her purrs. For Liz the prospect of life without her had become almost unimaginable.

Because they wanted to have more freedom to travel, Arif and she had agreed that after Mitsi was gone, they shouldn't have any more pets. Perhaps if her death had come at a time when Liz was less shaken by other tragedies, she might have had the strength to adjust to not having a pet. Arif was as crushed as she was by Mitsi's death, but he was determined that they should try to get along without another pet. With Arif's mood swings, how was Liz to survive without at least a pet to understand and comfort her? Liz prayed that Arif would relent.

Liz's prayers were answered when, just three weeks later, a wonderful male cat turned up at their door. Even though Arif didn't want any more pets, he fell in love with Sherpa at first sight. With an affectionate cat to help cheer them up, things started to get better until Arif showed symptoms of having another colitis attack.

Now that Liz was all too familiar with the symptoms of an impending attack, she again pleaded with him to see another doctor. This time the thought of another attack had him so frightened that he consented to go to a doctor who had been highly recommended by a nurse friend of Liz. After his first appointment with Dr. Shapiro, Arif felt he was in good hands and even if he had to have surgery that things were going to be alright. It was as though he had a new lease on life. One of the first things Dr. Shapiro did was to lower the doses of steroids and other medications that Arif was taking. He was very honest with Arif and told him that he suspected that surgery was the only viable route. It was Dr. Shapiro who saved Arif's life.

In late July Liz's high school class was holding a reunion to mark the thirty-fifth anniversary since graduation. Normally, the reunions were held every ten years, but now that they were growing older, the decision was made to hold a celebration every five years. When Liz first received the invitation, she just ignored it. If Derrick were alive, she would have combined a trip to see him with going to the reunion. As mentioned before, the reunions had served as catalysts for her to visit Derrick. When the invitation arrived, it served as another painful reminder that all was not normal in Middletown. Derrick was not there--working, hunting, fishing, partying, eating, sleeping and loving.

Jill and some other friends from Middletown tried to persuade Liz to attend the reunion. When she explained the close association between the reunion and seeing Derrick, they understood. This was the first time that Liz hadn't responded to the reunion questionnaire. Normally she filled it out in great detail even if she didn't attend the reunion. Because of the overwhelming support she had received from so many of her former classmates when she lost Derrick, at the last minute she decided to write a letter to the class explaining why she couldn't be there and thanking them for all their support. She sent the letter to Jill for her to take to the reunion.

About a month later, one of her former high school teachers, who attended the reunion, wrote to tell Liz how her "poignant" letter had touched him. After that until his death, he and Liz corresponded regularly. She went to see him and his wife the next time she was in Middletown. He lost his wife in 1993, and Liz hoped that she was able to help him half as much through her letters as he has helped her with his.

In early August 1992 Arif and Liz were taking an evening walk when she heard the distinctive call of a bobwhite.

In 1991 the bobwhite had made its appearance in late June, so Liz had almost given up on it for the 1992 season when it suddenly appeared. Again, for almost ten days it stayed around their home, singing joyously in the mornings and early evenings. While the bird was there, she hated to leave home even to go to work. Its song brought back memories of growing up in the Midwest and her times in the country-side in Missouri and Oklahoma with Derrick. The summer of 1992 was the last time that she heard one in Sacramento even though she was always subconsciously listening for its song.

In early October, Ellen sold her place in Indian Hills and moved to Minneapolis to be close to her children. When she told Liz about her plans, she was torn between wanting to go there one last time or having as her memory of her last visit those magic days she spent there with Derrick. If Arif hadn't been ill, she would have gone to visit Ellen and all her precious memories there. Even though Liz was extremely pleased that Ellen was moving to where she had so many loved ones, the thought of the property where Liz had such treasured memories being sold deeply disturbed her. The notion of never being able to return to her brother's home made her feel very desolate.

That fall Liz's professional meeting was held in Cincinnati, so she planned to go to Middletown on her way home from the meeting. One of her purposes in going was to establish memorials for her parents and Derrick at the Middletown Public Library. During the summer, Liz had been corresponding with the library director about the memorials, and her plan was to present him with the funds when she was to be in town at the end of October.

Since this was to be her first trip to Middletown since the funeral, she was having trouble facing the reality of having someone other than Derrick meet her at the airport.

Her cousin, Joanne, from Kirksville and her husband met and comforted her as she collapsed weeping into their arms. They knew how difficult this trip would be for her, and they were able to give the support Liz so desperately needed. They drove her to Middletown where she was going to stay with her cousin, Maxine. Since they wanted to go to the cemetery where Derrick was buried and the Catholic cemetery where her parents were, they went to both cemeteries before going to Maxine's house.

Driving into that cemetery and toward Derrick's grave was like living a nightmare. It was a wet, blustery autumn day, which added to the gloom. At first Liz was disoriented as they entered the cemetery, but when she saw the majestic oak tree, by then devoid of most of its leaves, she was able to tell Bill exactly how to get to the plot. As they parked, she was crying uncontrollably. Joanne took one of her hands and Bill the other, and they walked her to the grave. Then they both hugged her and stepped aside.

There before her was a marker reading "Derrick Matthew Hoffman, 1961 - 1991." Above the inscription was the Eagle Scout emblem. Her tears fell on the marker faster than the intermittent rain. There was only one bouquet on the grave. Liz recognized them as the silk flowers that Jill had put on the grave and photographed for her.

As she knelt in front of the marker, she recited to herself the comforting words of the poem, *Do Not Stand at My Grave and Weep*. As though she heard her, Joanne said, "Look at all the acorns. They are everywhere."

As Liz focused her eyes on the ground, she could see the acorns that were well camouflaged by the fallen leaves. Immediately she started gathering them and forming an acorn wreath around the marker. Somehow, they suited Derrick much better than silk flowers. She put some in her pockets to take to her parents' graves and to take home.

As they departed the cemetery, Liz was extremely grateful that Joanne and Bill had been able to accompany her that first time. When they reached the cemetery where her parents were buried, each of them placed acorns from Derrick's grave on theirs.

Joanne and Bill dropped her off at Maxine's where she was to stay for three days. Maxine, a paternal cousin, hadn't met Joanne and Bill, who were relatives on Liz's mother's side. All three were in their early 70's and seemed more like parents or aunts and uncles to Liz than cousins.

This was the first time Liz had ever stayed with Maxine. It was wonderful to stay in her cozy home rather than a motel. She let Liz drive her car, so every morning Liz got up at 6:00 and drove to the cemetery before breakfast. Usually she went again in the afternoon.

Seeing Paula was one of the highlights of the trip. She picked Liz up at Maxine's and drove her to the cemetery. On their way to the cemetery Liz put her hand on Paula's arm and said, "Paula, there's something I've been meaning to tell you, but I wanted to tell you in person rather in a letter."

Paula tensed up and said, "I hope it's not bad news about your health or marriage."

"No, no it's nothing like that. It's painful to me because Sue Hoffman's husband told me that you wanted me to have the hunting scene that you painted of Eric, and the next day when I went back to the house it wasn't there. The day before I saw it and checked it to see if it was signed. Not knowing who had painted it, much as I wanted it, I didn't ask for it. I think that Peter would have let me have it."

"I was hoping that you had it and just had forgotten to mention it," Paula said as she wiped some tears away. "Probably Matt or Byron threw it away."

"That first day as I entered the hall, it came to my attention immediately. I can't tell you how much I wanted it." Now Liz was crying.

Paula stopped the car at the cemetery and reached over and hugged her. "That's all right, at least we have our friendship and memories to share."

Liz and Paula dried their tears, got out of the car and walked to the Hoffman plot. Much to Liz's surprise, Alex and Justin, another close friend of Derrick's, joined them there. It was a wonderful meeting. On that somber October day, for about a half hour they stood around the grave telling stories about Derrick and laughing and joking. It was the kind of gathering that Derrick would have approved of and enjoyed. Justin commented that if Derrick had been there, he probably would have broken open a beer. It was far more appropriate to commemorate his memory with jokes and laughter than with tears.

After Alex and Justin departed, Paula asked Liz if she wanted to go to Derrick's place. Liz's heart quickened at the prospect, and she told Paula that there was nothing she wanted more than to go there with her. Paula said that her parents knew the people who were renting it and that she was sure that they wouldn't mind. As they drove the country roads to his place, Paula told her that she hadn't been there since his death. Obviously, this visit to Derrick's old place was going to be traumatic for both of them.

She told Liz about how she and Derrick had planned to start living together again the week that he was killed. Because she didn't approve of his drinking, she said that the night that he was killed, he was having one last fling before they got back together. He was to pick up something at her house the next morning. When he didn't turn up, she thought that he must have overslept. She was at work when she received word of the accident and his death.

They didn't stop as they passed the ditch where Derrick was killed. Her eyes brimming with tears, she told Liz about how she and a friend came to the site the day after the accident and found Derrick's reading glasses and some other personal effects scattered about in the tall grass and weeds.

She bravely made the turn into the driveway and toward the house. On their way up the driveway, Liz could see many of the trees that Derrick had planted. He would have been pleased to see how much they had grown. As they parked, a middle-aged man came down the steps and toward the car. Liz rolled down the window and said, "We hate to intrude on you like this, but I am Elizabeth Azmi, Derrick Hoffman's mother. My friend, Paula Carlson, and I wondered if we could look around the grounds."

Extending his hand, he said, "Welcome. I'm Joe Gleason. I believe I've met Paula before, and I know her parents well. You're both welcome to look around. I'll go in and let my wife know you're here. We'd like for you to see what we've done to the inside."

"We just wanted to see the grounds. We don't wish to intrude," Liz replied.

"I know that my wife would be very disappointed if you didn't come in," he said, walking toward the house.

Feeling that they had no choice, they followed Mr. Gleason into the house to meet his wife. When he told his wife who they were, she seemed thrilled to meet them. As they exchanged pleasantries, Liz couldn't help but notice that the Gleasons had done some extensive modernizing to the place. It no longer was a bachelor's quarters but a very comfortable, almost-modern home. As Mrs. Gleason proudly showed them around, Liz wondered what was going through Paula's mind as she saw the rooms in which she had lived with Derrick. Liz hoped that she wasn't making things too hard on Paula by having her take her there. It certainly was emotionally charged for both of them.

Even though so many changes had been made to the house that it made it difficult to recognize, the grounds remained pretty much unchanged. As they walked around the property, they both commented on how beautiful and park-like everything looked and how pleased Derrick would be if he could see it. When they let the Gleasons know that they would be leaving, they both invited them to return any time. Even though Derrick was gone, his hospitality lived on with the Gleasons. They left the property with a deep sense of satisfaction that the tenants loved the place and would keep it looking like a park.

On Liz's last day in Middletown she met with the library director to present him with the check for the memorials. It was gratifying to be doing something at long last to memorialize her parents. Books on specified subjects were to be purchased in their names with the memorial funds. For Derrick she had specified the purchase of books on scouting, nature, outdoor recreation, home remodeling, furniture restoration, and classic automobiles. Even though Derrick was not a heavy library user, she felt that the purchase of books on those particular topics for the library would have pleased him.

After establishing the memorials and placing floral arrangements on her parents' and Derrick's graves, she felt that her trip to Middletown had accomplished its purpose. Also, Maxine and she had a chance to have the best visit they had ever had, and Liz saw many of her dear friends. On her last evening, Jill and Raphael and Anne and Jeffrey and Liz had dinner at the same private club in Jefferson City where they had gone when Liz was there for the funeral. This time the occasion was far more joyous than the last. It was good to be with old friends and to talk about old times. All of them ate, drank, and laughed heartily that evening.

Liz was sad that she couldn't see Avis, but she felt that she had to respect Arif's wishes on the matter. It was particularly disturbing to her because Avis was well into her eighties. On her way home, when she was delayed in the Kansas City airport for five hours, she broke down and wrote a letter to Avis. In it she thanked her again for everything she had done for Derrick and brought her up to date on her brother's death, her trip to Indian Hills, and the establishment of the memorial for Derrick. After finishing the letter, regretfully Liz tore it up and threw it away. As much as she wanted and needed to mail it, she couldn't violate Arif's wishes. Oddly enough, just the act of writing the letter proved therapeutic.

As Liz sat in the airport, she felt apprehensive about going home. Ever since Arif was put on higher doses of his anti-inflammatory medication, her life had been a nightmare. Whereas normally they used to fight two or three times a year, now they were fighting several times a week over what she considered to be trivial matters. Much of the time she felt desperate knowing that there was little she could hope for as long as he was on that steroid medication.

Even though the new doctor, Dr. Shapiro, had cut back on his medication, Arif was still suffering from depression and mood swings. Although he succeeded in relating fairly normally with everyone else, Liz felt that she bore the brunt of his abnormal behavior. Often, she wished that she could go away somewhere, but knew that she could never leave someone she loved so much when he was so ill. Dr. Shapiro was hoping to have Arif strong enough physically to undergo surgery in December. Liz prayed that Arif and she would last as a couple until then. They almost didn't.

She hadn't been home from the trip more than an hour before they were arguing. No matter how careful she was about what she said, invariably she would say something to anger him. It reached the point where she didn't do much talking in his presence. There were times when she couldn't remember how wonderful life was before his illness. So many times during his illness, he tore her heart out by saying that he wished he could go to sleep and not wake up in the morning. With the losses that she had already endured, those utterances sent her into the depths of total despair. By mid-November life together became so intolerable for both of them that she came close to moving out just two weeks before the surgery. After a lot of prayer and soul searching, she decided to stay with him no matter what the consequences. She never regretted that decision.

On December 4, Arif underwent surgery.. Even though it was several months until he was completely tapered off his steroid medication, his temperament changed for the better almost immediately. The surgery was successful. He would have to live with an ileostomy for the rest of his life but within six weeks he was regaining his former strength and psyche. Liz was so thankful that after experiencing nearly three years utter hopelessness, she had the person she married back. They both had a new lease on life.

Liz looked at the clock to find that it was time to set her reading aside, check to see what Arif was doing and start dinner. She looked out to see that the wind was picking up and the snow intensifying. Arif was right; they might be eating at home on her milestone birthday.

So far, she had shed quite a few tears, but nothing compared to the last time that she read her manuscript so many years before. She resolved that if she couldn't finish read-

ing before she and Arif went to bed, she would get up after Arif fell asleep and finish it.

Chapter 13
1993 -1995

Arif's recuperation went extremely well, and after three years of just existing rather than living, thanks to Dr. Shapiro, they were enjoying life once again. After all the tension, frustration, sadness, and grief of those years, it was wonderful to cross the bridge from the depths of despair to near-normalcy and happiness.

It was a new normal because Arif had to cope with learning to deal with his ileostomy, a challenge which he approached with a great deal of courage and a very positive attitude. He returned to his engineering firm with much optimism and enthusiasm. Inside Liz there remained a deep sadness and a terrible grief to contend with, but all this was made much easier to cope with now that once again she had a happy, healthful and almost-normal home life.

On what would have been Derrick's thirty-second birthday, Liz was feeling very low when a dear friend of her family called. In all the years since Liz had moved from Middletown, Adele had never called. The only contact had been Christmas cards and Liz going to see her and her husband when she was in Middletown.

Adele had helped Liz's mother with housework and had helped take care of Liz when she was a baby. Even after Adele went to work elsewhere, she was always considered to be a member of the family. What prompted her to call on that day, Liz had no idea. It's the only time she ever called. When Liz asked her if she knew that it was Derrick's birthday, she said she didn't. Her call made getting through that sad day a little easier.

After talking to Adele, in a further attempt to comfort herself, she made two calls, one to Jill and the other to Diane Nelson. The next day a letter from Paula helped to ease the pain further.

About this time, she and Arif revised their living trust because so much had changed since it was last revised in 1990. Working on the revisions prompted Arif to make a comment that surprised Liz even though it shouldn't have. He was reflecting out loud on how correct he had been not to want to include Derrick in the financial distribution of their estate. He said that his overriding concern had always been that because Derrick wasn't married and had no children, anything he inherited would eventually end up going to one of the Hoffmans. Derrick's untimely death proved him right.

Liz wished that Arif had communicated this reasoning to her years earlier, but probably he had and she didn't comprehend it or didn't want to. Liz remembered Arif's displeasure when her father left one-third of his estate to Derrick. With that money, Derrick bought his house, which Peter Hoffman ended up inheriting. How right Arif had been while she had been so blind. Liz had been so sure that Derrick would eventually get married and have children. When she reflected on the disagreements Arif and she had over the years about not including Derrick in their will, the recent tragic turn of events made it all seem so inconsequential.

In the spring, Liz had cataract surgery on one eye. As a result, her eyesight became much improved, but the floaters, which worsened so much after Derrick's death, continued to obscure the vision in what used to be her best eye. The floaters remained a constant reminder of her loss.

The second Mother's Day without Derrick almost came and went uneventfully. Somehow Liz managed to forget that it was Mother's Day until Arif and she were talking to a friend who mentioned that her family was taking her out to dinner for Mother's Day. Her remark prompted Arif, who had also forgotten that it was Mother's Day, to turn to Liz and say, "Happy Mother's Day."

Liz astonished him and their friend by blurting, "No it's not. You know that I'm not a mother anymore." Then she started to cry.

When they were alone, Arif chided her for the outburst, and Liz tried to explain to him her sensitivities about Mother's Day. The next day when the friend called to apologize, Liz told her about having lost Derrick and apologized for her outburst. Also, she explained that Arif thought of Mother's Day more in a generic sense, whereas she took it too personally.

In June 1993 on the second anniversary of Derrick's death, Paula wrote about how her friends and parents were imploring her to stop grieving and to get on with her life. About a month later, Liz wrote to her that she too felt that she had grieved long enough and hoped that soon she would meet someone very wonderful with whom to spend the rest of her life. When in August Paula wrote that she had started dating someone very special, to Liz the news was very bittersweet.

As much as she wanted Paula to be happy, Liz dreaded the prospect of no longer having her and her letters for support. Also, if she remarried, Liz could no longer pretend that she was her daughter-in-law. Somehow Liz couldn't bring herself to face the fact that she would never have another daughter-in-law. Ironically, she never met Lynne, the only daughter-in-law she ever had. In spite of the feeling of impending loss, Liz wrote to Paula saying how happy she was for her. When, a month later, she wrote that she and Phil were planning to be married in March, Liz's dread of losing her deepened.

In October 1993 Liz attended a professional meeting in Boston, after which she stopped in Missouri on her way home. She stayed with Maxine and followed the previously -established pattern of driving Maxine's car to the cemetery every morning bright and early.

This time Paula and she didn't go to the cemetery or to Derrick's old place, but they met for lunch. It was good to see her looking so beautiful and happy. She had found a man who was very good to her son, Brad, which was of almost more importance to her than her own happiness. Fortunately, she seemed very happy and excited at the prospect of getting married.

Liz couldn't recall how it came up in the conversation, but she was stunned when Paula in a hushed tone said, "I know we've never discussed this, but I've known all along that Derrick had another will. I feel awkward discussing it here, but it's better than trying to write you about it. Have you heard anything?"

"Oh, yes. Arif caught wind of it at the Hoffman's the day of the funeral and feared that I was being drawn into some kind of trap by the Hoffmans."

Paula grasped Liz's hand across the table and with great empathy said, "Oh, Liz, that must have been so awkward for you."

"Believe me it was and still is. He didn't want me to go back to Derrick's place to be a drawn into their actions. I have to admit that the first time they took me to the property, I was shocked that only a day after Derrick's accident, they had removed so many things from the house. Why the hurry?"

"Yeah, Alex was very upset about it and called me about it."

"For Derrick I felt I had to return to the property before leaving town, so Arif reluctantly agreed to go very early the morning of our departure. We weren't early enough because Peter and Sue were already there packing and loading up the station wagon. They both seemed glad to see us, and Peter asked us to help him clean Derrick's office area. We thanked him and explained that we had a lot of things to do before leaving town and because Arif hadn't seen the place, we just wanted to take a quick look around before leaving. Of course, I didn't mention that I wanted to look for your painting. Oh, it was all so hurried and sad!" Liz couldn't hold back her sobs.

Paula gave Liz's hand a hard squeeze and struggled to control her tears.

Liz continued, "After we got back to Sacramento, Arif forbade me to ever have anything to do with any of the Hoffmans. For the most part, it's not been a problem for me, but I must confess that I had a good relationship with Avis and regret that I can't see her when I'm in town."

Paula responded, "Oh, I had no idea."

"As far as I know, she never said anything against me to Derrick, which enabled him and me to have such a close relationship. I'll always be indebted to her for that." Despite her discomfort with the topic, Liz further revealed, "While Derrick and I were driving from Dallas to Indian Hills, he told me of his deep love for you and that he had made provisions for you and Brad. I'm afraid that I should have asked him to elaborate, but instead I steered the conversation to a less morbid subject."

As Liz related what she knew, she prayed that Paula wouldn't be angry with her for not offering to assist in contesting the will that was made at the Hoffman's behest when Derrick became of age, designating Peter as sole heir. Paula brimmed with empathy and didn't appear at all upset or angered by Liz's revelation. Liz surmised that they both knew that at the time of Derrick's death, his personal life was in such turmoil that any claims on Paula's part would have been heavily disputed. Liz firmly believed that Paula loved Derrick for himself and not for any possible financial gain.

After witnessing Linda Gaspari's dramatic exhibition of grief at Hoffman's the day of the funeral, Liz had feared that it was a prelude to her trying to make a claim on Derrick's estate. Because of the messiness of Derrick's love life, Liz couldn't really blame Peter for destroying the other will, if one ever had been found.

Paula said something else that surprised Liz when she mentioned that Derrick often voiced the feeling that he didn't think he'd live to be 30. Perhaps he knew that sooner or later his luck would run out and he wouldn't always emerge from his accidents unscathed. Possibly he never mentioned this premonition to Liz because he didn't want to worry her. In fact, the only time he had ever mentioned anything to her about dying was when he told me about having provided for Paula and Brad in the event of his death.

While in Middletown, she went to the library to view a display of books that had been purchased with the memorial funds and add money to the memorials. It was gratifying to see the many fine books with their memorial bookplates and to feel that her mother and father and Derrick too would have been pleased.

Her trips to the cemetery were much the same as the year before. Mornings and afternoons would find her there. As her tears splashed on Derrick's marker, she recited *Do*

Not Stand at My Grave and Weep and sing *Those were the Days, My Son*. In spite of knowing that Derrick would disapprove of her crying at his grave, she couldn't control the tears. If she could visit his grave on a frequent basis, she was certain that she would be better able to obey the dictates of the poem and Derrick's wishes. Whenever she was overcome with sadness, she imagined Derrick saying, "Mom, please stop grieving. You can best remember me by being happy and living life to the fullest every day."

Because, again that time, the only flowers on the grave were the ones that Jill had put out for her on June 3, Liz feared that few people visited his grave. Jill assured her that several of Derrick's friends went there to pay their respects. Liz wondered if anyone from the family ever visited the grave. Avis had promised to keep flowers on Derrick's grave, and perhaps she did during the summer. With her husband's grave in the same plot, Liz was certain that she went, but now that she was in her mid-eighties, no doubt it was difficult for her to go there very often.

Liz was content not to go near Derrick's place. She didn't know how to find it without directions. Going there once with Paula was sufficient. More depressing than anything was going there and seeing how close to home he was when the accident took his life.

When Jill took her to the cemetery on the way to the airport, she told Liz how she made a habit of going there with her three-year-old granddaughter on Fridays at least once or twice a month to talk to Derrick. When her granddaughter inquired why Derrick was in the cemetery, Jill replied, "Because he didn't wear his seat belt." Paula also had mentioned how she would go to the cemetery to talk to Derrick.

As they approached the grave, Liz was surprised to see that some pheasant feathers had been stuck in the ground above the marker. They hadn't been there when she was there early in the morning. Jill explained that Alex had placed them there on his way to work to mark the beginning of hunting season. She added that he planned to use some of Derrick's old hunting blinds that season. The pheasant feathers were so much more appropriate for Derrick than the cone of silk flowers that Liz had placed on the grave the day before. Unlike the year before, there were no acorns with which to frame the marker. Since we had an hour's drive to the airport, Liz reluctantly said her tearful farewell and wondered when she would return.

One of Jill's friends, who rode to the airport with them, shared with Liz her recollection of her last meeting with Derrick. About two weeks before the accident, she and her husband were at Burt's Place when they ran into Derrick in the bar. With him was a stranger whom Derrick introduced as someone whose car had broken down near his house and who had approached him for assistance. Apparently, Derrick and the stranger soon determined that they would have to go to town for parts. On their way to the garage, Derrick suggested that they stop at Burt's Place for a beer, and several hours later they were still there. When and how the car ever got repaired remains a mystery.

While they were driving to the airport, Liz inquired "Jill, how is your relative Dave Ruhlen getting along? I hope he's been able to put his life together after being in the truck when Derrick was killed."

Jill sighed and replied, "Now there's a sad story. Dave was just getting back on his feet when six months after the accident, his father died suddenly of a heart attack at the age of 54. Can you believe that?"

All Liz could think to say was, "Oh, how tragic!"

"The irony is that in spite of losing his father so suddenly, Dave kept dwelling on Derrick's death. Soon after his father's death, he moved to St. Louis to try to make a new life for himself."

"Have you heard how he's doing?"

"No, not really. Now that Dwayne is gone, I don't know who to ask."

Upon learning of Dwayne Ruhlen's death, Liz reflected on how much Derrick's neighborhood changed in such a short time. Derrick used to talk about spending winter evenings at the Ruhlen's watching TV. Now Dwayne and Derrick were dead, and Dave had moved.

That was Liz's most recent trip to Middletown. After Liz left the hospital in 1994, she no longer attended professional meetings in the East and Midwest, so any future trips to Missouri would no doubt be with Arif to visit the University of Missouri, Columbia campus where they met and to visit friends and relatives in Joplin, Middletown and Kirksville. With so many places to go, they would spend, at the most, a day in Middletown. For many reasons, Middletown isn't one of Arif's favorite places. As was mentioned earlier, his experiences there have been unpleasant or traumatic or both.

Through their conversations and correspondence, Liz learned a lot from Paula that she didn't know about Derrick, such as that he was color blind, that Led Zeppelin was his favorite musical group, and that he loved to dance. She told Liz how good he was with young people and that he devoted time to working with the Boy Scouts. She said that he was the most appreciative person she had ever met. One time after his death when her son was ill with pneumonia, she went to Derrick's grave to tell him about Brad's illness. She said that she could feel him hold her and assure her that everything was going to be all right.

In March 1994, Paula got married. Fortunately, Liz's fears that she would lose touch with her after her marriage didn't materialize. When she wrote the week before the wedding and a week after her honeymoon, Liz realized how unfounded her fears had been. Their friendship continued to be strong. She wrote that she thought of Derrick every day and that he was the love of her life. She added that her husband, Phil, knew this and understood.

After Liz's retirement, when she told Arif that she had been corresponding with Paula from her work address and how much Paula's empathy meant to her, he was understanding even though he couldn't forgive Paula for having moved out on Derrick so soon after his surgery. Liz told him that she suspected that Paula had a compelling reason for doing what she did.

In 1995, her grieving took on a new dimension, one that she didn't anticipate. While Derrick was married and after, she never nagged him about when he would make her a grandmother. In fact, he was the one who talked about his desire to have children. Quite frankly, being a grandmother was never one of Liz's major aspirations. She figured that it would happen in due time, and as far as she was concerned there was no hurry. In fact, she recalled when Derrick and Paula were living together that Arif would tease her about being a grandmother to Paula's child. When he called her "grandma," Liz used to protest very emphatically that she wasn't Brad's grandmother. Perhaps she protested too much. Fate sometimes plays cruel tricks.

Now that the possibility of ever being a grandmother had been irretrievably taken away, Liz was full of regrets about not being able to be one. When their friends would babble on and on about how wonderful their grandchildren were, Liz felt a deep sense of having been cheated out of one of life's major joys. When some of her friends wrote at great length at Christmas about their grandchildren, she began to feel as though they were being insensitive to her situation when, in truth, Liz was the one being overly sensitive.

Rob and Derrick had no children, and now Liz had none. Arif and she had different, but what at the time seemed, good reasons for not having children. If something happened to Arif, Liz had no close blood relatives to lend her comfort and support. To her being left all alone was such a frightening prospect that she desperately tried not to think about it.

Not being able to dream of Derrick very often was a major frustration. The first dream came over a year after his death. In that dream Derrick looked very happy and was playing cards and dancing. Since she had never seen him dance nor heard him talk about dancing, she thought the dream to be out of character until she wrote to Paula about it, and she replied that Derrick loved to dance. Another dream soon followed of Derrick as a little boy. After that, every time she tried to dream of him, she would dream of Avis or Sue Hoffman instead. For several years, she dreamed of Avis at least once a month. The dreams weren't unpleasant, but they frustrated and upset her because Derrick wasn't in them. Often, she feared that the Avis dreams would never cease. The winter before starting to write this narrative, Liz had two dreams of Derrick within a three-day period. She doesn't know what triggered them and since then, she hasn't dreamed of him. One dream she found to be particularly upsetting because he was drinking in it.

So often she regretted not having called Derrick on the weekend of his accident. Probably she wouldn't have succeeded in reaching him, but if she had, perhaps she would better be able to put together the pieces of his last days. Because he told her that he felt that he could tell her anything, she was convinced that if she had asked him, he would have told her what was going on between him and Paula or Linda or whoever else. He might have said something to the effect of, "Hey, Mom, guess what? Paula and I are getting back together. She moved out on me to get me to stop drinking, and she went out with one of my best friends just to make me jealous. I really love her, Mom," or "Mom, remember what I said about Linda not being my type? Well, I was wrong, and I've asked her to marry me. I think you'll like her a lot." Since she found his love life to be so totally fluid and confusing, she probably would have focused the conversation on his career plans rather than his personal life and not know any more than she did now.

So many times she reflected on the unusual happenings immediately prior to and following Derrick's death. Was the foreboding that she felt on that weekend just a matter of coincidence? What about the physical manifestations -- her inability to sleep, the sore that so suddenly erupted on her lip and the twitching in her eye? It was the only time in her life that she had such a blister and her eyes rarely twitched. Was it a coincidence that Arif came home a day early? Otherwise, she would have been alone when she received word of Derrick's death.

The argument that resulted in her shouting and crying so shortly after Arif's return occurred at the exact time that Derrick was killed. For years she could still hear the chilling howl that the cat made that morning when Peter Hoffman called to inform them of Derrick's death. Never before or after did the cat make such a sound. Liz didn't imagine it--Arif also heard it. All these occurrences made her think that, subconsciously, she must have known that something terrible was about to happen.

Before Derrick's fatal accident, Liz never realized how common single-car, rollover accidents were. Now it seemed that rarely did a week go by, that she didn't read or hear of one. Growing up in Missouri, she was aware of how treacherous driving on gravel could be. She had memories of skidding on gravel roads as a result of riding her bicycle or driving too fast. More recently, Arif and she were driving on a gravel road in the Central Valley of California in perfect weather and daylight when suddenly they went too fast at the beginning of a curve, missed the curve, became momentarily airborne, and ended up in a field. Fortunately, Arif handled the crisis skillfully, and there was no deep ditch or traffic or other obstacle, so they landed and came to a stop upright with no damage to the car or them. For a moment, while they were airborne, Liz thought that they were going to meet the same fate as Derrick.

Since losing Derrick, Liz developed a great aversion to beer. Despite growing up around a lot of family and friends of German descent, Liz never developed a taste for beer, and after Derrick's death she found herself hating it. She felt that it killed her son and was the silent, unpunished killer of countless others. She knew that she shouldn't single out beer, when all alcoholic beverages are to blame, but because beer has the reputation of being not as strong, its use tends to be abused more than the stronger beverages.

Arif and she both retired in 1994. Before Arif's illness, she had never thought of retiring. All the personal tragedies that Liz suffered during the early 1990s played heavily in her decision to retire. Often Liz thought about the time in 1990 when she attended an international conference in Ottawa. Because she felt she couldn't afford to be gone any longer from home or work, she flew over both Middletown and Indian Hills without stopping to see either Derrick or Rob. Now that she had the time to see them, she no longer has them to see.

The only item Liz has from Derrick's home is the coaster set and holder, which is on a shelf in the great room of their new home at Lake Tahoe. It's the kind of home that

Derrick would have loved--all woodsy and rustic. The mallard-adorned coaster holder fits the decor perfectly and is one of Liz's most treasured belongings.

In her home in Sacramento there is a drawer containing her few mementos of Derrick. Items in the drawer include his birth certificate, an album of baby pictures, a rubber hammer that was his baby toy, numerous more recent pictures, a cancelled check which he endorsed (the only sample of his adult writing that she had), a gold pin that he brought her from Portugal (later stolen in a burglary), a postcard he wrote to her as a child, his obituary and acorns from his grave site.

Most of all, Liz has many wonderful memories, some of which are documented in this story. For some reason, God saw fit to take Derrick away from her and the many others who knew and loved him. She found this very hard to understand and accept, but she was also extremely thankful that he didn't have to suffer or go through life with permanent scars from an accident, commit suicide or do physical harm to anyone.

One significant comfort had been that through the experience she become aware of so many people who have lost one or more children. Whereas she used to feel so terribly alone in her loss, she learned that the world is full of walking wounded like herself. Many of these people are intensely religious, far more than Liz, but still are permanently scarred by their unnatural loss. To Liz these contacts proved to be far more healing than could ever be achieved through professional counseling unless the counselor had too suffered the same loss. Like so many of life's experiences, the loss of a child is something one has to experience personally to fully understand its horrific impact.

No doubt, many people who are acquainted with the circumstances feel that Liz had such a difficult time coping with Derrick's death because of the guilt she carried for not having raised him. Liz's contention was that guilt or no guilt, when one loses an only child, the loss is catastrophic. The close bond that developed between her son and her in the later years absolved any guilt she may have felt for the early years. Her main regrets were that she wasn't aware of the extent of his drinking problem and that time ran out while she was waiting for the ideal circumstances for him to visit them in Sacramento.

After almost five years, she still didn't have the courage to look through his album of baby and childhood pictures. Frequently she looked at his adult pictures and found great comfort in doing so, but somehow she became choked with emotion at even the thought of going through his childhood album. He was such a happy child, and that happiness is captured in those pictures. Why then should those pictures evoke such sadness? Perhaps it was because of all the hopes and dreams she had for him at that time for a happy, prosperous and long life--all of which were snuffed out forever on a country road in the Missouri heartland on June 3, 1991.

Throughout her narrative, Liz mentions taking pictures of Derrick. Derrick must have thought that she was really a photography enthusiast, because she can recall him making comments to that effect more than once when she was asking him to pose for the camera. She felt sick when she realized that no pictures had been taken at the reunion in Indian Hills. She realized that the last time she bought any film was in preparation for her 1989 trip to Middletown when she took so many pictures of him and Paula. Since Arif had no interest in taking pictures, she probably would never again engage in much picture taking now that she no longer had Derrick to photograph.

Looking through Derrick's adult pictures reminded her that she always felt that he physically resembled the Hoffmans and bore almost no likeness to her side of the family. Perhaps this was not entirely true, because when people who didn't know him saw his pictures, they almost always commented on how much he resembled Liz. No matter who he resembled physically, he was his own person. Even though he lived in Middletown in the shadow of the Hoffmans, he did not conform to their expectations and stood up to them for his own beliefs and way of life.

Liz was thankful that she and Arif were truly blessed with good health, abundant wealth, community recognition, and many wonderful friends, but there will always exist in her the deep, recurring internal pain that comes from having lost one's child.

Her purpose in writing this story was pluralistic. As mentioned in the first chapter, a major objective was to bring conclusion to the initial grieving process. Not having had anyone in whom to confide on a regular basis concerning her grief, she hoped that writing about her loss would serve as a substitute for being able to talk about it. Only time would tell whether this had been accomplished, but already she felt much better from having written about Derrick and her. She found herself experiencing a great reluctance to finish the story. Did this mean that she was still not ready to move on to the next phase of coping with her loss? She thought perhaps she needed to finish reading *The Thorn Birds* or revisit Indian Hills. Most of all, she regretted that her contact with Derrick was so limited that she had so little to write. In so many ways he was a stranger to her although during the last five years of his life, she felt that they were very close.

Even though she craved an end to the intense grief that had gripped her for so long, she never wanted to completely get over Derrick's death. She wished to continue thinking of him every day but to do so without such acute emotional pain. She wanted to no longer let Derrick's death keep her from living life to the fullest. It was time to focus on the present and the future rather than living in the past.

Another objective has been to make Arif better understand her feelings and despair. After reading what she wrote, it would be the answer to many prayers if he would embrace her and say, "Liz, I'm sorry you had to endure and suffer through so much alone. Now I understand."

A year ago when Arif and she traveled through Dallas on their way home from Boston, something very wonderful happened. When Liz looked out of the plane window at the Dallas skyline, as usual she was overcome with emotion and trying very hard to hold back the tears when Arif put his arm around her and held her tight. While he held and soothed her, she let the tears flow freely, releasing her pent-up grief. Nothing was said, and nothing needed to be--it was a beautiful moment of understanding. She prayed that it was a beginning to the understanding that she craved so much.

A third objective was to record events as she remembered them while they were still fresh in her mind so that as long as the manuscript exists, the story of her relationship with her son would live on.

A fourth objective was to overcome the anger Liz sometimes felt when she thought of how much Derrick hurt the ones who loved him with his fast living and penchant for partying. Sometimes she had difficulty suppressing the anger she felt about having been robbed of her immortality. Looking back on the last year of his life, she felt that he was trying to come to grips with his drinking problem, but life is fickle sometimes and cuts short one's best intentions.

If Derrick's example could prevent similar tragedies, then she would feel that all was not in vain. When, less than two years after Derrick's fatal accident, one of his close friends, Flipper Hussmann, had a similar accident under similar circumstances that left him paralyzed, she thought, "when will they ever learn?"

Liz didn't know if she would ever have written this story if she hadn't been inspired by the movie *A River Runs Through It*. She saw it only the year before and in it saw many parallels between the character of Paul, portrayed by Brad Pitt, and Derrick. Brad Pitt even reminded her of Derrick in physical appearance. In the movie two brothers rebelled against the strict upbringing by their minister father, but one brother, Norman, coped in a constructive way, whereas Paul followed the path of self-destruction. The movie moved her to tears.

It is appropriate that this story should be finished on January 31, 1996, on what would have been Derrick's thirty -fifth birthday. "Son, I will think of you every day, but I will try no longer to weep. I will always deeply treasure the memories of the precious moments we had together. Even though I will continue to listen for the bobwhite's song and carry an acorn from your grave in my purse, I must find a way to stop being morbid and dwelling on the past and instead go forward with a zest for life and a firm resolve to emerge from this ordeal a stronger, better and more caring person."

Chapter 14
1996 - 1997

On February 26, 1996, Liz sent a draft of this story to Paula. On March 9, she received a shocking reply, which left Liz totally stunned. At first, upon quickly skimming the letter, Liz was so sickened by its contents that it was several weeks until she could bear to read it thoroughly.

Now, it has been almost a year since she received the letter. The fifth anniversary of Derrick's death had come and gone and what would have been his thirty-fifth birthday had passed. Liz wanted to complete this chapter for the fifth anniversary, but a combination of anger, sadness, and guilt prevented her from doing so. Now the goal was to finish it for the sixth anniversary.

Although it would be extremely gut wrenching, Liz detailed the contents of Paula's letter. If she had tried to summarize what Paula wrote, much of the impact would have been lost. The letter did nothing to weaken their friendship. They continued to correspond regularly and affectionately as they had for the past five years.

Her letter, dated March 6, 1996, was a torrent of pent-up pain and emotion with hardly any breaks for paragraphs. She began by warning that the letter was very long and extremely difficult to send. She advised that if Liz could not bear to read the first seven pages she should skip to the end where she had included some important information that might help cure a persistent cough which Arif was experiencing.

She began by saying that reading the story assured her that Liz was truly a wonderful person. Paula said if she had been Derrick's mother and Derrick had told her the stories that he told Liz, she would have had no respect whatsoever for her as a girlfriend. She could fill in many of the blanks for Liz and for quite some time had been wrestling with herself to do so. Perhaps it would be better that she didn't tell Liz because she would hate to speak poorly of Derrick and lose her as a friend. She said that Liz knew how much she loved him and how hard his death was on her, but she couldn't live with herself if she didn't clear up the night she left him as well as a few other stories.

Paula wrote about how she stood by Derrick so many times when the going got tough, and looking back, now she realizes how naive she was to believe that her love for him could cure him. Although she believed he loved her, he loved his beer more, and he absolutely could not handle his liquor. She spent many months praying and trying to overcome her guilt for not telling Liz, and for having left him. If she had been as close to Liz as she is now, she would have asked her for help. Not even her parents, with whom she is so close, had any idea the pure hell she had gone through with Derrick until it was all over.

What she needed to clear up most for Liz was the hernia surgery episode. Derrick was extremely apprehensive about the surgery. Paula did everything to reassure him that it would be all right. When he came home totally inebriated the day before the surgery, it upset her terribly because Dr. Aquino had made him promise that he would not drink the day before surgery. As usual, when Derrick was intoxicated, he became very hateful and belligerent, knocking her around. She endured it and prayed that he would never do this to her again or to her son. She gave Derrick credit for never having let Brad see him hit her.

Then she went on to reveal that the abuse had occurred many times before, and each time she prayed and convinced herself that it would never happen again. Paula voiced her concern that Liz would have no respect for her for remaining in an abusive relationship. She described some of the earlier incidents of abuse.

The first time it happened was when she didn't want him to drive because he had too much to drink. That time he drove off, leaving her bleeding on the curb. When Alex and Justin found out about it from one of Paula's girlfriends, they were furious with Derrick and begged Paula to leave him.

Paula detailed how one Thanksgiving morning, Alex stopped by and made Derrick leave the house until she could get her things together and leave. It had been a horrible night spent cowering in the bathroom with Derrick going crazy and shoving her around, beating the wall, and slapping her. Fortunately, Brad was staying with his father.

Apparently, they made up soon because on December 23 of the same year she and Derrick planned a surprise birthday party for Alex. Before the party, Derrick came home drunk and revealed that he had been with his buddies at Joe's Alibi and was sick and tired of hearing how pretty she was. In his rage, he shoved her outside, tossed her keys in the snow so she could not flee in her car, and held her face in the snow, vowing that he would mess up her pretty face. To this day, the left side of her face serves as a constant reminder to her of that terrible day. It was so severely frostbitten that it hurts in the winter and is nearly impossible to cover with makeup during the summer when her face is tanned.

That same night he put several holes in the walls and doors. Later, Paula hung pictures over the holes and proceeded with the party as if nothing had happened. As usual, Derrick apologized, cried and swore off drinking. She couldn't leave him--it was Christmas and she couldn't do that to their families.

Back to the hernia surgery--the surgery went well, and she took him home and cared for him. She couldn't recall how long he was off work, but she remembers the last couple of days vividly. When she called home from work to check on him, she could detect that he was drinking, but didn't say anything for fear of making him angry. In the letter, in parentheses, she confided that after the third beating, she learned to keep her mouth shut out of fear.

Paula recalled one night when Derrick came in late and she laid in bed pretending to be asleep. He yanked her from the bed and started hitting her, calling her a tramp and slut "just like all the other women in his life." She didn't know what triggered it, but she found out later that he had been at a bar drinking and carrying on with several other women. End of parentheses.

When he threw her against the wall, she hit the doorframe and passed out. When she regained consciousness, he was crying and begging her forgiveness. Later, when she was diagnosed with a concussion, she told her doctor and family that she had slipped on a rug and hit her head. Only a few close friends of both parties knew the real truth.

Paula detailed how as the days after his surgery passed, she was becoming progressively more afraid because she would come home to find him drunk and belligerent. Derrick was to get his stitches out on a Friday. When she offered to go with him to have the stitches removed, he said that she had already missed too much work. Deferring to his wishes, she asked him to call her after the stitches were removed, which would be shortly after 10:00 a.m.

All day she didn't hear from him and kept trying in vain to reach him. By the time she left work, she was sick with worry and started calling his friends to see if anyone knew where he was. Finally, one of his friends informed her that he was celebrating getting his stitches out. This upset her no end. Needing to talk to someone, she called her girlfriend, Melissa, who asked her to join her for dinner in Springfield. Paula agreed to go to Springfield because she thought that she might find Derrick there. While in Springfield, they drove by some of Derrick's haunts, but didn't see his truck.

When she returned to Middletown, she still couldn't find him until she saw his truck in front of one of the trashiest bars in town, the kind of place he would have killed her for, should she have gone in. Consequently, she cried all the way home. Since Brad was staying with his father that night, she went to bed in his room.

She described how when Derrick returned home in the middle of the night, he entered in the manner of a raging bull. Since the door was locked, instead of using a key, he broke a window to get in. First, he went straight to their bedroom, which made her think that she was safe and could discuss with him in the morning how she couldn't take any more of the bars and the beer. She would give him the choice between her and his beer. Suddenly, he burst into the room and was on top of her, screaming that she didn't care about him, didn't take him to get his stitches out. All the time he was using his fist on her, and the more she struggled, the harder he hit her.

She told how she just laid there and took it, praying that he would kill her and get it over with. When he picked her up and threw her, she didn't give him the satisfaction of pleading or crying, nor did she pass out. Then he grabbed her purse and Brad's medication and started throwing everything around, demanding to know who her boyfriend was and where she had been. When she told him that she had been home waiting for him except when she had dinner with Melissa, he retorted that she was a lying slut and accused her of being out drinking and dancing with other guys. Later, she found out that he had been dancing and carrying on with other women.

Somehow, she managed to run from Brad's room to the living room even though her knee hurt so badly that she could hardly bear it. She begged him to quit kicking and hitting her because she feared that her knee was broken. He picked up the answering machine and told her to find all the messages that she claimed to have left. They weren't there, so it was obvious that they had already been erased. Derrick started throwing things and picked up a footstool and threw it at her head. When she used her arm to shield her face, the stool hit her below the elbow with such a force that it broke. In desperation, she picked up a piece of sharp, splintered wood and shielding herself with it, told him to let her go.

Finally, he told her to get out. She grabbed her keys, made the mistake of putting the wood down, and headed for the door where he stopped her, threw her on the couch and hit her in the eyes, ribs, and jaw. Praying not to seriously injure him, she summoned up all her courage and strength and kicked him near the area of his stitches. He doubled over in pain, giving her enough time to run to her car. After she locked herself in the car, he ran out and started beating the windshield. He was cutting up his hands, and blood was flying everywhere. As soon as it was safe to do so, she peeled from the drive and sped to Gary and Marsha's house.

She awakened Gary with the horn. Even though Gary and Derrick were like brothers, when Gary realized what

Derrick had done, he wanted to beat him the way Derrick had beaten her. She told Gary that she had to get out and get help for Derrick before he killed someone.

The only way she knew to help Derrick was to press charges against him, and hopefully the police would see that he got the help he needed. Going to the police was the most humiliating experience of her life. She described how they photographed her legs, face, torso, and the hair that was coming out by the handfuls. Because she was so humiliated, she refused medical treatment.

Then the police took her back to the house to get her things. Fortunately, they found Derrick passed out. She succeeded in persuading them to leave him undisturbed while she got some of her and Brad's most essential belongings. The next morning a convoy of her friends and some of Derrick's friends went to the house and helped her pack the rest of her things while Gary kept Derrick away from her. After that, Derrick ended up spending several days in jail. She reasoned that he was probably best off in jail because when her father found out about her cracked rib, dislocated kneecap, and cracked arm, he was totally livid.

By that time, she understood why Lynne's father hated Derrick so much, and why he had Derrick put in jail. Derrick had put Lynne through the same kind of hell. Earlier, when Lynne tried to warn her, Paula didn't believe her and reasoned that Lynne was envious of her good relationship with Derrick. In addition, she found out that Derrick had beaten Tammy and another girl friend, Amy.

Amy was the other woman to whom people referred. Derrick dated her for about a year. Paula described her as old enough to be his mother. A few weeks after his death, Amy looked Paula up and told her that the morning of the day he died, Derrick stopped by her house and told her, "This is my last binge. I love Paula too much to live without her. She is to give me her answer about trying again tomorrow. If she says yes, I will get the help I need, continue with counseling, and get some serious help, as long as she will be my wife. She is truly the love of my life."

She concluded the first portion of her letter, saying that for so long she felt responsible for his death, and that it took her a long time to realize that God saved her from him and from herself.

She went on to say that she had some other things, which she wished to clear up, the first being about her and Alex.

She said that she didn't start dating Derrick until months after she and Alex broke up. She admitted having strong feelings for Derrick while she was still dating Alex and that she dated him while he was separated from Lynne but before their divorce. She said that she jeopardized her morals because she was so crazy about him.

Also, she wanted to clear up the story about Trevor and her. She said that Derrick was seeing Linda long before there was anything between Trevor and her. Trevor pursued her and often ended up where she was, which upset her because he was supposed to be Derrick's good friend. One night she and one of her girlfriends had gone to Burt's for dinner when Trevor and one of his friends came in for a drink and joined their table. When Derrick arrived on the scene, he jumped to conclusions. She admitted that when she found out about Linda, she was hurt, and in trying to get back at Derrick, she had gone out with Trevor a few times, but didn't date him seriously until after Derrick's death when she went with him for 18 months. He, too, was an alcoholic but not an abusive one. She credits him with having helped her get through some very trying times after Derrick's death.

As for Brad, she said that Derrick spoiled him with material things, whereas she spoiled him with love. She didn't want Derrick to help her with any of her expenses, especially when it came to Brad, because she feared that people would label her a gold digger the way they had Lynne. Consequently, she and Derrick split the bills equally, and, since his house was paid for, Paula paid for the groceries and the phone bill.

The last thing she wanted to clear up was that Derrick and Linda split up two weeks before his death. She knew about this because Derrick had called her and informed her that Linda had gone back to her ex-husband. By that time, he and Paula were close phone buddies. She described Linda as an alcoholic and a drug user and obviously a liar as well.

She wrote about how she felt that God took Derrick to spare her the heartache as well as to spare Avis and Liz from the day that he killed someone. When Alex and Justin found out that she and Derrick were getting back together, they begged her not to because they feared for her well-being. Although Derrick was a wonderful person sober, he had a Dr. Jekyll and Mr. Hyde personality. In fact, the only time he wasn't mean when he was drinking was when he smoked marijuana. It took her a long time to figure this out, because he knew how much she detested drugs and did his best to conceal them from her.

Then she told me that her Aunt Rhoda had passed away recently and how she was the only member of her family who knew about the problems Paula had with Derrick's drinking. Rho's husband too had been an alcoholic, so she knew what Derrick was putting Paula through. Just as Rho's husband had overcome his addiction, Rho thought that Derrick would also. Because she knew how much Derrick and Paula loved one another, she always stood beside them.

When Derrick was killed, Rho vowed to Paula that the first thing she would do when she got to heaven would be to slap Derrick for hurting Paula so much by getting himself killed.

Paula described how she held Rho's hand and watched her die. Knowing that her aunt would tell Derrick off for her helped her bring closure to this very sad chapter of her life. She said that she knew it sounded strange, but it helped her to know that someone, who knew so much about Derrick and her, and knew the truth and had heard both sides of the story, was there with him.

After recommending a brand of vacuum cleaner with a special filter that might help cure Arif's cough, she ended by asking forgiveness for the things she had to tell Liz and expressing hope that it would help bring closure to a very trying time of Liz's life. She said that if she ever writes a book, she will entitle it "The Bobwhite Doesn't Always Sing.'

Liz's response to her letter was pitifully inadequate. How could she find the proper words to express her shock and revulsion at Derrick's actions? The essence of the letter was that Liz still loved her and would never be able to make up to her for Derrick's abusive behavior. Liz expressed regret that Paula and she hadn't been in touch while she was having problems with Derrick and ended with the hope that Paula and she would be friends forever.

How differently this story ended before Paula read it and wrote her response--it's almost as though it were two different stories about two different people.

For almost five years, Liz had been obsessed with trying to put together the missing pieces of her son's last days. Perhaps that was Liz's real reason for having written this book. Paula's letter contains a lot of missing pieces to the story, pieces, which Liz wasn't content to leave buried with Derrick. It also provides clues concerning his tumultuous love life. Additionally, it provides an answer to why God chose to take Derrick away. Thank goodness Derrick killed only himself.

It killed her soul to know that her son physically abused women when he was drinking. Liz suspected that there was a lot he wasn't telling her about his break ups with his wife and girlfriends, but she had no idea that he had it in him to physically abuse anyone. Derrick's father had never physically abused Liz, and, as far as she knew, there was no history of physical abuse in the Hoffman family or her family. This revelation was almost more difficult for her to cope with than his death. Whereas, prior to receiving Paula's letter, Liz wasn't plagued by guilt, now she found herself wondering if his coming from a broken home was the cause of Derrick's drinking and being jealous and abusive.

Liz wrote this book in the hope of bringing closure to her initial period of grief. This had been accomplished, but now she had to wrestle with the guilt that had surfaced as a result of her probing into secrets that should have remained buried with her son. Paula tried to protect Liz by not telling her, but when she read the book, she had no choice but to tell her side of the story.

Liz reasoned that perhaps it was her fate to continue to pay for the biggest mistake of her youth, that of marrying too young. Because of her sheltered, almost puritanical upbringing, she felt she had to get married when, at age 19, she lost her virginity to Peter Hoffman. It wasn't until six years later when she met Arif that she experienced true love. Unfortunately, Derrick turned out to be the innocent victim of her mistake.

She was thankful that Paula had forgiven Derrick, and Liz treasured her continuing friendship. She was thankful for the golden times Derrick and she shared, the memories of which she had to help get through the dark moments of doubt, regret, and anger. Whenever she became guilt-ridden, she remembered that he said that he loved her and felt closer to her than to his father, appeared to enjoy spending time with her, seemed to be very proud of her, and expressed appreciation for her support of his career goals. That's all she had to cling to and make her feel that she didn't fail him completely. Were the things he said to and his affection for her to be believed or just an act?

In her letter, Paula speaks of the responsibility for Derrick's death which she felt for several years until it became clear to her that God took Derrick away so that he wouldn't end up killing her or someone else. Now Liz found herself plagued with guilt. She was sure that Avis found herself wondering if she was in some way responsible for Derrick's drinking. No doubt Peter has wrestled with guilt. Sue Hoffman probably wonders what more she could have done to intervene.

No doubt there are many others who were close to him have found themselves feeling in some way guilty and asking what they could have done differently. After a great deal of soul searching, Liz became convinced that if Derrick could come back sober, he would not place the blame for his actions on any of his loved ones.

This brings to mind again the movie *A River Runs Through It*. Toward the end of the movie, the Reverend Maclean, revealing in a sermon his inner feelings about his son Paul's death, proclaimed that even though we can't always understand or help troubled loved ones, we can always love them. Similarly, even though Liz sometimes found herself terribly angry with Derrick, she would always love him.

Somehow, once again, Liz would have to pick up the pieces and go on; she owed that to Paula and the many others who have confidence in her; to the memory of her parents, Rob, and Derrick; and especially to the love of her life, her beloved Arif. The one thing that was making life worth living for her was that ever since Arif's surgery, he and Liz had enjoyed the best relationship of their entire married life. With the strength of his love and support, she could face almost anything.

When she started her book, she had no idea how it would end. If she had, it's doubtful that she would have written it. Now that it was written, Liz found it painful to read. What had been accomplished? What message did it bear? If it could help just one person better cope with the loss of a child or one person seek professional help for a drinking or abuse problem, it would have been worth writing.

Having read this book has made Arif far more supportive and understanding concerning her loss. That, in itself, made it worth writing.

Finally, the process of writing this account made Liz realize that even though what happened to her was terrible, how much worse it would have been if Derrick had ended up killing someone. She thanked the Lord for having spared her and Derrick from that fate.

Chapter 15
1998

When, in May 1997, Liz finalized Chapter 13, she felt that the book was finished, and, difficult as it would be, she would manage to go on with her life. The June 3, 1998 anniversary of Derrick's death came and went with her experiencing no inclination to add to the book. At last Derrick's story was finished, and, ugly as it was in part, it had served its purpose in getting her back on track with her life. Through writing it, she had reached some kind of closure.

Then on June 18, 1998, Liz made a trip to Missouri to attend her cousin Joanne's fiftieth wedding anniversary. She dreaded visiting the farm where she had spent such a happy day in 1989 with Derrick and Paula but felt that she had to put such selfish feelings aside, because of what it would mean to Joanne and Bill for her to be there. In vain, she tried to persuade Arif to make the trip with her, but he kept telling her that she was crazy to travel so far to attend a hectic event that would lend little opportunity for a real visit. Even though Liz knew he was right, she felt that after all the times Joanne had been there for her when Liz needed her, she should be there for Joanne and Bill on such a special occasion.

Her cousin George had let her know about the planned celebration six months in advance. A month before the event, however, she still didn't have plane reservations mostly because of Arif's strong feelings that she shouldn't make the trip.

With time getting short to make her reservations, again she brought up the subject with Arif. "Honey, I can't wait any longer to get my tickets for the trip. If I do, either there won't be anything available or the price will have gone sky high."

"Well, I was hoping that as time passed you would come to your senses about this trip. Why is it you're always wanting to go back there?"

"How many times do I have to tell you how Joanne was with me when mother died and so many other times when I needed her?"

"Yes, I understand that, but I feel that it would be better for you or us to visit her and Bill when it's not a special occasion."

"Arif, I feel really strongly about making this trip."

"You must have your reasons, but I hope you don't come back an emotional mess as you have so many times before."

She kissed him and said, "I won't. You'll see."

He shook his head and said, "I hope I don't have to say that I told you so."

Because of Arif's lack of enthusiasm about the trip, Liz was starting to have forebodings about going. Nonetheless, she got reservations and forged ahead with the plans. Even after she had plane reservations, Arif persisted in being negative about the trip. By the time she was to leave Sacramento, she was dreading going.

She flew into Jefferson City where she was met by dear friend, Anne Bishop, with whom she stayed the first night. Her husband, Jeffrey, was out of town, which gave Anne and her an opportunity to have a wonderful visit. Anne insisted that Liz drive her car while she was in Missouri. Liz had planned to rent a car, but Anne talked her into using the car since she could drive Jeffrey's personal car while he drove his government car.

The next day Liz drove to Middletown where she was to stay with her cousin Maxine. As she approached the city limits on the access road from the interstate, the first familiar place she saw was the cemetery where Derrick was buried. She had been driving along in a reasonably cheerful mood until the cemetery loomed before her and drained her of all happiness. Even though she hadn't been there for five years, she immediately spotted Derrick's favorite oak tree and drove directly to his grave.

Seeing his grave was traumatic enough, but it deeply disturbed her that there were no flowers on it. When she wrote to Jill about the planned visit, Liz told her not to worry about putting flowers on for the seventh anniversary because she would be there soon after to do it herself. Neither were there any flowers on Derrick's grandfather's grave. Only a planter of bedraggled geraniums stood by the Hoffman monument. It looked so deserted and forgotten. Even the majestic old oak didn't look as healthy as before. It looked as though it had undergone some kind of tree surgery. In a spasm of grief, Liz dropped to her knees and showered Derrick's marker with tears.

After talking to him and crying for about fifteen minutes, she forced herself to leave to drive five miles to the Catholic cemetery where her parents were buried. Again, she arrived to find no flowers on their graves. Their markers had sunk so far into the ground that they were almost totally covered with grass.

While Liz was trying to clear the grass from their markers, a man approached and introduced himself as the cemetery caretaker. In the course of their conversation, he mentioned that this was the first year that there had been no flowers on her parents' graves. She explained that a dear friend of her parents kept flowers on the graves, but now that her health was failing, Liz needed to make other arrangements. He informed her that a monument company in Middletown provided a service for a fee of keeping silk flowers on graves. After obtaining the name and address of the monument company from him, she inquired if anything could be done to raise her parent's markers. For a very nominal sum, he offered to reset them and said that he would try to have it done before she left.

While the caretaker and she were talking, Maxine drove up. As they hugged, she said that she thought she might find Liz at the cemetery. She was there that day because it was the seventh anniversary of her brother's death. After spending some time with her at Bill's grave, Liz told her that on her way to her house, she was going to stop by the monument company to make arrangements to have flower service for Derrick and her parents.

By the time she reached Maxine's, she was feeling really gratified that so much had been accomplished as a result of her chance meeting with the cemetery caretaker. Maxine and she spent the rest of the day catching up on everything that had occurred since the last time Liz had stayed with her almost five years earlier. Maxine was now in her late seventies and was doing remarkably well considering that she lived alone. She kept herself busy volunteering at the hospital, reading, seeing friends and keeping up her house and garden. It was clearly obvious that she loved having Liz stay with her. In spite of Arif's trepidations, the visit was off to a good start.

Early the next morning, after visiting Derrick's grave, Liz made the drive to Kirksville for Joanne and Bill's golden anniversary celebration. Even though it was a Saturday, traffic was quite light, so she arrived over an hour before the appointed time. On her way to Kirksville, she drove by the farm, but didn't stop because of the dread of revisiting the site of one of her happiest days with Derrick.

Joanne's daughter, Connie, had called Liz in Sacramento to ask her to stay on the farm with her and her husband. After explaining how difficult it would be to go there again, Liz told her that she had reservations at a motel in Kirksville that she hadn't confirmed with a credit card, so she could remain flexible. Connie was very understanding and repeated how happy it would make her if Liz would stay on the farm. Rather than stay at home, Joanne and Bill were going to spend the night at the country club in Kirksville where several other family members were staying.

It was so wonderful to be there with Joanne and Bill on such a beautiful occasion. Joanne's health had been tenuous for several years, so Liz felt that it was a miracle that she had lived to celebrate her fiftieth. She looked so pretty and seemed full of energy for the occasion. For a gift Liz took some silver teaspoons that Liz's grandmother had taken from the farm in 1899 when, after her husband's death, she was forced off the farm by his family. It gave her goose-bumps to be returning the teaspoons to the farm after almost 100 years. Clearly, the teaspoons were a very meaningful gift to Joanne, Bill, and their children.

It was obvious that everyone would be disappointed if Liz didn't stay at the farm that night, so Liz decided to conquer her hang-up and do it. Joanne and Bill's disabled son, Carl, and Liz returned to the farm early that evening, while everyone else stayed at the country club to gab. Since she had never spent any time alone with Carl, it was a good opportunity for her to get to know him better.

As Carl and Liz approached the farm, she had a sudden urge to get out of the car and run in the opposite direction. All too soon they were turning into the long driveway. Carl informed her that it would take him several minutes to negotiate the ramp to the house and that he didn't want any assistance. Nervously, she went ahead and put her suitcase in the designated bedroom upstairs. The heat upstairs was quite stifling, so she looked around and found a window fan to turn on. She felt more at ease upstairs because all her memories of Derrick were downstairs and in the yard.

After waiting several minutes, she thought she should check on Carl. He was still in the car and emphatically said that he didn't need any help. Outside it was much cooler, so in the waning light, Liz decided to walk around the yard. So many ghosts from the past seemed to be there with her--her grandmother, George and Joanne's father and stepmother, Liz's mother and father, Rob, her mother's sisters, Derrick-- for so many years the farm had been a gathering place for the family.

Much to her surprise, instead of feeling upset, she was finding comfort in being there. She found herself thinking about the week she had spent on the farm in 1951. That was the last time she had stayed overnight there. That was shortly after Joanne and Bill were married, and now they were celebrating their fiftieth. Liz had been a little girl, and now she was almost sixty.

Just then a cat ran across the lawn, which reminded her of how, as a child, she loved to go to the farm to play with the cats and kittens. She tried to find the cat, but it had gone into a shed. It was becoming quite dark and a few lightning bugs were making their appearance. Hearing the screen door slam brought her out of her reverie. Carl had successfully negotiated the long ramp leading to the front door and was now inside. It was starting to lightning and there was a scent of rain in the air, so she reluctantly returned to the house.

Before going to bed, Carl and she chatted about the stock market and sports for about an hour. In spite of the heat, Liz slept quite well and awakened feeling very refreshed. The sun was already out, and there was no sign of any rain having fallen from the night's teaser storm. When Liz joined the family for breakfast at the table where Derrick, Paula and she sat in 1989, rather than sadness and loss, she felt a sense of comfort. She felt as though she had come home. She was feeling so at peace that she ended up staying at the farm talking to Joanne, Bill, and many family members until mid-afternoon. What she had dreaded so much had turned out to be an uplifting experience.

Upon returning to Maxine's, there were messages from Paula and Jill. It was a relief to hear from Paula, because, even though we were regularly in touch through letters, Liz didn't know if she would want to see her. The next day Liz was to meet Paula for lunch and Jill for dinner.

That evening she and Maxine ended up stopping by Liz's parents' former home. Several times over the years Derrick had expressed a wish to see the old home place, but Liz had always been reluctant. Driving by and seeing it looking well maintained had always been enough for her. As they were driving by on their way home from dinner, Maxine saw the owner in the yard, so they stopped to chat. Mr. Railing was delighted to see them and really wanted them to see the house. Upon entering, Liz could smell new carpet and paint. Mr. Railing explained that a water pipe in the upstairs bath had broken several weeks before and he had to replace all the wallpaper, paint, carpet and tile. The place was like a show place. How pleased her parents would have been. It really gratified Liz to see it looking so nice and to know that Mr. Railing loved the place so much.

He had purchased the home from her parents' estate and had lived there ever since. On this trip, so many things were falling beautifully into place for Liz.

After visiting Derrick's grave early the next day, Liz was to meet Beverly Deming, a dear friend of her mother's, for breakfast. Beverly is the one who placed flowers on Liz's parents' graves all through the years. She and Liz corresponded usually once or twice a year. Once Beverly paid a visit to Liz and Arif in Sacramento. Whenever she visited Middletown, Liz usually met her for breakfast or lunch. This time, as a small token of appreciation, Liz had brought along a freshwater pearl necklace, which she had bought in Aruba to give Beverly.

When Liz entered the lobby of the restaurant, Beverly was already waiting for her. Even though she had to be in her seventies and was in frail health, she looked much better than Liz had expected. It was a hot day, and she looked neat and cool in her colorful shorts and matching top.

After embracing each other, Beverly said that she had a surprise for Liz at the table and motioned for her to follow. Liz couldn't imagine what the surprise could be. She followed her to a table in the far corner of the room where a very familiar figure was sitting. Suddenly Liz felt as though she was in the middle of one of her dreams about Avis Hoffman, but this was very real. Beverly was leading her to where Avis was sitting. She turned to explain that she had mentioned to Avis that Liz was coming, and Avis expressed a desire to see her. She said that she hoped she had done the right thing by bringing Avis along.

She was sure that Beverly could detect Liz's shock at her surprise. Liz couldn't remember if she had even mentioned to her that after the funeral Arif had mandated that she have no further contact with any of the Hoffmans-- probably not, because Liz would have no reason to share that kind of information with her. All the years Liz had known Beverly, she had no idea that Beverly and Avis were friends. Liz found out later that she had been Avis's hairdresser for over 30 years.

With all these thoughts racing through Liz's mind, she decided that once again fate had intervened and that if Arif ever found out, he would understand. For the past seven years, Liz felt that she had some kind of unfinished business with Avis, so she just couldn't walk out.

Trying not to act too flustered, Liz managed a nervous smile. After seven years, Avis appeared to have shrunk a little but looked as proud and determined as ever. She smiled broadly as Liz sat down. Almost immediately, Liz's misgivings washed away, and she felt comfortable and knew she was doing the right thing.

The three of them sat at the table for close to two hours, talking about Derrick, Liz's parents and mutual acquaintances. Avis had lots of pictures of her grandchildren and great grandchildren to show them. In the course of the conversation, when she mentioned that she was eighty-eight, Liz couldn't help but marvel at how strong she appeared to be both mentally and physically. She said that she was still doing most of her own housework and yard work. As they sat there, Liz thanked fate for arranging this meeting. Even though they engaged mostly in small talk, it was a kind of closure. She felt that this chance meeting would put an end to all the tormenting dreams that had plagued her for almost seven years. Also, she knew that fate had intervened to let her thank Avis once again for not turning Derrick against her.

Avis seemed pleased that Liz had made arrangements for flowers to be kept on Derrick's grave. She explained that she didn't go there much because she found it too depressing, and she would be there on a full-time basis soon enough. They talked so long that Liz was worried that she would be late for the early lunch that Paula and she had scheduled. As they were parting, Avis asked Liz if she had seen Derrick's memorial tree in the park. Liz told her she hadn't and asked her where it was. She said that she couldn't remember exactly how to get there but that Jill or Alex could tell her. Liz left, promising her that she would go to see it. Also, Liz thanked her once again for all she had done for Derrick. The words of appreciation obviously pleased Avis.

Driving to the lunch appointment, Liz kept marveling at all the coincidences that kept occurring every step of the way on this trip. The meeting with Avis seemed more than just a mere coincidence.

Lunch with Paula was short but gratifying. They met at the Red Dog where they had lunch with Derrick in 1989. Paula brought Brad along, so Liz finally got to meet him. He seemed like a very nice, studious young man. Lately, he had a lot of problems with seizures, so Paula hadn't been able to leave him alone for months. That afternoon she had to take him for blood tests, which was why Liz and she didn't have much time together. He was responding well to some new medication, so hopefully his and her life would be back to normal soon.

Paula looked beautiful as always but didn't seem as carefree and happy as the last time Liz had seen her, which is understandable after what she had been through with Brad. When she asked Liz if she had seen Derrick's memorial tree in the park, Liz replied that she hadn't but would like to. She said it was difficult to describe where it was, but that Liz should drive past the creek and keep going until she came to a parking lot. She offered to drive Liz to the airport, but Liz told her that she was driving Anne's car. They parted, promising to stay in touch.

That evening, when Liz was having dinner with Jill and Diane Nelson, Jill inquired if she had seen the memorial tree in the park. Liz replied that Paula and Avis had mentioned it and she intended to try to find it the next day. Jill's directions as to how to find it were as vague as Paula's. That evening Jill did not seem her normal, bubbly self, but then she hadn't seemed herself since, five years ago, when she had a mastectomy. Ever since, she kept herself insanely busy, so much so that she has lost touch with many of her friends.

After dinner they went to Jill's house where Liz got to see Raphael and Alex. Alex looked as handsome as ever. He told Liz that he was a heavy equipment operator for the highway department and on the side was learning to be a silversmith and making jewelry for Jill's new shop. For the time being, he was living at home and was between girlfriends. After Liz returned to Maxine's, she realized that she forgot to ask him how to find the memorial tree.

The next day her flight out of Jefferson City was at 5:00 p.m., so Liz planned to stay in Middletown until early afternoon. She was up early to go to both cemeteries. Upon visiting her parents' graves, she was delighted to find that their markers had been reset. What an improvement! While she was there, it had stormed almost every day, so she wasn't expecting the work to be completed. Everything about this trip had gone so well--almost too well.

After breakfast with Maxine, Liz stopped by the library to give the librarian a check for her parents' and Derrick's memorials. One more thing accomplished! Arif would be pleased and surprised to hear how well things had gone. Everything just seemed to fall into place. There were so many of Liz's friends and friends of her parents that she had stopped by to see without calling ahead and found at home. Now about all that was left to do was to find the memorial tree in the park where Derrick had worked for so many years. Liz hadn't been there since Arif and she went there after the funeral. It was another of those places that she found difficult to go without Derrick.

Because the park was not well marked from the south, Liz missed the turn her first time by. As she wanted to spend some more time with Maxine and stop by Derrick's grave again, she debated if she should try again. Since she had about an hour to spare, she decided to turn around. The sign was very visible from the north, so she had no problem making the turn. Upon entering the park, she started to drive toward the creek when she saw someone at the maintenance shed. Hoping that whoever it was could tell her where the memorial trees were, she turned in and parked. Walking quickly over to the building to get out of the hot sun, she entered and started to introduce herself.

"Excuse me. I hope you can help me find a memorial tree. You see, my son used to work at this park and..."

The man, who appeared to be in his late fifties or early sixties, interrupted her, saying, "Aren't you Derrick's mother?"

"Yes. But how did you know?" she asked incredulously.

"I was Derrick's supervisor. We met before a long time ago and also at the funeral home."

"And your name is?"

"I'm Mark LaGrange. Welcome," he said, smiling and extending his hand.

Grasping his hand, Liz responded, "Nice to see you again, Mr. LaGrange. Now I remember Derrick talking about you, and I think I remember meeting you after Derrick's other supervisor, Mr. Stinson, died."

"Call me Mark. If you don't mind, I'll drive with you and show you where the tree is."

"That would be ever so kind, but I hate to put you to any trouble."

"It would be my pleasure."

They got in the car, and Liz started driving toward the creek. As they approached the creek, she said, "I remember Derrick showing me that footbridge."

"It must have been the other one. This one is new. The other one was washed out in a flood," he explained. "I sure miss Derrick. He was like family. Firing Derrick was the hardest thing I ever had to do."

Liz looked over to see that Mark was crying. "Why did you have to fire him? Derrick never told me that he was fired."

"It was his drinking. It was just terrible. He'd come to work and go to sleep under a tree. It reached the point where I couldn't get any work out of him. He'd tell me that he drank too much coffee the night before and couldn't sleep."

"I feel so awful that I didn't know what was going on. Sometimes I tried to find out from Jill Aquino, but she would just say, 'Boys will be boys'."

"She and Raphael have two real good kids and then they have Alex who's been a big disappointment."

"I thought perhaps he had matured. Last night when I saw him, he seemed happy about helping in his mother's new shop."

"He's a real heart break for his parents. And then there's Flipper who's a paraplegic now."

"I heard about that. How sad and unnecessary. I guess nothing was learned from Derrick's death," Liz lamented.

"One time, Derrick invited the wife and me to a party at his house. You wouldn't believe what went on there. We left the first chance we got, and we never went back. Turn here and park up by the third tree," he directed.

Now they were in a part of the park with which Liz was unfamiliar. She parked the car, and after they got out, Mark pointed to a line of mid-sized trees in the distance. "Derrick planted all those trees."

"Yes, he used to be so proud of what he planted. I have pictures of him standing in front of some of those trees," she recalled.

They walked in silence to the trees. "This is the tree. I think Derrick would like it," he said as he blew his nose and wiped his eyes.

In front of the young oak tree was a stone marker reading, "In loving memory of Derrick Hoffman from Jenine, Trevor, and Mark LaGrange."

"Oh, it's lovely," Liz murmured. "I didn't know that you had done this. Thank you so much."

"It's strange," he replied. "None of the Hoffmans ever thanked me except Sue."

"Sue was always good to Derrick. She's different from the rest of the family," Liz observed.

"You have no idea how difficult Byron Hoffman was when he was head of the Parks Commission. He really made my life miserable."

"He always struck me as being terribly arrogant," was Liz's response.

"Sometimes, when Derrick would get upset with the Hoffmans, I would tell him to cool it so he wouldn't jeopardize his inheritance."

Changing the subject, Liz said, "I'm so glad that I'm getting to see this tree. You don't know how much it means to me. I didn't realize that it was a gift solely from your family. When Paula and Jill talked about it, I thought it was from a group of Derrick's friends."

"After I fired Derrick, we remained best of friends. He was like family to Jenine, Trevor and me."

"It was for the best. He really did well at his job in Jefferson City," she mused

"And then there was his personal life--what a mess. All the fights, the moving in and out."

"I know. I was always hoping that the right woman would come along and get him on the right track."

"You know what he was doing in that ditch, don't you?"

Liz's heart jumped. "No, what do you mean?"

"He and his friend were taking out mailboxes. They had just knocked over a mailbox. It's just too incredible. Derrick was trying to get his truck out of the ditch and didn't make it," he related between sobs." If Derrick had been in his old truck, which was heavier, he probably would have made it."

Liz stared at him in disbelief. All these years she thought that Derrick had fallen asleep at the wheel or had skidded. Instead, it was a prank gone wrong! Now they were both crying.

"And Dave Ruhlen walked away unscratched. From what I hear to this day Dave has never got a grip on himself. He's pretty much become a drifter and bum."

Suddenly, Liz's whole world came crashing down again. Any closure she had found was obliterated in a few short seconds. Everything was fresh and painful again. Her mind was whirling, her head spinning and heart racing. She thought she was going to faint. She was boiling over with shock and anger. How could this be happening? Why didn't anyone tell her before? Why didn't Paula or Jill tell her? Why, oh why? Was she the only one who didn't know? Was everything she thought she knew about Derrick a lie? She had to pull herself together, say goodbye to Mark, and get out of that park and that town.

As she drove back to the maintenance shed, she couldn't control her tears, nor could Mark. He kept repeating what a wonderful person Derrick was and how he was part of their family. Liz thanked him for showing her the tree. Before they said goodbye, he revealed that he had retired from the park and that it was a real coincidence he was there that day since he didn't go there very often.

With great difficulty, Liz drove back to Maxine's. She was crying so hard that her glasses were getting steamy, making it very difficult for her to see to drive. At Maxine's, because her time was getting short, she didn't get involved in telling her what she had just learned. She had a bite of lunch, packed and bid her goodbye. She was thankful that Maxine didn't notice her puffy eyes and tear stained face. As Liz drove away from Maxine's, she wondered if Maxine knew. Middletown is such a small town that news travels fast leaving few secrets to survive.

She didn't have time to stop at the cemetery. Perhaps, under the circumstance that was just as well, because for the first time in her life she was experiencing deep anger toward Derrick.

Her drive to Jefferson City to return the car to Anne was not uneventful. For the first time in her life, she had a tire blow out. After the events of the morning, the blowout really shook her. Traffic was extremely heavy on the interstate, and she had a great deal of difficulty controlling the car while trying to pull onto the shoulder. She must have been so distraught and preoccupied that she had hit some kind of debris when she drove through a construction zone about a mile before the blowout occurred. No one stopped to help her, so she ended up having to walk over a mile on the highway shoulder in the blazing heat to get help. Because she was wearing sandals, sand and cinders from the shoulder got under her feet, causing her feet to bleed. From a truck weigh station she called Anne, who came to get her.

The flat tire cut into the time Liz was to have had with Anne before the flight. She did find time, however, to relate to her what had happened. Anne's first reaction was that it couldn't possibly be true. Her recollection was that Derrick was alone in the accident, but Liz reminded her that Dave Ruhlen had walked away from the accident unhurt. Liz found herself wondering if Anne had known what happened and was putting on a really good act. Upon her return to Sacramento, Arif's initial reaction was much the same as Anne's--that it couldn't be true. Then he reminded her about the foreboding he had about her trip.

Where Liz lives in a fairly rural area between Auburn and Sacramento, mailbox vandalism has been such a chronic problem that some people have resorted to getting post office boxes or building mailbox stands out of bricks or concrete blocks. Liz always figured that the perpetrators were teenage pranksters, but the thought of someone Derrick's age doing it never had crossed her mind. It was something teenagers did when they got bored or drunk or belligerent, but not something that an adult would do. Then she remembered that on one of her visits, she noticed that Derrick's mailbox had been knocked over. She thought that a vehicle had accidently hit it, but Derrick said that someone in the neighborhood did it on purpose. Apparently, it was a common occurrence, and, apparently, he was a perpetrator as well as a victim.

For the first month after her return, Liz was churning inside. She found herself back where she had been seven years before, full of pain, disbelief and despair. Closure once again seemed elusive. What went through her mind was that she could ask Paula or Alex or so many others about the cause of the accident, but why would Mark La-

Grange lie to her? After wrestling with the idea, she never asked anyone for any more information about the accident. She found herself wishing that she had taken Arif's advice and never made the trip--that she had never found out what really happened. She also wondered what other shocking facts about Derrick were still buried in Middletown, waiting to be revealed. She felt as though she was in the aftershock zone of an earthquake and couldn't escape.

Just about the time she was starting to feel somewhat better, the following letter came from Mark LaGrange. He must have gone to some trouble to obtain her address. His letter started the churning all over again.

Dear Elizabeth,

I want to thank you for your kindness toward me during the visit you recently had to the park. I was never given a word of kindness by any of the Hoffman family, except by Sue.

Since you were here I have been thinking of Derrick. He mentioned you often and even thought about coming to work for you, but couldn't cut his ties in Middletown.

His relationship with Trevor, Jenine and I was one of family and not as an employee.

I certainly hope I didn't hurt you when I talked about Derrick, but thought you wanted to know the truth about his death.

Again thanks for coming by and may the Lord make peace in your heart.

Sincerely,
Mark LaGrange

Again, for a couple of weeks after receiving his letter, she was an emotional and physical wreck. She talked quite openly to her friends about her unsettling trip. Her stomach was chronically upset. Then she couldn't explain what happened, but she woke up one morning feeling better and continued to feel better. Perhaps feeling ill all the time made her fear that she could cause herself permanent damage by being constantly angry and depressed. Her dear friend Roberta Bundy, whose son committed suicide, was now terminally ill with bone cancer. Liz always suspected that her illness was brought on by the loss of her son. Once Roberta confided in Liz that she suspected the same. Consequently, when Roberta and Liz were together, they no longer discussed their lost loved ones. Perhaps learning what really happened made Liz so angry that she became determined not to let Derrick's selfish actions cause her irreparable physical or mental harm. For Liz it turned into a battle for her survival.

After returning, Liz didn't have any more dreams about Avis. It appeared that her unfinished business with Avis was at long last completed. Apparently, Liz needed to thank her once again because she had always been so good to Derrick and she had never spoken poorly to him about his mother. It was in her power to have poisoned Derrick against her, but she never did. When Liz called Beverly before leaving Middletown, the conversation turned to the meeting with Avis, and she said that Avis always spoke favorably about Liz to her.

Often Liz found herself thinking about Dave Ruhlen the neighbor who walked away from the rollover physically unscathed but was left mentally a shell of a person. Why did he let Derrick drive drunk or were they both drunk? Was he awake when it happened? Did he encourage Derrick to take out the Beasley's mailbox or did he try to prevent it? What secret did he have to live with? What caused him such long lasting torment? Oh, so many unanswered questions. When these thoughts crept in, her survival instincts kicked in and dictated, "No, Liz, don't even think of going there! No matter what you found out, nothing would change the outcome. You've come too far in your battle to survive to give in to these self-destructive thoughts."

Liz hadn't answered Mark's letter and possibly never would, or alternatively she could write him a short note at Christmas. Because she had come this far and struggled so hard to rebuild her life, at this late date, she didn't wish to become a casualty of an accident that occurred on a country road over seven years ago. She didn't wish to be a victim of her son's thoughtless behavior. Perhaps, as Mark expressed it, the Lord had made peace in her heart

Since starting this book in 1995, it has had many titles, which reflected Liz's frame of mind as the story unfolded. The first was *D*; next *So Close to Home*; then *The Bobwhite's Song*; followed by *Son, You were my Sun*; followed by *Those were the Days, My Son*; followed by *Three Red Roses*; then *When Time Ran Out; One Last Fling* and, finally, *Continuing Aftershocks*. Most likely there were others, which she forgot.

Once again Liz found the peace that comes with closure. There are some things, however, that she would always regret. One of her worst regrets was not having asked more questions and probed more into Derrick's affairs while he was alive. Would the outcome have been different if Paula had contacted her or if Liz had contacted Paula during that tumultuous last year before his death? Of course, Liz would always deeply regret waiting for the circumstances to be ideal for Derrick to visit Arif and her.

Although she always regretted never knowing Derrick's side of the story concerning the described incidents of drunkenness, physical abuse and mailbox vandalism, she took great comfort in knowing that Derrick was responsible only for his own death. It could have been so much worse. He could have killed Paula or Lynne or Tammy or Linda or someone else while in a jealous rage or he could have killed Dave or some others while driving drunk.

She derived immense comfort in knowing what a wonderful person Derrick was when he was sober. Raphael Aquino and Mark LaGrange both told her that they loved Derrick like a son. He felt a great responsibility toward Avis and helped her and others, both old and young. So many people thought the world of him. He was held in such high regard by his supervisors and colleagues that the company for which he worked closed all day the day of his funeral. Not very many people have over 600 persons attend their funeral. What a wonderful tribute to one so young!

Finally, if what it takes for there to be no more chapters to this story is for her never to return to Middletown, then so be it. At last, all her business there was finished.

Chapter 16
2009 and 2019

In September 2007 Arif and Liz went to Middletown for her fiftieth high school class reunion. After vowing not to return, she reluctantly gave in to the requests of several of her high school friends to join them at the reunion, and, for the most part, she was glad she did.

Arif had never been to Middletown for a happy occasion, so it was gratifying to see him having a good time at the reunion. In spite of being so reluctant to attend, Liz ended up having a better time than she ever could have imagined. Arif said that she acted as though she was running for class president all over again.

The worst moment of the trip was their first visit to Derrick's grave. Upon arriving in town, the first place they went was the cemetery. Without the oak tree to guide her, Liz was having trouble locating his grave when her eyes were drawn to a tall patch of grass and weeds in the otherwise well-manicured cemetery. With trepidation, she walked toward the unkempt area to find that it was Derrick's totally overgrown marker. With tears welling in her eyes, she dropped to her knees and started frantically pulling up the grass. Arif joined her in clearing the area around the marker.

Fortunately, because the ground was fairly moist, the grass was easy to remove. Because she was so upset, she couldn't figure out why the marker was overgrown. Arif pointed out that because there were flowers on one side of the marker and some pheasant feathers stuck in the ground on the other side, it was impossible for the person doing the mowing to mow close to the marker. Liz suspected that Alex had placed the feathers there, but it could have been any of Derrick's numerous friends. It was obvious that they needed to remove the impediments, so they removed the flowers and feathers, leaving the marker looking clean but naked.

Looking around the Hoffman plot, she saw Avis's marker indicating that she died in 2003 at age 90. To Liz's surprise, there were no flowers on any of the Hoffman graves. She wondered if Sue, Byron or Matt, all of whom lived in central Missouri, ever came to the cemetery. She doubted that Peter, who lived in Albuquerque, had been there since Avis's funeral. The entire plot looked neglected.

After visiting Derrick's grave, Liz was afraid of what they would find at her parents' graves. Much to her relief, everything was in good order. Their markers hadn't subsided since she had them reset, and there were two containers of silk flowers on the monument. Before leaving the cemetery, they went to see where her cousin, Maxine, was buried. It was Liz's first time in Middletown since she died. As they stood by her grave, Liz thought about her having been executrix for Liz's father's estate and what a wonderful support she had been through other difficult times. After her death, Liz had no relatives living in Middletown. After migrating from Germany, Liz's father's family moved to Middletown in the late 1890s, and now, 110 years later, no one in the family was left there. All that was left were tombstones.

Not seeing Jill and Raphael was a great disappointment. The last time Liz had seen Jill was in 2002 when she and Diane Nelson came to visit in Sacramento. Over the years, Jill had become very reclusive. She didn't attend the reunion, and Liz didn't get to talk to her until the last day they were in Middletown. Earlier when Liz talked to Raphael, he said that Jill was attending an out-of-town soccer game with one of their grandchildren.

When finally Liz was able to get ahold of Jill, Jill started out by saying, Oh, Liz, what a day I've had! I'm totally pooped. I hope you don't mind if we put off getting together until the next time you're in town."

Liz wasn't quite prepared for what she was hearing. Being that it had been almost ten years since Liz had been in town, somehow she expected Jill to suggest that she and Arif stop by for a few minutes either that evening or before they left town in the morning.

"Jill, for your information I'm not planning on returning soon, if ever."

Jill's unemotional response was, "Oh, my, I'm sorry to hear that."

"When we went to the cemetery, we found Derrick's marker totally overgrown, and Arif pointed out that was because the silk flowers on one side of the marker and the pheasant feather arrangement on the other side made it impossible for the person doing the mowing to mow close to Derrick's marker." Just talking about it was causing Liz to weep. "All we could do was to remove all the impediments and leave it bare."

When there was no offer of help from Jill, Liz continued, "I was hoping I could get Alex's phone number from you so I could ask him to make sure the marker didn't get overgrown again."

"He's hard to get ahold of by phone. Next time he stops by I'll ask him to check on Derrick's grave periodically."

The rest of the conversation was devoted to her grandchildren and their activities. When Liz told Diane Nelson about her disappointing contact with Jill, Diane told Liz not to take it personally because Jill treats all her old friends that way. That was the last communication Liz every had with Jill.

A highlight of the trip was going with Arif to the park where Derrick had worked. It was a golden September day, and the park shone in all its early-autumn splendor. They took their time walking the paths, stopping to admire some of the old growth oak and maple trees along the way. They found Derrick's memorial tree, which appeared to be thriving. They walked along the creek, and Liz pointed out the spot where her girlfriends and she used to skinny dip in their high school days. The park has one of the prettiest settings in central Missouri. It was easy to understand why Derrick loved it so much.

Liz left Middletown with the nagging concern that Derrick's marker might become overgrown again. With Maxine gone, she really didn't know who to ask to check on the grave. There was no listing for Alex in the phone book. With their parents buried there, why did the Hoffmans let things get so neglected? Sue had such a close relationship with Avis and Derrick, so Liz had assumed that she would visit the graves.

After the monument company discontinued its flower service, Diane Nelson had been placing flowers on Derrick's and her parents' graves. She had her hands full being caregiver to her husband, so Liz didn't want to impose on her to go to the cemetery several times during the growing season. Liz would just have to hope that by not having any flowers or other impediments on the grave, the mowing would get done. It saddened her to think of the area around his grave devoid of the oak tree, acorns, pheasant feathers and flowers. Perhaps Derrick would prefer his marker to be overgrown rather than naked. How naïve she was to think that her affairs in Middletown would ever be satisfactorily settled.

Looking back over the eleven years since she had added anything to Derrick's story, Liz's life had been exceedingly good. In fact, one good part of that trip was a brief encounter with her niece, Linda. Since my sister passed, Linda lived with her dad's family in Wisconsin so I didn't see her much. She told me that she had come back for a visit and Alex asked her to go through Derrick's things with him. When they did, she said they found the article about the medical library being named after me from the Midland Gazzette and an envelope half addressed to me. There was no note, but from what she said, it looked like Derrick intended to send it to me.

Arif and she have had a wonderful retirement, spending much of their time at their beloved Lake Tahoe where they have many wonderful friends and engage in a multitude of social and recreational activities. Many significant honors have been bestowed on them. If, in the 1990s, anyone had told her how happy she would be in the new century, she wouldn't have believed it. Back then, she believed she would never know true happiness again, but how wrong she was. Every day she gave thanks for Arif and her having been given a second chance at happiness. It made them so much more appreciative of each other.

Things keep happening to remind her how vulnerable she still was and perhaps always will be. She never knew what would trigger waves of sadness to wash over her. When they attended a Boy Scout event honoring several Eagle Scouts, suddenly she was teary eyed and had to excuse herself to find refuge in the restroom. That was the last Boy Scout event they attended.

A few years ago, she was at a charity benefit where she saw a dear acquaintance who was in her mid-nineties. She and Liz chatted for a couple of minutes, and then she inquired, "And how is that dear grand baby of yours?" For Liz it was a struggle to hide her shock and dismay. Her first reaction was to say, "You must have me confused with someone else for I have no grandchildren." What she ended up saying was, "Just fine" and quickly changed the subject.

More recently when she answered the phone, and a male voice said "Hi, grandma. How are you?" she knew that the voice at the other end didn't have a wrong number but was a perpetrator of the Grandparent Scam. Still, she found it painful to say, "I have no grandchildren." before hanging up. That was the only time anyone other than Arif had ever called her grandma.

It continued to surprise her just how many of their friends and acquaintances had lost a child. Among their close friends, she knew at least four couples who had lost adult male children either to suicide and/or substance abuse. Knowing and interacting with these courageous parents made her feel less alone and gave her the inspiration and determination to carry on.

It was over three years since she last heard from Paula. Although Liz intensely misses hearing from her, she doesn't blame Paula for wanting to break with the past and trying to build a new life. The last time she wrote, she talked about how, after her divorce from Phil, all she had was her son, her work and her dog. She said that she was unlucky at love and wasn't inclined to try again. For so long she was like a daughter-in-law to Liz, so it was difficult to have lost her. Liz remains deeply thankful that Paula was there when she really, really needed her. Now Liz has developed the strength to go on without her support, but she had hoped that they'd be friends forever. She said to herself, "Paula, wherever you are, please know that you continue to be very dear to me, and I wish you the very best."

"Derrick, please forgive me if in any way I contributed to the apparent lack of trust and low regard you held for women. Until your death, I knew only your side of the story. Since your death, I have only others' versions of the story. Without your being here to defend yourself, I hope I'm not judging you too harshly. While you were alive, I should have been more perceptive and have asked more questions. I failed you there, and I'm truly sorry for having let you down. I want you to know that even though you have deeply angered me and caused me extreme pain and agonizing guilt, I forgive you and will always love you. I say this with a smile in my heart and a bobwhite song in the corners of my mind.

After dinner Arif and Liz played a couple of games of pool and then watched the second half of a movie they had started the night before. It was after 10:00 by the time they turned out the lights. It didn't take long before Arif was lightly snoring. Liz waited a little longer before she quietly got out of bed and tiptoed back to her reading. Purky soon joined her and filled the room with purrs.

After a couple hours, she finished and reluctantly closed the manuscript, stretched and sat back with a feeling of great satisfaction. It was the first time that she had been able to read what she had written from beginning to end without becoming overwhelmed with sadness. Somehow this time, as she read, she almost felt as though she wasn't personally involved in the story. Why she was drawn to reading her manuscript the day before turning eighty she didn't know, but she felt extremely thankful for having done so. It reminded her that when she felt overwhelmed by the trials of aging that in the past putting her thoughts down on paper had helped her through what seemed to be insurmountable challenges and might do so again.

It was almost 1:30 a.m., and she needed to get some sleep before her big day. She turned out the lights and tiptoed back to the bedroom where she found Arif still sound asleep. She crept under the covers and moved towards his warmth. As she snuggled up to him, he surprised her with a kiss and murmured "Happy Birthday. Is it still snowing?" Before Liz could answer, he had gone back to sleep. She sighed contentedly and went to sleep thinking about how lucky she was to have had Arif to love for over 55 years.

Author's Note

So often couples who experience the loss of a child end up getting a divorce. In my story, Liz and Arif came ever so close to experiencing that fate. Even though they both let each other down, they endured as a couple and were given a second chance for happiness.

After losing her son, Liz didn't think she could ever be happy again, but much to her astonishment, some of the best and happiest years of her life and marriage were yet to come.

For many years, the writing I have done for publication has been on the origin of Nevada place names. *The Bobwhite Doesn't Always Sing* is a story that represents my only work of fiction. Often the early works of fiction writers reflect their personal experiences. This book fits that pattern and is based on true events.

It is a story of bereavement, life-threatening illness and a long, tortuous search for closure. I hope you find solace and understanding if you need that, or at least a good read that touches you in some way.

Mary B. Ansari
Indian Hills, NV
March, 2020

About the Author
Mary B. Ansari

During the 25 years that Mary Ansari was a member of the University of Nevada, Reno faculty, she held a variety of administrative positions in the University Library. She was tenured in 1973 and promoted to professor in 1983. In 1994, she retired as Director Emerita of Administrative Services and Branch Libraries. During her tenure at the University, she published widely in library and place name literature. She was national president of the Geoscience Information Society, and the society's Distinguished Service and Best Reference Book awards bear her name.

With her husband, Nazir, she has been a major benefactor to education, human services, and the arts in Nevada. She is trustee and secretary-treasurer of the Nazir and Mary Ansari Foundation, a charitable foundation seeking to improve people's lives through support of human services, education, the arts and culture in northern Nevada. In 2007, she and her husband were recognized by the University of Nevada's Board of Regents as Distinguished Nevadans and were honored as Outstanding Philanthropists by the Sierra Chapter of the Association of Fundraising Professionals. The University of Nevada, Reno's Map Library bears her name. She has served on several public boards.

Mary received a Master's degree in Library Science from the University of Illinois and a Master's in Business Administration from Western Michigan University. She received a Doctorate of Humane Letters from the University of Nevada, Reno. Mary and her husband reside in Indian Hills, Nevada, USA. This is her first and only novel.

Also available
by Mary B. Ansari, L.H.D.

Nevada Heartland
The Place Names of Carson City,
Douglas, Lyon and Storey Counties, Nevada

Also available in limited quantities:

The Place Names of
Douglas County, Nevada

The Place Names of Lyon County, Nevada

Mines and Mills of the Comstock Region,
Western Nevada

Available at: LeRue Press
280 Greg Street #10
Reno, NV 89502
Lrpnv.com
thebookgallerynv.com
amazon.com
barnesandnobleinc.com